ROOSEVELT HIGH
An Annie Mercer O'Dell Story

By
Kenneth Lee McGee

To My Extended Family

I want to thank all those people who helped make this story come to life.

Chapter One

"Annie Mercer O'Dell, what a *surprise* to see you in my office!" Vice-Principal Daniel Kemmerick said with all the sarcasm he could muster. He took off his suit coat and hung it casually over the back of his chair. He shook his head, ran his fingers through his prematurely graying hair and then sat down heavily.

Annie made direct eye contact, raised her hand in the air, used her most charming smile and said, "I didn't do it, Mr. Kemmerick. I swear I'm innocent!"

Mr. Kemmerick leaned back in his black leather desk chair. "Why is it that I don't believe you, even though I don't yet know what you're talking about?"

"Mrs. Etheridge sent me down here because she caught me, I mean allegedly caught me, going into her desk."

"What were you searching for in her desk, I mean *allegedly* searching for, Annie?"

She looked outside, tried to suppress a grin, but without success. "I might have been looking for a paper that an unnamed friend of mine turned in, and needed to get back because of some misinformation contained in alleged paper."

"Your friend has no name." Mr. Kemmerick swiveled his chair to look outside at two students as they ran across the parking lot with the security guard chasing, but losing ground. "How has he made it this far in life without a name?" Mr. Kemmerick asked as he turned back to face Annie. He frowned at her and said, "I know you're talking about Mace. Just cut the crap and tell me what happened. I guarantee he won't be in any trouble. The basketball team will need him once the season starts."

Annie stared at Mr. Kemmerick. He stared back. Fifteen seconds passed.

"All right." He held up his right hand as if being sworn in as a witness in a courtroom. "I give you my word."

"Okay, as long as Mace won't get into any trouble," Annie said but then stared at Mr. Kemmerick.

He sighed. "Fine! Cross my heart. Pinky swear. Whatever

you kids do nowadays."

"Okay, Mace told me he wrote this paper for her class after he got pissed off at her for insulting his mother because she refused to give old lady Etheridge a loan..."

Mr. Kemmerick had to stifle a laugh as he thought about the sixty-five-year-old teacher. "Annie! Her name is Mrs. Etheridge, not 'old lady Etheridge.' Now continue."

"Anyway, Mace wrote a few things he later regretted and I promised I would try to get it back. So I wasn't really breaking into her desk. I was simply trying to retrieve something that didn't belong to her in the first place."

"What am I gonna do with you, Annie? You know it's wrong to *allegedly* go through a teacher's desk, right?"

"There were extenuating circumstances!"

"Do you still have the paper Mace wrote?"

Annie reluctantly pulled the paper from under her sweatshirt and handed it over to Mr. Kemmerick. He began to read the paper and involuntarily began to chuckle. Annie smiled innocently as her eyes darted around the office. She wondered if Mr. Kemmerick still kept his computer password on the back of his college diploma, which hung on the wall along with his other plaques and photographs.

"I won't call your father this time, Annie. I'm sure he has enough *thieves* to catch already, but please don't break into her desk anymore."

"I promise I won't. Unless I have..."

The bell sounded ending the last period of the day at Theodore Roosevelt High School. Annie looked at Mr. Kemmerick and he hooked his thumb toward the door.

"Get out of here. If I have to call Detective O'Dell, he won't appreciate it. Take Mace's paper with you and give it back to him. Please tell him to be more careful in the future."

"Thank you, Mr. Kemmerick," Annie said as sweetly as the most skilled actress could and then jumped out of the chair.

Annie ran out of his office and headed outside to the quad area where she met up with her seventeen-year-old friends Mace Franklin, Elaine "Lainey" Novicki and Cindy Mackens.

"Well, are you suspended or anything?" Mace asked as he dribbled the basketball he carried everywhere. "Tell me quick 'cause I gotta get over to the courts. Got a pick-up game startin' soon."

"No, he just warned me to behave. What did you write exactly? Mr. Kemmerick almost laughed out loud while he read it. Here, he gave me back your paper." Annie handed the paper to Mace, but Elaine grabbed it instead.

"We need to read this first." Elaine and Cindy huddled together to read Mace's paper.

"Believe me, Annie. You don't want to know. What do I owe you?"

"The usual fee. A ride home when I need it and whatever I want to eat at Darby's next time we're there."

Elaine and Cindy laughed. "You called her 'more wrinkled than a ninety-year-old prune.' No wonder Mr. Kemmerick laughed."

Annie poked Mace in the arm. "You should know better."

"I was upset, okay." Mace bounced his basketball at Annie.

"Oh, and don't tell Daddy about today, okay." She caught the ball and threw it back at Mace. "He will try to interrogate me if he suspects anything."

Detective Keith O'Dell, now in the robbery division, had over twenty years of experience with the city of South Hampshire's police force. He had raised his only child, Annie, by himself since her mother, Amy Catherine Mercer O'Dell, passed away when Annie was five. Father and daughter remained very close even though Annie sometimes caused him aggravation because of her tendencies to get herself into situations that might appear to be a little *shady* to the outsider. Annie, sixteen years of age, five feet two and a half inches tall with short, naturally curly brunette hair and brown eyes, had a bit of Nancy Drew in her personality. She sometimes used her skills and influence to help her friends out of sticky situations—for a nominal fee, of course.

Mace caught the ball and dribbled it through his legs. "Now why would your father suspect you of any wrongdoing, Annie O'Dell. Would it be because he knows his only daughter so well?

3

Is Mr. K. going to tell Principal O'Dell?"

Annie shook her head. "No, he doesn't tell Grandpa when I get into trouble. He owes me because of how I helped him catch the thief stealing money from the cafeteria."

"So your grandfather doesn't know about any of the mischief you've been in?" blonde-haired Cindy asked.

Elaine flipped her shoulder-length brown hair out of her eyes, removed her glasses and held them up in the sunshine. "Oh, God! I hope he doesn't."

"Grandpa still thinks of me as sweet and innocent—his little angel!" Annie smiled and pretended to dance like a ballerina as everyone watched.

"You might be sweet, Annie, but innocent. I don't buy that for a second."

Cindy and Elaine both smacked Mace on his arms.

"Ow! What was that for?"

Elaine frowned at Mace and said, "Annie wasn't talking about sexual innocence. Although she is innocent about that. She means her grandfather doesn't know about her sleuthing."

"You mean snooping," Mace said over his shoulder as he sauntered away, still dribbling his basketball. "I will see you fine ladies tomorrow."

"Bye, Mace. I hope you win your game," Cindy said.

Annie rolled her eyes and then shook her head at Cindy. "It's just a pick-up game. They probably don't keep score."

Elaine read the second page of Mace's paper and laughed.

"What's so funny?" Cindy asked.

"He described Mrs. Etheridge as a combination of Helen Keller and Lizzie Borden without either of their good attributes."

"Give me that," Annie said as she grabbed the paper. "Did he actually use the word attributes?"

Chapter Two

Built in 1930, the large three-story building located just west of the downtown area of South Hampshire was home to Theodore Roosevelt High School. Made of locally quarried limestone and covering a whole city block, the impressive building could be very intimidating to new students. It normally took them a week to learn their way around the building. Some of the upperclassmen intentionally gave freshmen wrong directions. They tried to intimidate and frighten the new students with fantastic stories. One urban legend, that still made its way around school every fall, was the story of the freshman boy who got lost never to be seen again until twenty years later when a janitor found his mummified body underneath the stage in the theater. Most incoming freshman were skeptical and doubted the story's veracity, but there were always a few who believed.

The school's athletic teams were called the "Rough Riders," even though most students didn't remember Teddy Roosevelt had been the president at the turn of the century. The school symbol was a sword, but most students didn't know or care. The school board of education once commissioned a study to determine the actual time it took for a student to get from a classroom on the ground floor at the south end of the building to the farthest classroom to the north on the third floor. It was determined to take nearly ten minutes to travel that distance with students in the hallways. So, of course, the board recommended only five minutes between classes. The result of this was hallways filled with students rushing about to get to their next class on time. Teachers had gotten used to students being tardy. Especially freshmen who were still learning their way around.

Although the city of South Hampshire had always had a mixture of ethnicities, Roosevelt High had been predominately Irish, Italian and German in the beginning. Over the years that had changed and now the student population was composed of almost an equal split between Caucasian, Hispanic and African Americans. Hispanics were moving into the city faster than any other ethnic group. One section of SoHam was known as

5

Chinatown, even though its residents were from China, Japan, Korea, Vietnam and other far eastern countries. Roosevelt High experienced its share of racial tension, but for the most part, the groups tolerated each other. In the fall of 1996 the school was going through a period of détente.

A poll taken by the school newspaper, The Rough Rider Bulletin, revealed that only forty percent of the students thought the old building was haunted. Of that forty percent, only five percent claimed to have actually seen apparitions. Of that five percent, only one student claimed to recognize the apparition they saw.

"Are you absolutely sure, Susan?" Elaine stood with her pen poised over a small notebook as she interviewed Susan Brainerd for a followup story.

"Positive! It was the ghost of John Belushi. He was dressed in a samurai costume. I'd swear to it on my mother's grave!"

"But, Susan, you're mother isn't dead," Cindy reminded her.

"Well, if she was, I'd swear on her grave."

"Thanks, Susan. We'll talk to you later." Elaine rolled her eyes, as Susan turned to walk away.

Elaine Novicki, the editor of the school newspaper, looked at her best friend, assistant editor and staff photographer, Cindy Mackens, shook her head and sighed.

"No story there, Lainey!"

"There is a story, but I don't think Susan would appreciate being labeled a psycho in the paper."

"I did get that picture of her in the biology lab. She looked kinda nuts in that shot."

Elaine smiled at Cindy and then sighed again.

"Lainey, what are you thinking about?"

"Thinking about what we can use for the lead story."

"There's always the parking lot issue."

"I think everyone has had their fill of whether or not the school should knock down the old garage building to make more space for kids who drive to school."

"How about a story about the band?" Cindy asked.

6

"Which band? Not the marching band, I hope."

"Oh, come on," Cindy said as she grinned. "I heard a lot of positive feedback about the story of the freshman, tuba-playing girl who fell down at halftime and couldn't get back up."

"Her parents called the school and complained to Mr. Kemmerick. He threatened to give me a detention if I ever printed a story like that again."

"Annie took those pictures, not me."

"Don't ever let her borrow the camera again," Elaine warned Cindy. "Now, which band are you talking about?"

"The only band that counts, Fridays At Five. I got some new pictures of Kenny Colwell when he was home. We could talk to that girl he knows."

"Emmy Colasanti?"

"Yeah. She might have something interesting to tell us."

Elaine and Cindy couldn't make up their mind and decided to wait until tomorrow when the whole staff met.

"Hi, Cin. Did you finish that report for Mr. Kolinski's class?" Elaine asked as she and Cindy stood by their lockers before class started the next morning.

"I finished it, but I doubt I'll get an 'A' on it. I had to kinda fill it with smoke to get the amount of words he wanted. Do hyphenated words count as one or two?" Cindy asked.

"I would count them as two, but who knows?"

"Good morning, ladies! How are the two most beautiful girls in school, who have lockers on either side of mine, doing this beautiful morning?" Mace Franklin was all smiles as he appeared out of the mass of students crowding the hallway and greeted his friends.

"Morning, Mace. How was your night?" Cindy asked.

"It rocked. I met Trish at the library and then we went to her house to study, if you know what I mean." He shoved his basketball into his locker.

"You do know her father is a judge, right?" Elaine asked.

"I know it. He likes me. He thinks I am a fine example of a serious student with ambition and a bright future ahead of him."

"Has he ever actually met you?"

"So weak. I expect better from you, Cindy Mackens."

"Seriously, Mace, did you finish your paper for class?"

"I did and I expect it will set the standard for the whole class."

"So you copied it from the encyclopedia."

"No way! I bought it from The Geek. I mean Lendall Greenwood, that fine young man with the brilliant mind."

"How much did that set you back?" Elaine asked.

"Fifty and it was worth every penny," Mace answered.

Elaine and Cindy smacked his shoulder.

"What was that for!"

"You are incorrigible, Mace Franklin. You should know better."

"I'll see you ladies for lunch, and I mean ladies in the finest sense. You are both looking fine today. Did I mention that?"

"Bye, Mace!"

"You know I was just joking about my paper."

"We know. The Geek charges a hundred bucks, and you are too cheap to part with serious cash like that."

Mace Franklin had been friends with Elaine Novicki, Cindy Mackens and Annie O'Dell since second grade. Mace came from a single-parent home. His mother Elisabeth was a vice president at a local bank, and supported her two sons without help from their father. His father deserted the family after the birth of his second son, Keyshon. Mace hadn't seen or heard from Bill Franklin in over ten years, aside from a couple of birthday cards. Keyshon had never seen his father.

The Novicki and Mackens families lived across the street from each other in the upper middle class neighborhood of Cumberland Heights. They had lived in their respective homes since the girls were four years old. Elaine was an only child while Cindy had an older brother, Marshall, who was away at college, and a twelve-year-old sister, Maddy, who constantly drove Cindy nuts.

8

Chapter Three

"Mister Sullivan!" The entire class jumped as their teacher pounded his desk with his large fist.

"Yes, Mr. Vidmar."

"I asked you once before to please pay attention and leave the social commentary for after class."

"Sorry, Mr. V. I was just telling..."

"That's enough!" Mr. Vidmar pointed to the door. "You can visit Mr. Kemmerick for the rest of the period. I'll let him know you're on your way."

Matt Sullivan had a reputation as a troublemaker. He was the only son of Cormac Sullivan, who owned several bars and The Hungry Lion, a successful restaurant, in the South Hampshire area. The elder Sullivan was rumored to be "connected" and Matt exploited that to his advantage with the other students. Matt was a frequent visitor to Vice-Principle Kemmerick's office. On his way to the school office, he came across Victoria Madison, a senior cheerleader with a penchant for bad boys.

"Hey, Victoria! Where are you headed?" Matt asked.

"I got sent to see Kemmerick. How about you?" Victoria replied.

"Same place. Wanna make a stop on the way?"

"What have you got in mind, Matty?"

"I thought maybe we should check out the girls' bathroom and see if it's clean."

"Does that line ever work?" Victoria rolled her gray eyes.

Matt grinned. "It did last week on Amy Porter."

"You know she's a freshman, right?"

"So what? She is a very mature freshman." He held his hands in front of his chest.

"I think I will pass on your offer for now, Matt. If you want to ask me out on a proper date, though, I might have a different answer."

"Your answer is always 'no,' Victoria. No matter what the question."

"Maybe you need to rephrase your question then," she

teased with a flip of her long blonde hair.

Mr. Kemmerick was mildly surprised to see Victoria Madison waiting in the office to see him but was used to Matthew Sullivan's numerous visits.

"Come on in, Victoria. Matt, you can cool your heels out here until I have time to see you."

Victoria followed Mr Kemmerick into his office.

"What can I do for you, Miss Madison?"

"Mr. Kemmerick, it is impossible for me to make it from my locker to my Algebra II class on time. I have too many people to talk to on the way, and I need more time."

"Did you ever consider walking and talking at the same time?" he asked sarcastically.

"I do, but there just isn't time. Will you please sign my excuse." She batted her eyes and smiled at Mr. Kemmerick.

He rolled his eyes as he reached for a pen. "Please try to make it to class on time from now on."

"I will try, Mr. Kemmerick. I promise I will."

After making a few calls and killing time, Mr. Kemmerick called Matthew Sullivan into the office and pointed to a chair. Matt slumped into the chair.

"Did you and Mr. Vidmar have another disagreement?"

"Not so much a disagreement, but merely a slight difference of opinion." Matt waved his hand to show his indifference. "He thought I should pay attention to his boring class, and I had better things to do."

"Do you want to transfer to another class, Matt?"

"Like what?"

"Well, we don't have a bartending class yet."

"Hey!" Matt sat upright. "I'm never going to be a bartender. I'm the guy who will be hiring the bartenders."

"Please try to get along with him. Your father really would like you to graduate this year."

"I kinda like it here, though. I like watching the fresh young girls every year. They need me to show them around."

"Just wait here until your next class, Matt, and try to get along. I don't want to call your father again."

10

"I don't blame you, Mr. K. I don't like talking to him, either."

After the last class of the day, the newspaper staff met in the journalism room.

"Has anyone seen Maris?" Elaine asked. "We need everyone at this meeting. I'll give her another minute, but then we need to get started."

Maris Miller ran into the room out of breath.

"Sorry I'm late, Lainey. I got busy talking to Bert Hodges and lost track of time."

"Why were you talking to him, Maris?"

"He asked me for help with his paper for English. I told him not a chance in hell, but he kept bugging me."

Bert Hodges happened to be a senior athlete who had gotten by doing a minimum amount of work.

"Okay, let's get busy. We need to decide what the lead story will be."

The staff buckled down to work and decided to go with a story about Fridays At Five. Kenny Colwell, the lead singer and guitar player, was a graduate of Roosevelt. Two of the other guys in the band were Roosevelt grads, also. The band would soon acquire international rock star celebrity, and Elaine wanted to capitalize on their status as local legends.

"Okay, who knows Emmy Colasanti?" Elaine looked around the room.

No one seemed to know her.

"She is a friend of Kenny Colwell, and I need a volunteer to interview her. You know, see if she has any juicy stories to share. Something to interest the kids."

"I'll talk to her." Randy Braun raised a hand to volunteer.

"Do you know her?" Elaine asked.

"She's in my history class. I don't know her that well, but I know her sister, Diane. My older brother, Christopher dated her. I'll talk to Emmy and see if she will help us. Don't expect too much."

"Why not?" Cindy asked as she twirled a finger through her hair.

11

"I don't know if I've ever heard her talk to anyone. She's really shy."

"Do your best," Elaine instructed him and then moved onto other business.

The next day before first period, Randy stopped by Emmy's locker. He introduced himself and mentioned the class they shared.

"I'm on the school paper and we're doing a story on Kenny Colwell."

Her blue eyes sparkled when he mentioned Kenny's name.

"Do you know him? I heard someone say you live in the same neighborhood."

She answered in a voice that sounded childlike, "We both live in Raynor Park."

He realized she was quiet and shy, but she did know Kenny Colwell. She agreed to meet him after school at Darby's Dogs.

"Hey, Emmy! Over here," Randy hollered as he spotted her walk in later that afternoon. He stood up and motioned to get her attention.

She waved to Mr. Darby, who smiled at her and then joined Randy in a booth.

"Hi, Randy." She dropped her backpack and took off her faded army jacket.

He noticed she wore a top with the Darby's logo.

"I work here part-time and I have to start at four today," she explained.

"That's cool. Do you want anything to eat? Maybe some pop?"

"A root beer would be nice."

Randy ordered a root beer for each of them, and Mr. Darby didn't charge him since he was with Emmy.

"What can you tell me about Kenny Colwell for the paper?" he asked as they sat in one of the red vinyl and stainless steel booths that were a trademark of the locally owned teen hangout.

"We've been friends since I was seven. I used to practice with the guys and go to the shows," she said without adding she

12

would sometimes join the band on the stage and sing with them.

"What is he really like, Emmy? Has he changed much since they are now famous?" Randy asked with his pen poised over his notebook.

"No, he's still the same guy as before. You'd never know he was famous or anything."

"Does he talk about life on the road much? You know, the girls and stuff? I'm sure a band like his is faced with plenty of temptations, if you know what I mean." Randy raised his eyebrows and grinned.

Emmy shook her head. "If you're looking for something negative about him, you've come to the wrong place. Kenny Colwell is my friend and always will be. I'm not telling you anything to hurt him."

"I'm sorry, Emmy. I had to ask."

"It's all right," Emmy said and then took a sip of her root beer.

Randy and Emmy talked while they drank their root beer and Emmy shared some humorous stories. Not exactly the dirt the paper hoped for, but enough for a good story. Randy seemed to get the impression Emmy and Kenny were maybe more than just casual, or even close, friends.

"Thanks for your help, Emmy. I like the story about him tripping over his guitar cord and making it appear as part of the act."

"Please, don't say anything about his ears."

"I won't, Emmy." Randy smiled at her. "I'll talk to you in Mr. Culbertson's class. Maybe we could do something after school one of these days."

Emmy bit her lip and didn't answer.

Chapter Four

There were two public high schools in South Hampshire—Roosevelt and a newer school, Abraham Lincoln High. There was also the Catholic school, St. Raymond's. Football season at Roosevelt High was an important part of the school year. The Rough Riders were one of the best teams in the state, year in and year out. Head coach, Roger McMahon, a former linebacker in the NFL for the Green Bay Packers, had been at Roosevelt for over twenty years without ever suffering through a losing season. Guys who made the varsity team were accorded the stature of gods to some of the younger kids. Roosevelt and St. Raymond's were bitter rivals when it came to football. Between the two schools, they had won twelve state championships—six apiece. The schools played each other during the regular season, but were in different classes for the playoffs. There had been two years when both schools won the championship in their respective class.

The fast-growing, adjoining community of Crest Ridge built a high school in 1985. Before that the kids in Crest Ridge attended Lincoln. Crest Ridge Central earned a well-deserved reputation for having the worst football program in the conference. They had never had a winning football season in the brief history of the school. They had never beaten St. Raymond's and only once did they win against Roosevelt. The city of South Hampshire built a stadium back in the fifties for the local schools to use for their important games. North Park College also used the stadium as their home field. Each high school had a football field on campus, also —except for St. Raymond's. They played all their home games at Memorial Stadium. When Roosevelt and St. Raymond's played, the stands were packed with close to eight thousand fans.

Annie, Mace, Elaine and Cindy were eating lunch in the cafeteria one day when Diana Ahronson and Damon Barclay walked past. Diana waved and then she and Damon headed outside to the Quad.

Cindy mentioned, "You know if we took a vote for the most popular girl in school, Diana would win in a landslide."

14

"She'd get my vote," Mace said with a mouthful of the hamburger he was inhaling.

"Don't talk with your mouth full." Annie punched him in the arm. "Don't you have any manners?"

"I don't think Hollywood could come up with a more perfect high school student," Elaine added after she finished her salad. "She's a senior, a cheerleader, member of the student council, senior class secretary, involved in every possible club and committee imaginable, and besides all that, she's smart, pretty and a caring person." Elaine raised a finger for every point she brought up.

"She's as friendly to the freshman as she is to the high and mighty seniors," Annie said.

"Hey! Be careful what you say about us high and mighty seniors, kid. Remember you're just a junior," Mace teased Annie.

"She never seems to have a harsh comment to make about anyone," Cindy said and then sighed.

"You sound like you're in love with her, Cindy," Annie joked. "Just once I'd like to hear her get pissed off and swear like..."

"Like you do when your Grandpa isn't around," Mace teased.

"...a sailor is what I meant to say before this creep interrupted me."

"She was voted the homecoming queen last year and this year she's got to be the odds-on favorite to be prom queen," Cindy reminded everyone.

"I'd vote for you, Cin," Mace said as he grinned.

They waited for his punch line.

"What? Why are you all staring at me?" Mace held out his hands as if in protest.

"We're waiting for a smart-ass comment," Annie said as she frowned at him.

"Can't I vote for Cindy if I want? After all I think she's the most beautiful and... smart... and... intelligent."

Annie and Elaine started coughing, while Cindy beamed with pride.

"What a load of bull..."

Mr. Kemmerick walked past at that moment. "Do you mean manure, Annie?"

"Yes, Mr. Kemmerick, isn't that what I said?" Annie put a finger in her mouth and tried to look innocent.

He shrugged, shook his head and kept walking.

"As I was saying," Mace continued. "I think Cindy is..."

"She's not doing your Sociology paper so just forget it, Mace." Elaine threw a French fry at him.

Mace caught it in his mouth. "More, please."

"Knock it off!" Annie punched his arm with more authority this time.

"Hey! That's my shooting arm. Be careful." Mace rubbed his arm even though it didn't hurt.

Diana Ahronson, a natural blonde with a trim figure, was the oldest of four kids. Her younger sister, Danica, was only seven. Her two brothers, Chad and Charles, were in eighth and seventh grade respectively. They both pestered their sisters to distraction. Especially Diana, who constantly had to warn them to leave her girlfriends alone.

"What about Damon?" Cindy asked dreamily. "I think he's absolutely gorgeous."

"Close your mouth and stop fawning over him," Annie said. "He and Diana are practically engaged. Besides his mother is making sure he marries someone from a 'respectable' family." She used air quotes.

"She should after what his sister did."

"What did she do?" Mace asked as he grabbed the last of the fries from Annie's tray.

"Don't you remember?" Elaine asked. "She eloped with a guy from the 'wrong' side of town. It was quite the scandal."

"Yeah, because she was knocked up," Annie said and then giggled.

Damon's older sister, Deirdre, disappointed the family when she eloped with a "commoner" by the name of Gavin Rogers. Being two months pregnant factored immensely in the elopement.

16

"Derrick Keasling told me that Damon actually complained about the way his mother got on his case about who he had to date," Annie said and then nodded. "That's right. He complained. That means he's almost human like the rest of us."

Diana's boyfriend, Damon Barclay, was the only son of the wealthiest family in South Hampshire. The Barclay family could trace their ancestral roots back to the early days of the country. Legend claimed the cherry tree George Washington supposedly chopped down belonged to Claymore Barclay. Of course, unlike the cherry tree, Claymore Barclay was not a myth.

"He does drive a used car to school," Elaine said.

"That's right. Poor guy. He has to drive a five-year-old BMW 535i. Maybe we should take up a collection for him," Mace said as he waved to two of his friends from the basketball team.

"Come on, Mace. Cut him some slack. He doesn't flaunt his money like some other kids do. It you didn't know he was a Barclay, you'd think he was just another regular guy." Annie stood up for Damon.

"Has anyone heard where Diana is going to college?" Cindy asked.

Elaine opened a container of red seedless grapes. "I heard she hasn't decided yet. Damon is going to Princeton like his father and grandfather. I'm sure he wants Diana to join him."

Annie said, "I know for a fact she's considering Princeton, Stanford, Northwestern and even North Park."

"And how, pray tell, is it that you know this for a fact?" Mace asked as he turned his back to the group as three girls walked past.

"I kinda checked her file last week," Annie admitted.

"Your Grandpa is going to expel you if he ever finds out how you go through the confidential files," Elaine warned her. "What else did you learn?"

"Damon is definitely going to Princeton regardless of where Diana goes."

"Didn't the Barclay family start North Park?" Cindy rested her chin in the palm of her hand as she thought about Damon.

"I think so. Why?"

17

"You'd think Damon would go there."

"Yeah, he could go for free." Mace turned back to the group.

"Look who's talking! You're gonna get a scholarship to play basketball there. And, by the way, those girls are sophomores." Annie thwacked the back of his head.

He grabbed Annie's arm and twisted it. "So?"

"They're a little young for you. If Trish only knew how much you flirt with other girls, you'd be burnt toast."

"Was that a reference to my heritage? You wee Irish lass."

"That's the worst Irish accent I ever heard." Annie laughed.

The present day Barclays lived on an estate which formerly consisted of over a thousand acres. At one time it had stretched from the banks of the Kinmundy River north for several miles. Now it had been reduced to a mere forty acres. Much of what was formerly Barclay woods and farmland was now "The Barclay Estates" an area of exclusive homes for those who could afford the entry fee.

"I heard that Mrs. Barclay didn't approve of Diana at first," Cindy remarked.

"Why wouldn't she?" Elaine asked.

"Because her parents have jobs. At least that's what I heard."

"Jobs? Aren't they both doctors?" Annie asked. "I'm sure I've heard that."

"Her father is a heart surgeon, or some kind of surgeon, and her mother has her own psychiatric practice. I wouldn't call that having jobs. More like careers." Elaine ate her last few red grapes before Mace could snatch them.

Cindy stood up to take her tray back. "I still think they are a fabulous couple. They're kinda like normal kids like us."

"Are you calling Annie normal?" Mace asked. "God help us if she's normal."

"Shut up, Mace, before I pound lumps on your head," Annie threatened.

Chapter Five

Randy Braun was senior class president and head of the organizing committee for the class sponsored Sweetheart Ball to be held on September twentieth. The committee started planning for the dance in their junior year. The ball was now only a week away.

"Let's get started. We have a lot of work to do," Randy said. "Diana, has your committee decided on a band yet?"

"Well, since it was impossible to get Fridays At Five, we have decided to go ahead with the local band we were considering. I have seen them play and they are really good. They are exactly what we need. They are called The Notable Exceptions and Kenny Colwell recommended them."

"So, we are sure about this band?" Randy asked.

"It's a done deal. We gave them a deposit and signed the papers," Diana answered.

Randy turned and asked, "Elaine, Cindy, how about our decorations and the refreshments?"

"We're just about set. We need a few more donations for the refreshments. The gym is all ours after the last class on Thursday, and we have fifteen volunteers to help turn our beautiful gym into paradise. Piece of cake!"

"How about ticket sales?"

Maris Miller and her boyfriend, Grady Harris, were in charge of tickets.

"We have sold over three hundred tickets so far and since Damon's father is covering the cost of the band and rental of the gym, we should be able to raise over four thousand dollars. We have normally sold another hundred tickets on the day of the dance so we're counting on that."

The committee met for over an hour to finalize plans for the annual Sweetheart Ball. This had been a traditional fundraiser for the senior class for many years. They would crown a king and queen from the senior students. Now that the band had been booked, all the committee members could relax. That was the final hurdle. The committee had held out hope that Fridays At Five would be able to play, but they were on tour and would be in North

Carolina. The Notable Exceptions had agreed to be a last minute replacement, if needed, over a month ago.

The next week passed quickly and after working long hours Thursday and Friday the gym had been transformed.

"Wow! We did it! The gym looks better than ever," Randy said as he stood back and admired their work.

"We never would have done it without your help, guys," Elaine thanked them.

"As long as the school doesn't burn down we should be set." Randy looked at the time. "We have an hour and a half before the doors open. Should be enough time for everyone to run home and get ready."

"Maybe for you, Randy, but we girls might be a little late. We need to fix..."

Elaine listed all the things the girls needed to accomplish to be ready for the dance. The guys stared with dazed expressions.

"Better get a move on, ladies! I know Trish will be ready on time," Mace said and managed to stick his foot in his mouth.

"Mace Franklin! I will be ready when I'm ready. You will wait all night if I say so," Trish Eiffert said angrily.

The girls snickered as Trish put Mace in his place.

At seven o'clock the doors opened and a few minutes later the students began to arrive. Most of the tickets had been sold to couples, but not all. There were many girls who had come to the dance alone or in groups hoping to meet some guys. Unfortunately, the single girls outnumbered the single guys by a large margin. In addition to the normal couples like Diana and Damon, Grady and Maris and Mace and Trish, Elaine and Randy Braun were together. Cindy was asked to the dance by Kyle Norris. Victoria Madison and Matt Sullivan showed up together, much to everyone's surprise. Annie O'Dell came by herself mainly just to watch everyone. She didn't date often but had gone out occasionally. She even went out with Matt Sullivan once just to prove she could *handle* him. Her father had not been very happy when he discovered his daughter's plan.

"Cindy, you are looking fine tonight!" Mace said.

"You clean up pretty good yourself, Mace. Where's Trish?"

"She had to make a stop in the little girl's room. Hey, there's Lainey. Whoa! Did her father see that dress? I am shocked he let her out of the house looking like that."

"Hey, guys," Elaine said.

"Hey, Lainey. Mace was just commenting on your dress."

"What did he say, Cindy? Probably something about my father."

"I was just expressing my concern as a lifelong friend about the revealing nature of your dress."

"If you're so concerned, why are you staring at my chest?" Elaine asked.

Cindy and Elaine teased Mace about his concern.

"You guys look different tonight. That's all," Mace said.

"Yeah, we actually wear bras now, Mace. We have matured unlike one of our friends," Cindy said as she watched Annie sneaking a glass of punch.

The band started playing and the dancing began. Mace was an enthusiastic dancer and rarely left the dance floor. When he wasn't dancing with Trish, Cindy and Elaine corralled him. Even Annie O'Dell managed to grab Mace for a couple dances.

"My! My! My! don't you look fine tonight, girl," Mace said as he smiled at Annie.

"Thank you, Mace. I like your sport coat."

"Is this your first time at a school dance, Annie?"

"No, I came to the dances last year. I even came with Matt Sullivan once. That was the night he picked a fight with Bert Hodges, and they both got suspended."

"I remember that now. You tried to break up the fight, and I had to pull you away from them."

"Yeah, my chest hurt for a week." Annie punched Mace in his side. "That's for trying to feel me up last year."

"I did no such thing. Where did you get that dress? It sure looks good on you."

"I borrowed it from Maddy Mackens. The dress shops don't have my size."

"You mean they don't carry miniature sizes."

21

"Do you want me to slug you somewhere else where it might affect the future of your unborn children? And stop trying to look down my dress, creep."

"I was not looking."

"Not much to see anyway. Hey, did you hear about the random locker searches?"

"Yeah! I heard yours got searched first."

"Grandpa was just trying to prove a point."

"What? That you're the most hardened criminal in the school?"

"No, he just wanted to show that I had to follow the same rules as everyone else."

"Did you manage to get all the fake IDs out."

"Yeah, I stashed them in your locker. Make sure I get them back Monday."

The dance continued smoothly for the next hour. Annie O'Dell kept her eyes peeled for any signs of trouble. She noticed some of the younger girls going outside with some of the seniors. They came back inside without any apparent harm. Annie was standing by Mace when she noticed Bert Hodges and Todd Delaney pull a couple of girls toward the exit. She knew that Dawn Matuzak had a bad reputation, but it was the other girl that set off an alarm in Annie's brain.

"Mace, did you see that?"

"See what?"

"Delaney and Hodges just pulled Emmy Colasanti back there. They are probably sneaking a drink or a smoke."

"Emmy!? Are you sure? I knew her sister was kind of a slut, but I didn't think Emmy was that kind of girl."

Annie punched Mace in the arm with force. "She's not! That's why I know something is wrong. Those guys and Dawn Matuzak are going to take advantage of her."

"Dawn Matuzak is a tramp. Why do you care what happens to her?"

"How dense is that skull of yours? Is there any brain activity in there at all? I could care less about Dawn, but I'm worried about Emmy. I don't think she realizes what those guys are planning. Come with me and be quiet."

Annie waved at a group of guys. Then she and Mace hurried to where she knew Delaney was headed. They stopped and Annie peeked around the corner.

"What can you see?" Mace asked.

"Mace, be careful! You almost knocked me over."

"Sorry, Annie."

"Bert and Dawn are kissing and Todd has his hand on Emmy's arm. Be quiet and follow me."

Mace followed quietly. All of a sudden Todd grabbed the bow on the back of Emmy's dress. Emmy turned around, slapped Todd and broke away. She paused long enough to slug Todd and then ran toward the main gym passing Annie and Mace before running into two freshmen boys.

"Come back here, you little bitch! You're nothing but a tease," Delaney shouted.

"Mace, watch Bert and don't let him do anything," Annie yelled.

"What are you going to do, Annie?"

Annie didn't hear Mace because she was moving toward Todd Delaney. Annie stuck her foot out as Todd ran past trying to catch Emmy Colasanti.

He fell on his face and cried out, "What the hell!?"

"Did you trip and fall down and go boom?" Annie mocked him.

"Why you little..."

"Not so fast there, Todd!" Mace suggested.

"Are you gonna stop me?"

"We might help him a little," someone with a deep voice said calmly.

Delaney rose to a knee and saw three large football players standing behind Mace and Annie. He slowly got to his feet, backed away and said, "We were just teasing her."

"Try someone else next time, bozo!" Annie warned him.

Annie turned to the football players and gave them high-fives. "Thanks, guys. I appreciate it."

"Anytime, Annie. You know we got your back."

Annie turned to Mace and he put his hands on her shoulders. He could feel her trembling.

"Are you all right, Annie?"

She put a hand to her chest and felt her heart racing. "I'll be fine in a minute. I'm sure glad you were with me."

"Did you think I would let you do that by yourself? You aren't Wonder Woman, you know. Come on, let's get back to the dance."

"Did you see and hear how little Emmy Colasanti handled Todd and Bert. She showed some guts for a tiny girl."

"You aren't much bigger yourself. You should keep your eyes open for Todd and Bert. They might try something to get back at you."

"Bert won't. He's not really a bad guy, but Delaney is a bully. He won't try anything unless I'm alone, and I always have my little friend with me." Annie pulled out a can of pepper spray from her purse.

Mace and Annie headed back to their friends. Annie looked for Emmy but didn't see her in the crowd. Annie noticed a couple of the football players sticking close to her. She waved and gave them a thumbs up sign. She danced with Mace again and they talked as they shared a slow dance.

"How did you get here? Did you get a lift?" Mace asked.

"No, I walked."

"Well, you're not walking home. You're riding with Trish and me."

"Thanks, Mace, old pal. I hope Dad doesn't hear about what happened. He'll ground me for life for pulling a stunt like that."

"Okay, everyone! Listen up," Randy Braun hollered into a microphone. "I'm going to announce the winners of the king and queen contest. Can I have a drum roll please?"

The drummer played a weak drum roll and got a mock cheer from the crowd.

"Okay, your Sweetheart Ball king for 1996 is... Derrick Keasling! Come on up here, Derrick."

Derrick made his way to the stage.

"And now! Drum roll, please. Your 1996 Sweetheart Ball

24

Queen... Rachel Lowery!"

The band started playing as Rachel made her way to the stage. Rachel received her crown and she and Derrick faced the crowd while the cameras captured the moment. They shared a dance and then Derrick gave Rachel a kiss for the cameras.

"I thought Diana and Damon were shoo-ins," Annie said.

"Diana will be prom queen and maybe even homecoming queen. Those are more important," Cindy explained.

"I suppose, but Derrick and Rachel make a nice couple," Lainey said.

"They aren't a couple, Lainey. Derrick's still going out with Clarissa Morgan."

"You know what I mean, Annie. Maybe next year you will be queen of the dance."

"Yeah right! Next year's queen will be Kristen Keasling. They should just give her the crown now. She's the prettiest girl in school."

"And all along I thought you were, Annie," Mace teased.

As the dance wound down, Annie spotted Emmy Colasanti talking to Derrick and Kristen Keasling. Annie didn't really know Emmy, except by sight. They had never been friends and hadn't had but maybe three or four classes together at Roosevelt. Annie thought she should keep an eye on her at school, if she could. Todd Delaney might just be dumb enough to try to get revenge. Annie caught a ride home with Mace and Trish. He stopped in the street in front of the O'Dell's ranch house.

"Thanks for the ride, Mace. Trish, you looked great tonight in case I didn't tell you. Don't let Mace do anything he shouldn't."

"Don't you need to get in the house, little girl? I think it's past your bedtime."

"Remember to take Trish straight home, Mace. You never know. I might have put a tracking device on you somewhere."

Annie got out and ran up the sidewalk to her house. The porch light was on and she knew her father was waiting up for her. He didn't have a chance to see her before she left because he was still at the station. Annie dashed up the porch steps, opened the unlocked door and stepped inside. She tossed her coat and purse on the bench in the entryway and ran over to the couch where her father was about to fall asleep.

"Daddy! I'm home. If you want to take any pictures, do it quickly because I'm taking this dress off in ten seconds."

"How was the dance, sweetheart? Get it? Dance sweetheart. Sweetheart dance."

"You are funnier than Groucho Marx," Annie said as she rolled her eyes.

"Thanks, sweetie."

"He's dead, remember, and dead men aren't funny."

"Did you dance with many guys? First hand me the camera, please. Then you can answer my questions. It's on the counter. I want a few pictures of my little girl in her first dress."

"Daddy! This isn't the first time I've worn a dress. Just maybe the first time I've had such a fancy dress to wear."

Dad took some pictures and Annie turned her back to him.

"Will you unzip this for me? I want to change into my pajamas. I'll be right back."

"If you need help unzipping the dress, who zipped it up for you?"

"Daddy! You shouldn't ask me that."

Her father unzipped her dress, and she ran to her room. She returned three minutes later. She jumped on the couch next to her father. She told him all about the dance and the guys she danced with. She wasn't sure she should but she went ahead and told him about what else happened.

"I saw Bert Hodges and Todd Delaney grab Emmy Colasanti. That slut, Dawn Matuzak, was with them."

"Annie Mercer, watch your mouth."

"Well, she is! Or should I say whore? Would 'slutty whore' be a better description?"

Her father frowned.

"I knew there was only one reason those two guys would be taking Emmy outside, and I knew it wasn't because they were going to study."

Dad asked, "How did you know that girl wasn't going along willingly?"

"Because I kinda know her. She is an innocent angel, just like me, Daddy."

"Innocent? Okay, I'll buy that, but an angel." He shook his head. "Who do you think you're talking to? Your grandfather?"

"I grabbed Mace and we followed. We watched for a second. All at once Delaney grabbed her and Emmy slapped him. She hit him and he let her go. She took off running with that jerk chasing her. I told Mace to watch Bert and I stuck out my foot and tripped Delaney. He fell flat on his face. He tried to get up, but I stopped him."

"Just how did you stop him? Did you pull your hairbrush out and point it at him?" Dad interrupted.

"Are you gonna let me finish?"

"Pardon me. Please, continue, by all means." He lifted his hands in surrender.

"Mace made sure Bert wasn't going to do anything, and I took care of Delaney."

"What would you have done if this Delaney kid tried to grab you? Did you even think about that?"

"Oh, did I forget to mention the three football players who were with me as backup? I guess I did," Annie said as she grinned at her father.

"That's my sweetheart."

"I told them earlier to keep an eye on me, and if I signaled, they were to back me up."

Detective O'Dell hugged his daughter and she gave him a kiss.

"I'm going to bed now. Good night, Daddy."

"Good night, sweetie. I'll see you in the morning. We have to do some grocery shopping."

"Okay, but not before ten, all right. I need my sleep."

Detective O'Dell waited a few minute sand then made sure the doors and windows were locked before he headed to his bedroom. He sat on the edge of the bed and looked at the picture on his nightstand. "She's growing up, Amy Catherine. I'm doing the best I can, but I sure wish you were here."

Chapter Six

When Annie O'Dell saw Todd Delaney at school on Monday, he tried to scare her. She ignored him and he got upset.

"Just wait, O'Dell. You won't always have your friends around to protect you."

Just then Matt Sullivan walked up behind Todd.

"Please tell me I didn't just hear you threaten Annie O'Dell. She's my friend, by the way." Matt's usually friendly face changed to a menacing look.

Todd turned around to face Matt. "I was just kidding, Matt. I'm not going to do anything."

Matt grabbed Todd's shoulders and squeezed until he saw pain in his eyes. "That would be a wise decision and from what I've heard, you don't often make wise choices. Consider this a warning, Delaney. If anything happens to Annie O'Dell, anything! I will be looking for you and I won't be nice." Matt shoved Todd against the lockers as everyone watched. Annie heard some snickers from the other kids.

Todd took off and Matt put his arm around Annie's shoulder. "I heard what happened at the dance. You were really brave, Annie, if a little foolish. What if the football players were late getting there? Did you think about that?"

"I knew they were there, Matty. I was careful."

"Please keep your eyes open, Annie. I wouldn't want to see you get hurt."

"How is your Uncle Riordan doing?"

"He's doing all right. I hope Detective O'Dell knows I don't hold it against him for putting Uncle Riordan back in prison. He made a mistake and deserved what he got. Say hi to your father for me. You need anything, Annie, you let me know."

Friday was Roosevelt High's big football game against the Crusaders of St. Raymond's. Neither team had lost a game yet this year. Over eight thousand fans filled the stadium to capacity. It had been four years since the Rough Riders had beaten their arch rivals, but this year they had a good chance. The offense was vastly

28

improved over the previous year, but it had been the play of the defense which gave them hope. The defense, led by a sophomore middle linebacker named Tony Bertucci, had shutout three opponents so far. His play had made an immediate impact on the team and he had three years to play on the varsity. Elaine, Cindy, Mace and Annie were at the game together.

"Where is Trish? This is the big game," Annie asked as she grabbed a handful of buttery popcorn from Mace's bucket.

"Her jerk of a boss scheduled her because two of the other girls quit just so they could go to the game. Can you believe that crap?" Mace whined.

"Well, you have us to keep you company, Mace, old buddy," Annie said as she chuckled.

"Yeah, well. Who's gonna keep me company after the game? Do I have any volunteers for that duty?"

"Sorry, Mace, but I gotta go straight home," Elaine said.

"Yeah, me, too. I gotta watch Maddy later," Cindy replied as she grabbed some popcorn. "Why did you put so much butter on this?" Cindy wiped her hand on a napkin.

"You got a lame excuse, too, Annie?" Mace asked.

"Nope! I don't have to be home until midnight. I can keep you company, Mace."

"Annie, you do know what he's talking about, don't you?"

"Yeah, Annie, he wants to make out." Elaine and Cindy warned Annie even though they trusted Mace totally.

"So what? I've been kissed before."

"Annie Mercer O'Dell! You have never kissed anyone other than your father and grandfather."

"How do you know?" Annie asked as she grinned. "Maybe I kissed a boy that you don't know about."

"Like who?" Cindy asked.

Elaine shook her head. "No you haven't."

"I'm not telling," Annie said.

Mace sat back and listened. He ate a handful of popcorn and then wiped his hand on his jeans. "It doesn't matter who, or if, Annie has any experience kissing a guy."

"Why is that, Romeo?" Elaine asked.

"Because I am the best teacher in school for that kind of sex education."

"Oh, gross!" Cindy shook her head.

"Gag me with a spoon." Annie put a finger down her throat.

"You can't kiss Annie, you dolt," Elaine informed him. "We've all been friends for too long. If you try to kiss her, it will ruin everything."

"Yeah, Mace, you can't kiss Annie," Cindy added her opinion.

"Hey! Don't I get a say in this?" Annie poked Mace in the side as she stared at Cindy and Elaine. "Maybe I want him to kiss me."

"Get serious, Annie. You don't want your first kiss to be with him," Elaine said.

The game remained close throughout and in the fourth quarter the defense caused a turnover and the offense scored to go ahead. Roosevelt had a four point lead. The defense stopped the Crusaders on a fourth down play to take over the ball. There were only two minutes left. All the offense had to do was hang on to the ball and run out the clock. On second down the quarterback handed off to the running back who was hit hard and fumbled. A Crusader picked up the fumble and ran it in for a touchdown. The offense got the ball again but couldn't move it and the game ended with Roosevelt losing a heartbreaker.

"Man, we shoulda had that game," Mace said as he smacked the concrete wall as they left. "I pity the kid who fumbled the ball. That's gotta be rough."

"Did you ever blame yourself for losing a ballgame, Mace?" Elaine asked.

"Nah, basketball's a team sport. One guy can't win it by himself and one guy can't... Oh, I see your point. You're right again, Lainey. Must be nice to be so smart."

"I'll see you guys on Monday," Cindy said.

"Can you give me a ride, Mace?" Annie asked.

"Sure, Annie. Wanna get something at Darby's first?"

"Sounds good to means then we can go parking."

"Annie!" Elaine and Cindy yelled at her.

"What? I can't let a handsome star basketball player kiss me?" Annie teased.

"Yeah, you could do that. but you're gonna be with Mace," Elaine teased back.

"No respect! I lead the team in scoring, we have a winning season and still no respect. What's a man gotta do?" Mace wanted to know.

Elaine smiled and said, "We respect you, Mace."

"I'm waiting for the punch line."

"We will send flowers to your funeral if you get caught kissing Annie."

Just then Matt Sullivan walked up. He had heard part of their conversation. "What's this I hear about someone kissing Annie O'Dell?"

"Hey, Matty. Mace is taking me to Darby's. Then we're going to Swallow Cliff. Wanna come with us?"

"I don't think Mace wants me with you guys at Swallow Cliff," Matt told her.

"I meant Darby's! We aren't going to Swallow Cliff. Daddy would lock me away, if he caught me there, even if it was with my old buddy, Mace." Annie put her arm around Mace and held him close.

"What's that mean? Am I a eunuch or something?"

Annie smiled wickedly at Mace.

"Don't look at me like that, Annie. You don't even know what that means."

Annie reached up and whispered in Mace's ear.

"If I wasn't brown already, I would be blushing. Does your Daddy know you talk like that?"

"Are you gonna tell him?" Annie asked.

Matt was listening and looking around. "I'll go with you guys to Darby's if you don't mind."

Mace drove Annie and Matt followed them over to Darby's. When Mr. Darby saw Matt Sullivan, he came over to talk to him.

"Hello, Matthew. How is your father?"

"He's fine, Mr. Darby. I just want to get something to eat. I promise I won't cause any trouble. Can I talk to you for a minute, please? In private."

"Sure, Matty. Follow me."

They went in the back to talk.

"I heard Todd Delaney and a couple guys talking about trying to hurt Annie, and I thought if I was along they wouldn't be so stupid."

"That Delaney kid is a worthless piece of crap like his father. Even so, if he tries to start something in my place, you stay out of it, Matthew. You can't afford any more trouble right now, all right. You understand?"

"I get it, Mr. Darby. No trouble in your place, but if he tries something somewhere else."

"That's different. If he tries to hurt that child you do what you have to do. I will back you up."

Mr. Darby knew Matt had had a rough life at times and tried to protect him from the world of his father. Matt once saw Danny Darby getting attacked by three guys behind the store. He waded in and put two of them in the hospital. Mr. Darby made sure Matt was long gone by the time the cops arrived. Since none of the guys could identify Matt, he was never charged.

"Are you buying, Mace?" Annie asked.

"I'm buying for me. You're on your own, Annie."

"I'll buy for you, Annie. What do you want?" Matt asked.

"Chili cheese dog with onions, fries and a Coke."

"What? You on a diet or something? Only one dog?" Mace teased.

"It's late, okay."

Annie found a booth and saved it for the guys. They placed the orders and waited for the food. Mace and Matt weren't exactly good friends, but there was a respect for each other. Matt decided to tell Mace what he overheard at the game.

"You really think he might try something?" Mace asked.

"The boy is dense."

"You got that right!" Mace looked out the window and poked Matt in his side. "I guess he's even dumber than we thought."

Mace and Matt saw Todd and two buddies walking toward the door. Mace looked back at Annie to see if she had seen them. She had and she shook her head at Mace. Mace walked over to Todd and stood in front of him without saying a word.

"There are no football players here now, Franklin. Looks like you're outnumbered."

"Maybe not, Delaney." Matt walked up behind Mace.

Todd looked at the two guys in front of him, swore and then turned around and left.

"We're both taking you home tonight, Annie," Mace informed her as he and Matt sat across from her in the booth.

"Thanks, guys, but Daddy frowns on me having a threesome. One guy a night is his rule. At least till I'm eighteen."

She smiled gratefully for the guys concern. They stuck around at Darby's for an hour and then took Annie home. She invited them both inside.

"I'm home, Daddy, and I brought two guys with me. Is it all right if they both stay?" Annie hollered.

"You know the rules, sweetie. Only one guy a night." Detective O'Dell walked out of his room saw Mace and then Matt Sullivan. "Everything all right? Did Annie do something?"

"No, sir, but Delaney was doing some trash talking. We thought we would do some preventative maintenance." Matt always talked respectfully to Detective O'Dell.

"Him again. Thanks for watching her back," Detective O'Dell said as he slapped Matt and Mace on the back.

"We were watching her front, too, Detective O'Dell." Mace realized what he said. "Crap! I didn't mean it like that."

Annie and her father laughed at Mace's discomfort.

"Can they stay for awhile, Daddy?"

"Of course. You guys hungry? No, wait a minute that was a stupid question. You are always hungry, Mace. How about you, Matthew?"

"I'll make some popcorn, Daddy. You can go back to your room and finish your reports." Annie took her father's hand and led him out of the living room. "We will be quiet, and they won't stay past one, I promise."

"Good night, Annie. Holler if you need anything."

"Night, Daddy. I love you, and I won't need any help. I can handle these guys."

Annie kissed her father and he shook his head. Annie made popcorn and they drank Cokes. They turned on a movie and sat on the couch. Annie didn't realize Mace was waiting for Matt to leave and vice versa.

When Annie went into the bathroom, Mace told Matt, "Okay, we're gonna have to leave at the same time otherwise Detective O'Dell is gonna come out here and shoot us both."

"You're right, Mace. I know you're her friend and I'm not sure what I am to her. I'll leave first. You can hang around if you want. I'll check the neighborhood and make sure Delaney isn't around. If I see anything suspicious, I'll call a couple friends and come back here."

Annie came back into the room and Matt told her good night. She decided to hug him and he hugged her back. She looked into his eyes and he smiled at her. She smiled back and wished he would kiss her, but he didn't.

"Good night, Annie. See ya later."

"Good night, Matty."

Matt checked the neighborhood, but didn't find anyone hanging around. Mace left a few minutes later. He got a hug, but Annie didn't think about kissing him.

Chapter Seven

Three weeks had passed and Elaine, Cindy and Annie were walking down the hallway at school when they come around the corner and saw Victoria Madison standing beside Matt Sullivan. Their lips were locked together.

"Hey, Victoria! Hey, Matt! Be careful there. You don't want to start rumors. A cheerleader caught with the school bad boy," Elaine said as she shook a finger at the couple. "That won't help your reputation, not that your reputation is worth saving."

"We weren't doing anything, Elaine," Victoria insisted.

"In my house we call that making out." Elaine's smile was as phony as could be. "How about at your house, Cindy?"

"My parents call it communicating."

Matt was silent as he looked at Annie.

"Don't look at me, guys." Annie shrugged as she looked at Matt. "That doesn't happen at my house, remember?"

"Annie, you told me your father was dating again. Doesn't he ever bring his dates home?" Elaine asked.

"Sometimes, but they are careful in front of me. Virgin eyes, you know. I might be corrupted if I see someone kissing."

"We're on our way to lunch. Wanna join us, Victoria, or are you too busy 'communicating' with Matt?" Elaine asked.

Victoria waved them away. "I'll just stay here. We have more things to 'talk' about."

As the three girls were walking away, Annie turned to look back at Matt. He watched her and smiled as she turned around. He blew Annie a kiss. She pretended to catch it on her cheek and smiled, but then she pointed her finger at Matt, as if it were a gun, and blew him away.

Mace and Trish joined Elaine, Cindy and Annie in the Quad.

"Hi, Mace, what're you up to today? Where's your basketball?" Annie asked as she noticed its absence.

"Just hanging out with my favorite, best, absolutely gorgeous, smartest..."

"What do you need?" Annie sat on the table, leaned back

and used her hands for balance.

"Need? Why are you assuming I need anything?" Mace shrugged as he stood in front of the girls.

The girls stared at Mace in silence.

"All right, so I need something. Like you guys never ask me for favors. I need help with Algebra II. I'm lost."

"Cost you big time," Annie said.

"I'm willing to pay. You guys know me."

"Exactly my point. Payment in advance." Elaine held out her hand.

"Rough crowd! Can you help me after school today, Lainey?"

"No can do. Got a staff meeting until five. I can squeeze you in after that."

"Should I come over to your place?"

"Sure." Elaine nodded.

"Bring the dough," Annie said and then laughed.

"See you then. Right now Trish and I have some communicating to do. Later!"

Mace and Trish took off. Annie stared absentmindedly into space as Elaine and Cindy talked. Cindy nudged Annie's leg to get her attention.

"Earth to O'Dell. Come in, O'Dell."

"Huh, what?"

"Where were you? I asked three times already. Are you going to talk to Mrs. Shipley about graduating early?"

"Yeah, I'm supposed to see her after school today."

"What did your father say?"

"Well, uh." Annie scratched her knee and wouldn't look at either Cindy or Elaine.

"You didn't tell him yet. What are you waiting for?" Cindy asked.

"I have to pick just the right moment to talk to Daddy about it. He might not go for the idea. He still thinks I'm immature."

Elaine laughed and said, "He is a detective, Annie. He knows things."

"I'm not immature!" Annie scooted down and sat between

36

Elaine and Cindy. "Am I?"

"You're not immature. Just nosy, impulsive..."

"Don't forget devious and..."

"Some friends you guys are. See, this is why I need to graduate this year. I'd be lost around here next year. You will be gone. Mace and Trish will be gone. Matt will be gone. Who would I hang out with?"

"Matt? You would miss Matt Sullivan?" Cindy asked. "He's as bad as Rory Porter."

"He's not as bad as everyone thinks. He's been nice to me."

"If he's been nice to you, Annie, it's because he doesn't want your father to bust him."

"I can think of one other reason Matt Sullivan would be nice to our sweet little Annie," Cindy added without thinking.

Annie sighed because she knew exactly what Cindy meant.

After school Annie met with her guidance counselor Mrs. Shipley to talk about early graduation.

"Have a seat." Mrs. Shipley pointed to a chair as she read another student's file.

Annie fidgeted in the chair for a moment but noticed the file was Matt Sullivan's.

Mrs. Shipley laid the file on her desk. "What can I help you with, Annie? You said something about graduation. I looked at your file and you are well on your way to graduating with your class. I don't see any problem."

"That's the problem!" Annie jumped up and placed her hands on the desk. "All of my friends are in this years class. Next year I will be lost without them. Is there any way I could graduate this year? I have taken summer classes the last two years."

"Let me take another look at your transcript. How do your father and grandfather feel about this?"

"I haven't mentioned it yet. I wanted to check with you to see if it was even possible, and if so, just what steps I would have to take."

Mrs. Shipley perused Annie's transcript quickly. "Since you took extra English and math classes in the summer, you would have the required credits for those subjects. Are you sure you want to graduate early? You seem to really enjoy high school, Annie."

"I do enjoy it, but I want to move on. I want the challenge college will bring," Annie said. *I hope you believe that load of crap. Grandpa would see through it in a second.*

"I hope you aren't talking about older boys."

"No way!" Annie shook her head. *Though that would be one advantage of college.*

"You need to talk to your father and grandfather before you decide, but you have enough credits to graduate this year. As long as you take a full load next semester and pass everything." Mrs. Shipley looked at her transcript again. "You do realize you would give up any chance at being your class valedictorian. You have a perfect GPA but some of the students in this years class have higher GPAs because of their honors classes."

"I wouldn't be class valedictorian anyway. Jimmy Cho is ahead of me and that won't change."

"Talk to your father. Then come back to see me."

"Thanks, Mrs. Shipley. I will."

Annie headed home and got busy in the kitchen. She wanted to surprise her father. She was busy in the kitchen when he walked in the back door.

"Hi, Daddy! You're home early. How was your day?"

"It was all right, sweetie. Is that meat loaf I smell?"

"Yes! I made your favorites. Meat loaf, cheesy potatoes and baked beans."

"That can only mean one of two things. Either you got suspended from school, or you are pregnant. Now which is it? I demand to know, young lady." He pounded on the island for emphasis.

"We need to talk." She pulled him into the living room and they sat on the worn, but still comfortable couch.

"Confess! Now!" he insisted.

"Daddy, I'm only suspended for a week, and I'm three months pregnant. Am I starting to show? How do you always know my deepest secrets?"

"I am a real detective, remember? We have ways of finding out things." He laughed and then hugged his daughter.

"Go change and I will get dinner on the table. I really do have something to talk about," Annie said nervously.

"I knew I should have had that sex talk with you earlier." He stood up and smacked a fist into his other hand. "Three months, huh?"

She laughed and motioned for him to leave. "Scoot. Go put on your comfortable clothes."

Dad changed while Annie set the table. In a few minutes they were eating.

"This is really good, Annie. Did you change the recipe or something?"

"Just a little. Do you really like it?"

"Nah, I'm just starving. I would have eaten old baloney on stale bread and thought it was a gourmet meal tonight."

"That is on the menu for tomorrow. I knew I should have made it today."

After a few moments of silence as they ate, Dad asked, "Okay, now what's on your mind, Annie? It must be important for you to make meat loaf."

"All right, this is it. You know my friends—Elaine, Cindy, Mace and everyone."

"What are their names again? Do I have files on them?" He added another slice of meat loaf and more cheesy potatoes to his plate.

"Daddy!"

"Sorry, go ahead."

"They all have one thing in common. Do you know what it is?"

"They are all suspects in an armed robbery?"

"Yes, but that's beside the point," she said and then paused as she thought about how best to continue. "Okay, it's this. They are all seniors. All of my friends are seniors which means they won't be at Roosevelt next year."

"Roosevelt doesn't have a graduate program?"

"This is serious, Daddy." Annie frowned and continued. "I talked to Mrs. Shipley and I have enough credits to graduate this year. I want to graduate with my friends, so I can start college when they do. They are all going to North Park and since that's where I want to go it just makes sense that I start with them, so we can be together and have fun and..."

Dad leaned forward and put his hand over Annie's mouth to quiet her. "You had me at hello."

"What? Does that mean you'll let me?"

"Yes, I know you enjoy high school, but I think being with your friends would be better. Yeah, you can always make new friends but..."

"Oh, Daddy! Thank you! I love you! I mean I would love you even if you told me no but..."

"Yeah! Yeah! Do you want any more cheesy potatoes?"

"No, you can have the rest."

"Have you thought about all the things you will miss. Prom night, newspaper staff, having your grandfather around to see you everyday."

"I don't see Grandpa everyday. I get sent to the vice-principal's office where the troublemakers go."

"That's right, I forgot. By the way, have you seen Mr. Kemmerick lately?"

"Daddy! A girl has to have some secrets, even from her sweet father."

"Well, whatever it was couldn't have been too bad. You didn't get suspended or anything." He laughed but then pointed a finger at her and said, "Now about that pregnancy thing."

"Oh, Daddy."

Chapter Eight

Annie and Mace were walking to their first class the next morning. Mace could tell something had her all excited, but waited for her to say something.

"Guess what?" Annie asked Mace as they stopped.

"Let me see. I know. You won the lottery last night and want to share it with your best friend. Me!"

"Yeah, I did, but that's not the big news. Daddy agreed to let me graduate this year. Isn't that great?"

"What? Man, I was counting on having one year of peace and quiet at college before you got there. Why'd you have to go and ruin my day, girl?"

"And here I thought we were going to be roomies."

"Does North Park allow coed rooms now? Sweet!"

"Just because we're roommates does not mean..."

"Did your father really agree, Annie?"

"Yes, last night I made meat loaf..."

"You poisoned your father. Where did you bury his body?"

Annie smacked Mace on the arm. "Will you shut up and listen? He asked if I had thought about all the things I would miss, but I don't care about stuff like that. I would rather be with my friends at North Park. Where are Lainey and Cin, anyway?"

"They had to stop at the journalism room for something."

"Do you know why?"

"Nope. Didn't ask." He shook his head. "See you at lunch. I gotta run."

"Yeah, see ya, Mace."

In the journalism room Elaine and Cindy were talking to Mrs. Hart, their faculty adviser. They had to make a decision about the front page before school started.

"This has to go to the printer by nine o'clock," Mrs. Hart reminded the girls.

"We have to choose between these photographs," Elaine said as she looked at Cindy.

"I like this one better." Cindy picked up her choice.

"I agree."

"What about the story?" Mrs. Hart asked as she crossed her arms over her chest.

"We have triple checked the facts, Mrs. Hart. We have three sources who corroborated the story. I feel that we need to print it. The students deserve to know the whole truth."

After some more discussion, Mrs. Hart approved the story. The headline would cover the entire top of the front page.

"Local Teacher Named In Lawsuit"

Two days later the entire school was talking about the school paper. The article was about one of the new teachers in the school this year. Miss Teahan Solano had been named as a defendant in a lawsuit brought by some of the parents. She had been accused of working in a strip club in another state. Due to some detective work by Annie O'Dell and Cindy Mackens it had been discovered that Miss Solano did indeed work at the club—as an undercover operative for the FBI at the time. She did not work as a stripper, but rather as a cocktail waitress. The lawsuit was dropped and Miss Solano's reputation was secure. Unfortunately, her cover had been blown. She left without a word to her students. Mrs. Hart, along with the entire newspaper staff, was called into Principal O'Dell's office. They were reprimanded, but no further discipline was levied against them.

That afternoon there was more excitement at Roosevelt High. It involved Todd Delaney and even Annie O'Dell in a way.

"Todd Delaney!" Mr. Kemmerick shouted.

"Yes, Mr. Kemmerick. What can I do for you?"

"You can stop right there."

"Why? What's going on?" Todd asked as he shrugged.

"I believe you know. Now set your backpack down. It will go easier if you co-operate with us," Mr. Kemmerick said.

"Yeah, sure!"

Todd set his pack on the floor and took off running down the hall. Mr. Kemmerick shook his head at Principal O'Dell.

"Let's take that to your office, Dan. We can see for ourselves and hold the pack in the safe. I'll call his father and see if they will come in and talk."

After school that afternoon, Todd Delaney, his parents, along with their attorney, were in Principal O'Dell's office. They were discussing the copy of the trigonometry test Todd had in his possession.

"I swear I didn't know it was there. It was planted. Annie O'Dell put it there just to get me in trouble."

"Is that the story you're sticking with, Todd? Perhaps you should see this video first."

Mr. Kemmerick played a video which clearly showed Todd Delaney searching through Mr. Kennedy's desk.

"Would you like to explain this?"

"I was looking for a book Mr. Kennedy needed."

"Dan, would you call Mr. Kennedy in now. I believe he can settle this for us."

Todd slumped in his chair and waved his hand. "Don't bother. I stole the damn test." Todd looked at his father and then the attorney. "Lot of good you did. How much did you pay this shyster for coming here, Dad? He sure was worth it."

After some negotiation between Principal O'Dell, Mr. Delaney and the attorney, Todd was suspended for one week and he would be on probation when he returned.

Principal O'Dell talked to Mr. Kennedy later that day in his office. "How did you know he was going to steal the test, Jim?"

"Todd was bragging to his friends and Annie overheard him. She came to me. She offered to stakeout my room. She sounded excited about being a 'real' detective. I convinced her otherwise. I didn't want her to be involved in this at all. I set up the camera and just waited. It was easy. I wiped my desk down so only Todd's prints would show if it came down to that."

"Well, unfortunately, I don't think this will be the last of our troubles with young Delaney."

"I suspect you are right about that, Mr. O'Dell."

Principal O'Dell took a deep breath. "I'm going to have to talk to Annie. Her sleuthing is becoming more serious and it needs to stop."

Chapter Nine

Although Halloween was on Thursday, Elaine and Cindy decided to wait and have a small party on Friday. Friday worked better for everyone since the football game was scheduled for Saturday afternoon. Annie was bringing a very special "date" to the party—Keyshon Franklin.

Annie had been over at Mace's house in the dining room studying and they talked about the party. Keyshon overheard their conversation as he looked through the fridge for something to eat. When he heard about the party, he walked into the dining room and asked Mace and Annie, "Can I go to the party with you? I can wear my Batman costume. Please, can I go?"

Annie looked at Mace and answered, "We have to ask your mother, but if she agrees then you can go with me. We will go to the party together. Would you like that?"

"Yes, will it be like a real date, Annie? Will you talk to me?"

"Yes, I will talk to you and it will be like a real date except that you can't kiss me."

"I don't want to kiss you. I just want to have fun. Will there be games at the party?"

"I'm not sure, Keyshon, but there will be music. We can dance together."

"I've never danced with anyone before. I just dance by myself. I better start practicing right away."

Keyshon raced upstairs and a few minutes later Annie heard him playing some music. She looked at Mace and smiled as she moved her head in time with the music.

Mace closed his Algebra II book and asked, "What? You really want to take Keyshon?"

Annie nodded. "Let's ask your mom if it's okay."

At that moment Mrs. Franklin walked into the room. She set her purse and keys on the china cabinet. "Hi, guys. What did you need to ask about?"

"Hi, Mom. There's a Halloween party at Lainey's house Friday night and Keyshon wants to go," Mace answered.

"You don't have to take him with you. I'll be home Friday night. I'm taking him trick-or-treating on Thursday."

Annie told her, "We want to take Keyshon with us. I do, I mean. He sounded so excited when he heard about it. I told him we could dance together and he ran upstairs to practice. Please, can he go with us?"

Mrs. Franklin walked over, stood behind Annie and said, "You know he can be a handful at times. He's twelve now and not as easy to handle as before."

"He's always good for me," Annie said.

Mrs. Franklin thought about it for a moment. "Of course, he can go with you. That is so sweet of you, Annie."

"I'll make sure he has fun and all the other kids really like him. I bet all the girls will want to dance with him."

"You will need to have him home by ten. He will need time to settle down, or else he won't get any sleep."

"We can do that, Mom. I'll run him home and then go back to the party. Annie and I are gonna party all night long." Mace showed his mother a new dance move as Annie watched.

Annie shook her head. "Maybe I'll bring them both back by ten, Mrs. Franklin. He can be such a doofus at times."

"I know you're not talking about me, girl," Mace said as he froze into position like a robot.

On Friday Keyshon acted surprisingly calm as he got ready for the party. Mace wondered if he felt all right.

"Are you okay, little bro? I thought you would be more excited."

"I'm all right, but I am a little nervous about the dancing."

"I'm sure you will do okay. I've seen you dancing before."

Keyshon shook his head. "That's not it. I'm worried about Annie. What if she doesn't know how to dance? What should I do?"

Mace rubbed his jaw. "That's a good point, but I've seen her dance and while she may not be as smooth as you, she will do all right."

"That's a relief," Keyshon said as he wiped his forehead.

"I'll let you dance with Annie, too, but just once."

"Thanks, Keyshon. I appreciate that."

The guys got ready and drove over to pick up Annie. She saw the car pull in the driveway and was ready to go.

"I'm leaving now, Daddy. I'll see you later."

He looked up from his newspaper. "Hang on a second, Annie."

"What? Mace and Keyshon are here. I need to go," Annie said as she looked out the front window.

"I thought this was a Halloween party. Aren't you supposed to wear a costume?" Mr. O'Dell asked with a straight face.

"Very funny!" Annie answered. She was dressed as a black cat and even had a tail. "I decided just to wear my normal outfit for tonight."

"Be careful and don't let any of the guys pull on your tail."

"Oh, Daddy!"

"Bring me home some candy. My sweet tooth is acting up."

Annie ran out the door. Keyshon got out of the car and ran up the sidewalk to meet her.

"Hi, Annie, do you like my costume?" Keyshon asked.

"You look just like the real Batman. Are you ready to have some fun tonight?"

"Yeah, but I'm worried about the dancing. I might have to dance with all the girls because I am so smooth and such a good dancer."

"That's okay as long as you dance with me more than anyone else." Annie smiled at Keyshon and they got into the car.

"Where's your costume, Mace? You told me you were going to wear something."

"I am in costume," he insisted.

"Bull! You're wearing jeans and a Michael Jordan jersey. That's not a real costume."

"It's all I could think of."

"You are so lame. Is Trish going to meet you there or do we have to pick her up?" Annie asked.

"Lainey was picking her up, but I will give her a ride home."

They arrived at the Novicki home and rang the front doorbell. Elaine answered the door, looked at Mace and shook her head. "I guess we know who will win the best costume award," she said sarcastically as she shook her broom and scratched at the green makeup on her face.

"I'm Batman!" Keyshon told her enthusiastically. "And I'm going to dance with Annie. I'll dance with you, too, Lainey, but only once."

"I would love to dance with you. Don't forget to ask me later."

Keyshon held onto Annie's hand until he relaxed and got comfortable. He was shy around new people and there were some people at the party he didn't know.

"Who is that in that spaceman costume?" Keyshon pointed and asked.

Annie turned to see who Keyshon meant and laughed. "That's Barry Newton and I think he's supposed to be a computer."

Keyshon heard music playing and saw a few kids dancing in the family room. He looked at Annie and asked, "Would you like to dance with me?"

"I'd love to dance with you, Keyshon."

Keyshon took her hand and led to her to a spot in the middle of the room. He started dancing and soon had the attention of everyone in the room.

"Hey, Mace, Keyshon is a better dancer than you," Randy Braun teased.

"Yeah, just wait till I get loosened up. I'll show you some moves," Mace answered as she danced with Trish Eiffert.

Keyshon danced with as many girls as he could. When it came time to award the prize for best costume, Keyshon was the unanimous winner.

Just before ten Mace and Annie took Keyshon home. He got out of the car and ran inside.

"Mom! Mom! I won first place. I had the best costume and I won a prize! I got to dance with Annie and Lainey and a couple other girls. It was fun, but I'm tired." Keyshon talked as fast as he could until he ran out of breath.

47

"I'm so happy for you, Keyshon. Show me your prize?"

Keyshon held up his prize. It was a video of the movie *Batman Forever*. Mom immediately realized the costume contest was rigged, but she didn't let Keyshon know. She smiled at Mace and Annie.

"We're going to go back to the party, Keyshon. I had fun dancing with you. You've got some smooth moves," Annie said as she twisted her hips.

""You're not too bad yourself, Annie. Not as good as me though," Keyshon teased her.

Mace and Annie headed back to the party. By the time they got there, most of the kids were gone.

Annie told Elaine and Cindy, "Thanks for letting Keyshon win the prize. He was so excited."

They both shrugged and Elaine said, "We didn't say anything to anyone about letting Keyshon win the prize."

"Really? I thought because of the Batman video you guys rigged it."

"We didn't have to. Everyone loves Keyshon and he did have a great costume."

"But what about the video?"

Elaine smiled and said, "I bought it to give to my dad for his birthday. I don't think he'll mind that I gave it to Keyshon."

"That was so sweet of you, Lainey."

Chapter Ten

On November sixteenth the football season ended on a sad note as the Roosevelt Rough Riders were defeated by Winnetka North in the playoff semi-finals at the packed SoHam Memorial stadium. The game was close, but a costly turnover near the end decided the game. After the game there was a party at the Madison home. Victoria's parents were gone for the weekend, and she had been allowed to have a small party with a few friends. Word had gotten around about the party and soon the Madison house was overrun by rowdy teenagers.

"What am I gonna do, you guys? The house will be destroyed!" Victoria shouted to be heard above the noise, as she walked around with two guys from school.

"Kinda late now, Vicky. You should have known better than to print posters with the address and date," one of the guys said as he spilled some beer on the carpet.

The other guy added, "Don't worry, I'm sure your parents will understand. Besides, the cops will be here soon. I'm sure the neighbors will complain. Oh! I forgot. Your neighbors moved out."

"Lot of help you guys are!"

Elaine, Cindy, Annie, Mace and Trish were at the party. Elaine and Cindy were drinking pop, but Mace and Annie had a plastic cup of beer. Matt Sullivan was there with a bunch of friends. They tried to keep the party from being totally out of control. When the beer ran out, so did most of the kids. They literally ran out the door. Victoria cried as she surveyed the damage.

"See, Victoria. It's not too bad. I hope you've got lots of garbage bags," Matt said as he shook his head.

"My parents will kill me and never let me have another party," Victoria whined.

"If you're dead, you can't have a party anyway," Mace teased.

"Come on, Mace. Help us clean up," Elaine told him after she smacked his arm.

"Annie, does your father know where you are?"

"Kinda," she said with a shrug.

"What is that supposed to mean?" Mace asked.

"He thinks I'm staying overnight with Lainey, and that's the truth. I will stay at Lainey's tonight—just a little later than Dad knows though."

Mace shook a finger at her. "Girl, you better be careful. Remember, he's a detective."

"You're not gonna tell him, are you?"

"Your secret is safe with me. All your secrets are safe with me," Mace teased.

"Will you guys stop yappin' and start helpin', okay?" Victoria shouted as she stood watching everyone else working.

It took some time and hard work, but finally the house was back to normal. Everyone had left but Matt, Elaine, Cindy and Annie. Trish and Mace left just a few minutes before. The girls were about to leave when Annie realized something.

"Matt, are you spending the night here?"

"Yeah, Victoria asked me to stay. Why?"

"No reason. I'm just surprised. Have a good time."

Matt put his hands on Annie's shoulders and asked, "You're not jealous, are you?"

She looked up at him. "Yes, I am. I wanted to spend the night with Victoria and now my plans are destroyed."

"You can stay with us. There's room in her bed," Matt teased.

"Maybe in another lifetime, Matthew Sullivan."

Elaine tugged on Annie's arm. "Come on, Annie, we're leaving."

"Last chance to stay, Annie." Matt smiled as he teased her.

Annie shook her head and turned to leave with Elaine and Cindy. In Elaine's car they talked about Victoria and Matt.

"Can you believe Victoria is letting Matt Sullivan stay with her," Cindy said.

"Why not? He's okay," Annie mentioned from the back seat of Elaine's 1995 green Ford Contour.

Cindy turned in her seat to look at Annie. "How can you say that? Would you let Matt spend the night with you?"

"Sure, Daddy would let me... when I'm a hundred years old, maybe."

"Do you think this is the first time he has... you know?" Cindy asked Elaine.

"What's the matter, Cin?" Annie asked as she laughed. "Can't you even say the word?"

"I don't hear you saying it, Annie Mercer O'Dell!" Cindy exclaimed.

"Okay, she's a slut. Last year she was going out with Trevor Branwell and I heard rumors that she..."

"Don't be spreading rumors, Annie. Either you know it for a fact, or don't say anything," Elaine said.

"Well, I didn't take pictures," Annie replied.

They got to Elaine's house and Cindy looked to see if there were any lights on across the street at her house.

"It doesn't look like anyone's still up. Do you mind if I crash with you tonight, Lainey?"

"I don't mind. We can crash in the basement. Someone can have the couch and I'll get the air mattress out."

"Flip you for the couch, Cindy."

"You can have it, Annie. The air mattress is more comfortable anyway."

They tried to be quiet and not wake up Mr. or Mrs. Novicki. They fell asleep around three and slept till noon.

Elaine took Annie home, and Annie walked in the house. She found a note on her bedroom door.

Room for Rent... Cheap
Room abandoned by previous tenant
Call 915-555-6566

Annie knew she was in trouble unless she called her father. She wondered how much he knew about last night. She decided not to give anything away and deny everything as long as possible.

"Hi, Daddy. I guess you wanted me to call, huh?"

"Who is this? Is this the former tenant of the room across

51

the hall from me?"

"You know I was with Lainey and Cindy."

"You're gonna make me interrogate you, huh? Okay. What time did you get to Lainey's house?"

"I didn't look at my watch, so I don't know."

"Was it before or after midnight?"

"I was at Lainey's before midnight."

This was technically correct since her father dropped Annie off at the Novicki house before the game.

"I mean after the game. What time did you get there after the game was over?"

"I can't tell you that."

"Please judge, instruct the defendant to answer the question," Detective O'Dell said.

"Daddy, it was late, but I'm all right. Isn't that what's important?"

"You know I worry about you, sweetie. I'm glad you're okay. How many glasses of beer did you drink?"

"No, no, no!" Annie shook a finger even though she was talking on the phone. "You can't get me on a question like that. You're fishing and I refuse to bite."

"You are slick, honey. Are you gonna be home tonight?"

"Yeah, I've got homework to finish. What do you want for dinner? Not meat loaf, okay."

"Let's get a pizza. We can have some quality father-daughter time together. You order the pizza, and I'll bring home something to drink. What kind of beer do you like?"

Annie smiled at her father's attempt to trick her. "Let me think for a moment."

Her father heard some key strikes on her computer.

"I would like either some Murphy's Irish Red or Murphy's Irish Stout or maybe some Smithwick's, but if you can't find any of those favorites, good old Guinness Dry Stout will work."

"You're using your computer to look these up, right? I can hear you typing."

"I'm on the computer, but just to do my homework. I really like all those beers."

"You win. What kind of pop do you want?"

"We've got pop in the house. Get what you want to drink. I'll have a sip of yours to remind myself how awful beer tastes."

"I should lock you up in your closet until you're forty."

She laughed. "I'm pretty sure that's illegal."

"Okay, I'll release you at thirty. Consider it time off for good behavior."

"Can I get a bunch of tattoos while I'm incarcerated in the big house. I want a picture of a squad car on my chest, the names of all my lovers on my butt and…"

"I'll be home around six. Bye, honey. I love you."

"Love you, too, Daddy. See you later."

Detective Keith O'Dell was running a few minutes late, but he finally arrived home with a pizza, breadsticks and a six pack of Samuel Adams. He set everything on the island in the kitchen.

"I'm home, Annie! Where are you?"

"In my room. I just got out of the shower." Her bedroom door was open.

"Are you decent? Can I come in?"

"Give me one second." She tossed away her towel, put on a t-shirt and shorts, and came running out to the kitchen.

"How was your day, Detective O'Dell?"

"Well, it was like this see." He tried his James Cagney impression on her for the hundredth time.

Annie rolled her eyes.

"I busted the bad guys, see. And then I wiped out another bunch of bad guys, see, and I met this dame... Not working for you?"

"Not a big fan of John Wayne."

"It wasn't John Wayne. It was Cagney."

Annie gave him a blank stare as if she had never heard of James Cagney.

"Never mind! I got pizza and breadsticks. Some beer for me."

"I made a salad, too. Need something healthy to eat. I'm just a growing child, remember?"

"I need to change. Be right out. Pick out a movie and we'll

eat in front of the TV."

"Can we watch *Lassie Come Home* again? Please, oh, please! It's my favorite of all time." Annie clapped her hands and bounced up and down on her toes.

"Whatever you want, honey."

Annie glared in the direction of his room. She knew he wasn't listening.

"Daddy, I met this junkie in an alley this afternoon and he got me hooked on heroin. We're going to run away together and have babies."

"That's fine, sweetie. I'll be right out." He came back to the kitchen a few minutes later.

"Did you even hear a word I said?"

"Yes, Annie. You want to watch *Lassie Come Home* and you and your junkie friend are running away to have a baby. Was there something else that I missed? You didn't rob another bank today, did you? You know I hate it when you rob banks in broad daylight." He kissed Annie on her forehead. "Let's eat!"

They took the food out to the living room. Annie picked out a new movie to watch called *True Crime*. They ate as they watched it. Annie found it interesting because it was about a high school girl who did some sleuthing. Dad watched but was tired and sleepy, especially after a couple beers. He was drinking his third beer and set it on the coffee table. A moment later Annie absentmindedly reached for it and took a long drink. She set it back on the table and then looked at her father. He was frowning at her.

She realized she was busted and smiled innocently. "Oops! Am I busted for underage drinking, officer?"

"Yes! Annie, I know you have occasionally helped yourself to one of my beers but..."

"I plead guilty, judge, and throw myself on the mercy of the court. As this was the first offense I have ever committed please consider this in your sentencing.

He shook his head and sighed. "Fine. Your sentence is to make dinner all next week. Whatever I want."

"Fine, your honor. Since I'm already busted, can I..."

54

"Just finish that one. No more and it will be our secret."

"Yes, Daddy. I will try to make sure I attend my AA meeting this week."

They finished that movie and Annie popped in another one. She snuggled close to Dad and he put an arm around her shoulder. Soon she could hear him snoring. She slipped out from under his arm and stood up. She lifted his feet onto the couch. She found a blanket in the closet and brought him a pillow from his bed. Annie tucked him in and kissed his forehead.

"Night, Daddy. I love you," she whispered softly.

Annie put the leftover food in the fridge and made sure the house was locked and secured before she went to her room. She finished her homework and crawled under the covers. She read until she could barely keep her eyes open.

In the middle of the night, Dad woke up and after a moment, noticed the pillow and blanket and smiled. He got up from the couch and bumped into the coffee table. He swore under his breath as he rubbed his shin. He headed to his room, but first looked in Annie's room to check on her. She was sound asleep with a book in her hands and the light still on. He slipped in quietly, took the book, set it on her dresser and looked at her for a moment.

"You are looking more like your mother every year," he whispered. He turned off the light and went to his room. He looked at two pictures on the nightstand next to his bed. One was of his late wife, Amy Catherine. The other was the last picture ever taken of them all together as a family.

Chapter Eleven

"Why are you so excited today?" Annie asked as she and Mace walked into the school.

"In case you've forgotten, basketball season starts today," he said as he bounced his basketball off the wall beside the doors.

"Big deal," Annie teased. "Are you guys going to be any good this year, or will the team suck?"

"We're gonna be amazing. We should win the conference and probably the national championship."

Annie slipped inside just before the door closed and asked, "Do they even have a national championship?"

"No, but we'd win it if they did," Mace proclaimed.

Mace stood six-two in his bare feet and had cat-like quickness on the court. He had been the starting point guard for the last two years. He had also led the team in scoring those years.

"Do you have a chance to make the team?" Annie teased. "I heard there were some new guys trying out."

"I'm reasonably certain I'll make the team."

"Okay, I know you'll make the team."

"Thanks for the vote of confidence," Mace said as he high-fived Marcus Bell, one of the other basketball players.

"I know you're counting on getting that scholarship to North Park," Annie said.

"If I don't get it, I'll end up at Paul Frank Junior College. I've gotta stay in SoHam to help take care of Keyshon."

Roosevelt High had never been a basketball powerhouse like they were in football, but they had had decent teams. In 1987 they finished third in the class AA tournament. The guys in the starting lineup this year were all seniors. They had two guys six-six and the other two guys were nearly as big. They had been playing together since junior high.

The first five games of the season were easy wins by the Rough Riders. The real test was the game against perennial powerhouse Mannheim Catholic. Mannheim was a large private school in Chicago's south suburb of Hickory Glen. The two teams played once a year and this year's game was at Roosevelt. Mace's friends were in the stands to watch the game.

"Lainey, look at Victoria! She's flirting with those two older guys. They're probably in college." Cindy pointed even though Elaine could easily see Victoria.

"What difference does it make, Cindy? She flirts with every cute guy she sees."

"Then she shouldn't be a cheerleader. Cheerleaders are supposed to represent the school. They shouldn't be shameless flirts who sleep around," Cindy said.

Elaine and Cindy kept talking about Victoria until they saw Randy Braun and Kyle Norris walking toward them.

"Hey, guys! We're up here. We saved some seats," Cindy hollered at their dates and waved. Randy and Kyle joined them and kissed the girls.

"About time you got here. Where have you been?" Cindy asked.

"We had to stop for gas and it took forever to find a parking space. I wish they would hurry up and get rid of that old bus garage. We need more parking spaces. Does your mother know we are bringing you and Cindy home?" Randy asked."

"I told her," Elaine said.

A large cheer erupted from the student section as the Rough Riders sprinted out of the locker room. Mace led them as they began their warm-up routine. Mace looked up at the section where his friends usually sat and waved at them.

"Hey look, Lainey! There's Damon and Diana. Wow! I wish we had his money. Even a tiny part of it would be nice." Cindy sighed and seemed envious. "Doesn't Diana look fabulous? She has such nice clothes."

Randy and Kyle looked at Diana and then back at the girls.

"She's wearing jeans. What's the big deal?" Randy asked.

"Yeah, but those jeans probably set her back a hundred bucks."

"Who'd ever pay that much for jeans? By the way, where is Annie O'Dell?" Randy asked. "Isn't she usually with you guys?"

"She said her father was dropping her off, but she would

need a ride home," Elaine answered. "You have room, right?"

"Maybe," Randy said.

"Lainey, look!" Cindy poked Elaine's side.

"What? And stop hitting me. It hurts," Elaine said.

"Annie just walked in and isn't that... She's talking to Matt Sullivan! What's up with that?"

"I don't know," Elaine said as she shrugged and stared at Annie and Matt. "It is rather curious though."

"You don't think Matt gave her a ride here, do you?" Cindy asked as she kept watching Annie and Matt.

"No way! Her father would kill her."

Annie and Matt were talking about his family. They just happened to meet by the ticket booth and walked into the gym together.

"I gotta go find my friends, Matty. I hope your father feels better."

"Yeah, thanks, Annie. He'll be okay. I'll talk to you sometime," Matt said and then watched as Annie walked away. "I should talk to you more often, Annie O'Dell," he whispered. "Those are nice jeans."

Annie glanced over her shoulder and caught Matt staring at her. She grinned and then headed over to the section where she and her friends usually sat. She scampered up the bleachers and squeezed in between Elaine and Cindy. "Hey, guys! Thanks for saving my seat? Looks like a full house tonight, huh?"

"Did we need to save one for Matt?" Cindy asked as she stood up.

"Matt? No, why would we need a seat for Matty?" Annie shrugged.

"You tell us," Cindy said with her hands on her hips.

Annie looked back and forth between Cindy and Elaine. "Stop acting like that, you guys. I was only talking to him. We ran into each other and I asked about his father."

"What's wrong with his father?" Randy asked. "I saw him last week at The Hungry Lion."

"He was having chest pains and had to go to the emergency room last night."

"How do you know that?" Elaine asked.

"Lainey, do you really have to ask? I have my methods," Annie said as she watched where Matt chose to sit.

The game began and the Rough Riders controlled the opening tip. Mace controlled the offense and hit Marcus Bell in the lane for an easy shot. With a taller lineup than Mannheim, the Rough Riders dominated the boards and their aggressive defense forced several turnovers. The first quarter ended with Roosevelt up by nine points. Mannheim made some adjustments and staged a comeback in the second quarter. The Rough Riders were only up by two at the half. They ran to the locker room, sat by their lockers and waited for Coach Powell to join them.

"Mace, you need to move the ball better. Make quick passes to get their zone moving, then hit the seams..."

Coach Jeffrey Powell used the halftime to make small adjustments in the offense and exhorted his team to keep up the pressure on defense. As the second half got under way, Mace hit a couple of jumpers and the Rough Riders began to pull away. The final score was 59-49 in favor of Roosevelt. Mace had fifteen points and ten assists. His defensive pressure on the Mannheim guards resulted in over twenty turnovers.

Annie mentioned to her friends after the game, "You realize Mace is going to have trouble."

"Why? What kind of trouble?" Elaine asked.

"His head won't fit through the classroom doors."

"Oh, you're right, Annie. What are we going to do?" Elaine asked.

"Maybe we could deflate his ego a little," Annie said as she spotted Matt Sullivan talking to one of the cheerleaders. And it wasn't Victoria Madison.

"What are you plotting, Annie Mercer?"

Annie told Elaine and Cindy her plan. They were all going to the dance and Mace would be there as soon as he could. Annie told Trish her plan, and Trish was eager to participate.

Mace and his teammates finally joined the dance. They got some applause from the crowd. Mace saw Trish sitting with Cindy and hurried over to see her.

"Well, what did you think of the game? Told you we were going to win." Mace tried to kiss her, but she turned away. "Hey! I took a shower. Why the cold shoulder?"

"Do you realize you shot only thirty-nine percent from the floor and you guys missed six free throws. Your turnover-to-assist ratio was way too low. How do you expect to keep winning if you keep up this kind of performance."

Mace's jaw dropped. Trish had never talked about statistics before. Suddenly it dawned on him. "Fine! I get it. Where is Annie? She's the only one who could get these stats. Did she steal them from The Geek, I mean Lendall?"

Mace was talking about Lendall Greenwood the team statistician and resident school computer geek. After the game Annie had made her way to Lendall and used her charms to get a copy of the stats. She knew Lendall was shy around girls and had flirted with him shamelessly.

"Did I steal what from Lendall?" Annie asked as she returned from dancing with one of the guys from her English class. "Don't bother dancing with Grady," she said to Cindy. "He stepped on my feet more times than I can remember."

"Annie O'Dell! I know what you were trying to do, girl. Yeah, I'm ecstatic that we won tonight, but I know it's a long way till the end of the season. I promise I will keep my ego in check." Mace waved to a group of students. "It won't be easy, but I'll try."

Annie smacked his arm. "I'm going to break your head."

Just then a group of five younger girls came over to talk to Mace.

"I must go dance with my fan club. I'll be back after I sign autographs for everyone." He winked at Annie and rushed off to dance.

Annie sat and watched as Elaine and Cindy danced with their boyfriends. She noticed Damon Barclay and Diana Ahronson dancing together. Mace rejoined Trish on the dance floor. Annie was daydreaming—lost in her own little world until someone sat next to her.

"Why is the prettiest girl in school not dancing?"

"Oh, but she is. Right out there with Damon Barclay."

Annie pointed at them. "What do you want, Matty?"

"Would you dance with me, Annie?"

"Why aren't you dancing with Victoria? You two have been the most talked about couple in school since that night you slept with her after the party."

"Yeah, I did spend the night with her, but we aren't really a couple."

"Are you going to tell me nothing happened? Don't use that lame excuse that you're just friends. I've heard that bull before."

"I'm not going to lie to you, Annie, but you know how she is. She flirts with every guy she sees."

"Flirting is different than what you and Victoria did. I flirted with The Geek tonight because I needed something from him. Doesn't mean I'm going to sleep with him. At least not tonight. Can't guarantee anything past that, though."

Matt could tell Annie was upset that he slept with Victoria Madison.

"Christ, Annie! All I did was ask you for a dance. I'm not making a move on you," Matt said but didn't move away from Annie.

"Fine! I'll dance with you."

Matt and Annie danced together for the rest of the night. They talked and were having a good time. Matt could be very funny at times and Annie giggled like a young schoolgirl. The last dance of the night was a slow song. Annie looked at Matt warily.

"I'll behave, Annie. I won't hold you too close."

"I'm not afraid of you, Matthew Sullivan. Remember, I went out with you once."

"Yeah, but maybe you didn't notice the two plainclothes cops who were following us all night," Matt said.

Annie took a step back. "What are you talking about?"

"Your father had us staked out or whatever you guys call it. We were never alone the whole night."

"I don't believe you and it doesn't matter anyway."

"Can we just dance?"

"Fine."

Matt took Annie in his arms and they danced slowly as the

music played softly. Annie rested her head on Matt's chest as they danced. She felt safe in his arms for some reason. Matt leaned close and could smell the scent of her shampoo. It reminded him of strawberries.

"I need to find Lainey. She and Randy are giving me a ride home," Annie said after the song ended.

"If you can't find her, I'll give you a ride," Matt offered. "I don't mind and I've got a car tonight."

"Thanks, but she's over there with Cindy. I had a good time, Matty, even without any plainclothes cops around to protect me from you," Annie teased Matt and then ran over to join Elaine and Cindy.

"Are you ready to go, Annie, or is Matt taking you home?" Elaine asked. "He's watching us, or at least watching you."

"I'm not going home with him. We just danced a little. That's all. Don't make a big deal out of it."

"We're just concerned, Annie," Cindy said.

"I know, but you don't have to worry about me, or Matt, either. He's not as mean, or as bad, as everyone thinks. He's really kinda nice, and he's smarter than people give him credit for, too."

"Okay, Annie. You don't have to defend him so much. He may not be mean to you, or the girls he's interested in getting to know better."

"I know what you're getting at, Lainey, but it's not going to happen. Trust me!" Annie said with a little too much conviction.

Chapter Twelve

"What are you thinking?" Elaine asked as she and Randy Braun ate lunch in the cafeteria.

"I was trying to remember when I met you," he answered.

"Seventh grade. We went to different grade schools before that."

"That's right," he said and then grinned. "We were pretty competitive in junior high."

"What do you mean?" she asked as she opened a container of apple slices.

"We were the smartest kids in our class, and we tried to outdo each other for the best grades," Randy said as he touched Elaine's shoulder length brown hair and looked into her brown eyes.

"I was smarter than you," she said as she looked at his chin. "Did you shave this morning?"

"I wish," he said. "I might not ever have to shave. Just the way it goes. Where are your glasses?"

"I'm wearing my contacts today," she said.

They finished eating and Randy took care of their trays. He turned around and smiled as he saw several guys looking at Elaine.

Annie touched his arm and said, "Are you jealous that other guys think Lainey is pretty and kinda hot?"

"I'm not jealous. Lainey and I have been dating for a year and a half."

"Is it getting serious now? It wasn't in the beginning."

"Have you been talking to Lainey about stuff?" he asked.

"She mentioned it took six months before you ever kissed her, but now you're getting more aggressive. You're not pressuring her to do more than kiss, are you?" Annie asked as she looked up at him.

"I'm not telling you, Annie," he said as he frowned.

"That's all right. I know what guys are after, and you better be careful, Randy Braun."

"You better be careful, too. I saw you dancing with Matt Sullivan."

Annie blushed and then said, "We're not dating. You guys are."

They walked back toward the table and saw that Cindy had joined Elaine. Cindy Mackens was blonde with short-cut, layered hair. She had gray eyes. She was an inch shorter than Elaine and more slightly built. Most guys in school considered her prettier than Elaine.

Randy stopped walking, touched Annie's arm and asked, "Has Cindy ever had a real boyfriend?"

Annie laughed and then said, "No, she likes pretend guys better."

"You know what I meant," Randy said. "Has she?"

"No serious boyfriend. She's gone out with several guys. Why are you asking?"

"I heard she was seeing Adam Wozniak, and was wondering if she knew about his vices."

"What vices?" Annie asked as she led Randy in the opposite direction. "What have you heard? Tell me or else I'll change your grades."

"I haven't seen this personally, but I've heard from a few people that he likes to drink and has smoked pot a few times."

Annie looked at Randy and then at the table where Elaine and Cindy sat. "Don't say anything to Lainey or Cindy until I've had a chance to check this out."

He nodded and they rejoined their friends.

Bert Hodges' parents were away for the weekend, so on Saturday night he had invited a few couples over. Unlike Victoria, he had managed to keep his party private. Bert's part-time girlfriend, Dawn Matuzak, joined him. Bert only used Dawn as a last resort if he didn't have a date with anyone else. She would drop anything, or anyone, to please Bert.

Randy borrowed the family car for the night and picked up Elaine and Cindy. Adam lived down the street from Bert and walked to the party. Victoria Madison brought Todd Delaney with her. Bert's older brother was supposed to stay home, but as soon as his parents left, he took off to see his girlfriend. He wouldn't return until Sunday evening. Bert ordered some pizzas, and his brother bought the beer for the party earlier that day. The couples hung out in the family room and talked. No one drank too much, except maybe Todd and Dawn. Randy still resisted all efforts by the guys to have a beer.

"Come on, Randy! You can have a beer. One beer won't kill you," Todd insisted.

"No, thanks, I can do without the beer," Randy said.

"What a wimp!" The guys at the party were really getting after Randy.

Elaine rose to his defense. "Lighten up on him. I admire him taking a stand. All you guys drink because you think it makes you cool. Well, it doesn't."

The guys quit pressuring him and Randy resisted the temptation to drink. All of the other kids had some beer—even Elaine and Cindy. Todd started kissing Victoria while they were sitting together in a recliner. Soon they were making out.

Bert told Todd, "Go upstairs if you are going to keep that up."

"Which room should we use?"

"Stay out of my parents room. You know which one is theirs and stay out of my room, too. I'll be needing it soon."

Todd and Victoria headed upstairs. After a few more minutes, other couples had found places to have some privacy. Some of the couples left to go home. Elaine and Cindy found themselves with only Randy, Adam and Bert and Dawn in the family room.

"We're going upstairs now. You guys can stay as long as you want. I know Adam was planning to spend the night, Cindy. You're welcome to stay, too," Bert smirked as he led Dawn upstairs to his room.

"Cindy, what do you say about going downstairs to play some pool?" Adam asked.

"I'll play pool with you, but I'm not going to drink any more beer," Cindy told him.

Elaine and Randy were now alone in the family room. They moved to a couch in the corner of the large room and Randy kissed

Elaine. She kissed him back, and soon they were kissing passionately and he used all eight hands it seemed to Elaine. Somehow he managed to convince her to lay on her back. He moved next to her and kissed her while sliding a hand up her belly. They were still kissing when Randy slipped a hand under her top. Elaine didn't stop him until his hand was on her bra.

"Stop it, Randy! You know I won't let you do that."

"Come on, Lainey! We've been together for long enough. You can trust me not to go too far."

"You're already going too far! Stop it." Elaine shoved Randy off the couch and onto the floor.

"Ow! I hit my head."

Elaine looked over the edge of the couch. "Are you all right, Randy? I didn't mean to hurt you."

"I'm all right." He pulled her on top of him. They kissed and Elaine didn't object when Randy placed his hands on her hips.

Cindy and Adam were having fun in the basement. They were playing pool and not even kissing. Cindy won a game and they stopped for a moment. Adam moved close to Cindy and lifted her up to sit on the pool table. They had been talking for a minute when Adam kissed her. She didn't mind because he didn't try to do anything else. She kissed him back and he put his hands on her sides. She put her hands on his shoulders and they kissed again. This time Adam touched her more intimately and Cindy pushed him away.

"Stop that, Adam! I'm not going to let you do that."

"Come on, Cindy. I won't hurt you or try anything more."

"You've already tried too much. Now move back and let me go before I smack you."

"All right already!" Adam raised his hands in the air. "Geez, you'd think no one has ever tried that before."

"No one has gotten away with it yet. A couple of guys have tried."

Cindy jumped down from the table and ran upstairs.

Adam stayed downstairs and grabbed another beer from the fridge. "Geez! What a prude. All I did was touch her. I hadn't even tried to undo her top yet. Maybe I should have used my tongue when I kissed her."

Elaine and Randy were still on the floor, but now Elaine was on her back as Randy straddled her. Randy had his hands on her jeans in front and was trying to unsnap them.

"Randy, what on earth do you think you're doing?" Elaine asked rather calmly as she struggled to keep her emotions under control.

"I want to make love to you, Lainey. I want you to show me that you love me."

"Have you been drinking?" Elaine asked. "You've never acted this way before."

He shook his head. "I haven't touched a drop of alcohol, but I really want you to show me how much you love me." He leaned forward to try and kiss her again. "Show me, Lainey."

She pushed him away. "No, I can't do that!"

"Don't you love me, Lainey?" he pleaded.

"No, I don't, Randy! I like you and I like going out with you, but I'm not giving myself to you." Elaine pushed him again. "Get off of me this instant!"

Just then Cindy arrived; out of breath from running away from Adam. She had mistakenly thought he was following her. She saw Randy and Elaine and heard what Randy was asking Elaine to do. She picked up a book and held it above Randy. "Randy, get off of Lainey before I club you. I mean it."

Randy looked over his shoulder and put up his arm to protect himself. "Cindy, stay out of this. This is between Lainey and myself."

"I will not stay out of it. You get off of her right now before I hit you."

Randy stopped what he was doing and got up. He moved away from Elaine and Cindy, sat in one of the chairs and began to weep silently.

Cindy knelt next to her friend. "Are you okay, Lainey? Did he hurt you?"

"I'm all right, Cin. He didn't do anything. He was trying, but I wasn't cooperating." She looked around the room. "Where is Adam?"

"Downstairs, I guess. He tried to kiss me and I threatened to hurt him," Cindy said.

Randy sat in the chair dejectedly. He wiped his eyes and blew his nose. "I'm sorry, Lainey. I shouldn't have done that. I don't know what came over me."

Cindy helped Elaine up and they sat on the couch and stared at Randy.

"I'm really sorry, Lainey. I won't try anything like that again."

"Will you take us home, Randy, or do I need to call Mace or Annie or someone?" Elaine asked.

"You don't have to do that. I'll take you home." He stood up and looked for his coat. "I'm really sorry, Lainey."

"You better be, you creep," Cindy said as she glared at him.

Randy drove Elaine and Cindy back to Elaine's house. The girls sat in the back and didn't talk at all. He pulled into the driveway, parked, turned off the car and turned around to look at them. "I'm really sorry."

"We've heard that enough already," Elaine said. "Thanks for the ride home."

"Can I call you later?" Randy asked.

"You can call, but I might not answer."

Randy watched as the girls went into the house. He backed out slowly and drove home.

The girls sat in on Elaine's bed and talked about what happened.

"Was he drinking and you didn't know?" Cindy asked.

Elaine shook her head. "No, I think it was because we've been dating for so long that he thought he had earned the right to do more than kiss me."

"That's so bogus! What are you going to do? Will you break up with him?" Cindy asked.

"I'm not sure, but I might. We haven't been getting along as well as before. Maybe it is time to end the relationship."

"Adam is history," Cindy said rather nonchalantly. "No big loss."

Chapter Thirteen

"Annie! I'm home."

"I'm in my room, Daddy. You can come in."

Annie was on her bed studying. She was on her stomach, supporting herself with her elbows with her feet in the air. Her father came in and sat on her bed. He looked around her room. He hadn't been real strict with Annie about how she kept her room and it showed.

"How do you find anything in here, sweetie? It almost looks like someone robbed you."

She turned onto her side. "I know where stuff is. I know I should pick up my clothes, but I'm just lazy."

"You have a laundry basket here. Why don't you just toss your clothes in it? How difficult is that?"

Dad reached down and picked up some of her dirty clothes and tossed them into the basket. He grabbed another pile and realized it was her underwear.

"Daddy, will you put my underwear down."

"Sorry!" he said as he stared at the underwear before letting it fall to the floor. "I wanted to tell you who I saw today."

"Who?" Annie sat up next to her father.

"I was in the store, and ran into Elisabeth Franklin."

"How is she doing?"

"Fine. We talked while we finished shopping and I asked her if she would like to get a cup of coffee. She agreed so we grabbed a cup at the Donut Den next to the store."

"I hope you didn't have any frozen stuff in the car."

"Nothing that melted." He paused for a moment. "I asked her for a date tomorrow."

"What? You asked Mace's mother for a date! I can't believe it." Annie was totally surprised.

"Yeah! Why not? You don't mind do you?"

"I guess not. I never thought about it before. I suppose I shouldn't make a big deal about it. It's just a date."

Annie and her father ate dinner and were cleaning up the kitchen afterward.

"Daddy."

"What, sweetie?"

"I know you get lonely sometimes. It used to bother me when I was younger and you would go on dates. I guess I thought you didn't love Mom anymore. I knew she was gone and all, but I didn't think you should go on dates."

"I didn't for over three years after she passed away. It took that long to get over her death. I've never stopped loving your mother, though."

"I know that now, Daddy."

"I never got serious about anyone else, though. No one could compare to your mother."

"Daddy, I know you have slept with other women after Mom. It's okay. I don't mind, I guess."

"Annie!"

"Come on! I know about sex. I'm not a little girl anymore. I remember when I was eleven or twelve and we had 'the talk.' I don't know who was more embarrassed—you or me."

"I did the best I could, Annie."

"You did fine, Daddy. I didn't have to ask any of my friends about sex."

"It's not easy being both a mom and dad, too."

"Isn't that a line from a song?"

They both laughed.

"A Merle Haggard song, I believe. Anyway, I did what I could for you, honey."

"You have done a great job. Look at how I turned out. The perfect daughter."

"Yes, you are! Except when you..."

"Daddy!"

Detective O'Dell left the station just after five on Tuesday. He hurried home to get ready for his date with Elisabeth Franklin. He parked in the driveway and rushed into the house.

"Annie! Are you home?" he hollered as he hung up his coat.

"I'm in my room studying," she answered. "Are you and

Mrs. Franklin still going out tonight?"

"Yes, I need help picking out what I want to wear. Will you take a look in my closet for me? Can you find me a shirt and a pair of pants that don't make me look like a cop? I'm going to jump in the shower real quick."

"Okay, but you have to pick out your own underwear. I'm not doing that."

Annie checked her father's closet for a decent shirt. She rejected everything she saw.

"You need to buy some new clothes," she muttered.

Finally, she found a shirt she liked and a pair of dress pants that passed inspection. She set them on his bed and returned to her room. Dad finished his shower and got dressed. He walked across the hall to her bedroom.

"Well, do I look all right?" he asked as he stood in the doorway.

Annie got up from her bed and inspected him.

"Turn around. I want to see how they fit."

He did as told and then looked at Annie.

"You look all right, but you need to buy some new shirts. Everything you have in the closet just shouts 'cop.' You need some jeans. If you want, I'll go shopping with you one of these days."

"Thanks, I'll take you up on that. Can you tell I'm a little nervous?"

"No, really?" Annie teased. "It's just Mace's mom. You have known each other forever."

"Yeah, but this is different. I want to make a good impression."

"You already have, Daddy. She wouldn't be going out with you if you hadn't. Just relax and have fun. Remember you have a ten o'clock curfew and come straight home after your date. No stopping at Swallow Cliff and making out."

"How do you know about Swallow Cliff?" Dad asked.

"Oh, Daddy! I'm not a baby anymore."

"Have you been there before?"

"Of course I have. That's where I go with my friends to drink beer and fool around."

71

"Well, do you think your friends will mind if we go up there to kiss and neck?"

"Oh my God! Don't you ever use that word again. No one has used that term in a thousand years." She put her hands to her ears and said, "I'm going to pretend I never heard that."

"Sorry, should I say that we are going up there to 'hook up?'"

Annie rolled her eyes, sighed and said, "You are hopeless. Just stay away from there. I would hate for my friends to catch you talking to Mrs. Franklin like that."

"What are you having for dinner?"

"We've got stuff in the fridge. I'll be all right. Just go and have a good time. I'll see you later. Before ten!" Annie hugged her father and kissed his cheek.

He headed over to pick up Mrs. Franklin. He parked the car, checked the mirror and got out. Keyshon opened the door before Mr. O'Dell could ring the bell.

"Hi, Mr. O'Dell. Come on in. Did Annie come with you?"

"Sorry, Keyshon, but I came alone."

"That's okay," he said. "Mom is still upstairs getting dressed. She changed her clothes twice already. I think she's afraid."

"I am no such thing, Keyshon," Mrs. Franklin told him as she walked down the stairs and into the living room. "Hello, Keith. I'm ready to go if you are."

"You look very pretty, Elisabeth."

"Thank you. You look all right yourself." She smiled at him and then told Keyshon, "You go to bed when Mace tells you, okay?"

"I will, Mom. Have a good time, but no kissing. You have to be home by ten o'clock." Keyshon smiled because he remembered to say everything Mace told him to.

Mr. O'Dell rolled his eyes.

Keith walked Elisabeth out to the car and opened the door for her. He got in and backed carefully out of the driveway avoiding the metal basketball hoop.

"If it's all right with you, I thought we could go to Zelmo

72

Miller's. It's a local place and the food is great."

"That's fine with me. I've never been there before."

"It's kinda a cop hangout. Zelmo was on the force for years. When he retired he opened up this place."

It only took a few minutes to get to the restaurant. They were seated in a booth on the opposite side from the bar so they could talk privately and not have to yell to be heard. They placed their drink order and began to talk. The conversation never lagged and there were no awkward moments of silence. Two hours later they were finally ready to leave. When he brought her back home, she invited him in for coffee.

He walked her to the front door but then stopped. "I would love to come in for coffee, but Annie told me I had to be home by ten. If I'm late, she might ground me."

She laughed and said, "I understand totally. I had a good time tonight, Keith."

"Would you be interested in going out again? Like maybe tomorrow night? Unless you have plans or something." He didn't know what to do with his hands, so he stuffed them in his pants' pockets.

"I don't have any plans and I would love to have dinner with you again." She moved closer and waited for him to kiss her.

"I'm no good at reading the signs, but I would like to kiss you if that's all right."

"I understand. I haven't dated for long time and I would like to be kissed."

He smiled, kissed her good night and then headed home.

Annie was sitting on the couch watching a movie on TV when she heard the back door open. She checked the clock and hollered, "You're lucky you made it home on time. How was the date? Did you guys have fun and don't tell me if you kissed or anything."

He walked into the living room, sat beside her, put an arm around her shoulders and kissed her cheek. "We had a very good time and we're going out again."

Chapter Fourteen

Annie saw Mace before school on Wednesday. She hadn't seen him for a few days which was rather unusual.

"Hey, Annie! What's up?"

"Hi, Mace. How was your weekend?"

"Boring! We had a game Friday."

"I know. I was there, duh. Where have you been?"

"We had practice Saturday and Sunday. I did homework the last couple days."

"You know my father and your mother went out to dinner, right?"

"Yeah, I know. It's cool. They had dinner. No biggie."

"Don't you feel a little weirded out by it?" Annie asked.

"They're just friends. It's not like they're getting married or something."

"What if they did? You and I would be brother and sister."

"Does that mean we couldn't make out with each other anymore?" Mace teased.

"We could still do that, but we would have to stop sleeping with each other," Annie joked.

"Bummer! I gotta run. See you at lunch?"

"Yeah, bro. I'll see you then."

The week had been uneventful until after school that Wednesday. Annie got home a little early from school, and found her father and Mrs. Franklin on the couch together kissing. She tried to be quiet and sneak to her room, but Dad heard her.

"Annie, is that you?"

"Hi, Daddy! Hello, Mrs. Franklin. Sorry, I got home early." She stood there without looking at either of him. She shifted her weight back and forth from one foot to the other.

"That's all right. We weren't doing anything."

Is that what you call it? Annie thought.

"Elisabeth and I are going out for dinner again. Do you want to come with us?"

"Sorry, but I can't. I was going to study with Mace."

74

"I should get home, Keith." Elisabeth stood up. "I need to make dinner for the boys and get ready for tonight."

"I'll pick you up at six, okay?"

Keith and Elisabeth kissed briefly as Annie watched.

"I'll be in my room." She ran down the hall as if being chased by a grizzly bear.

"Do you want me to give you a ride later?" her father asked.

"Sure, Daddy. That would work."

Later, Annie didn't speak on the short ride to the Franklin home. She sat quietly and looked out the window as they drove along Widener Avenue with its shops and small businesses. Detective O'Dell turned onto Henning Street, which led to the residential neighborhood of Mayfield. The Franklins lived on Oakland Lane.

As soon as they arrived, Annie ran in the house and upstairs to Mace's room without saying anything to Mrs. Franklin, or even a goodbye for her father. She flopped onto Mace's bed and groaned.

"What's up with you?" Mace asked as he spun around to face her in his desk chair.

"I saw Daddy and your mother kissing on the couch when I got home from school," she told him as she grabbed his basketball and started spinning it in her hands as she tossed it in the air.

"So?"

"It was weird. I wasn't expecting it, so it seemed strange."

"Don't you like my mom?"

"Of course I do. That's not the point." Annie sat up and tossed the ball to Mace. "She has always been nice to me. You know how much I like Keyshon."

"Don't make it into a bigger deal than it is, Annie."

"You're right. It's just dinner."

"And kissing," Mace added with a grin.

Annie groaned and flopped onto her back.

Two hours later Annie's father and Mace's mother returned from their date. Annie and Mace had finished studying and were watching TV. Keyshon was already in bed asleep. Mace and Annie listened to their parents as they talked in the kitchen.

"I had a good time tonight, Keith. I'm glad you called."

"Would you like to try this again sometime?"

"If we can coordinate our schedules. We're both very busy."

"I'm good friends with the boss. Maybe I can get some time off," he joked.

Mace and Annie looked at each other.

"Okay. Maybe this might get a little weird, Annie."

"As long as they just go to dinner it should be all right."

"Has your father dated much over the years?" Mace asked.

"Not a lot. I don't know how much he did when I was young. I know he hasn't dated anyone real seriously in the last couple of years. What about your Mom?"

"She dated this guy for three or four years but they broke up about two or three years ago."

"Did you get along with him?"

"Yeah, I guess. He was good to Mom and treated me and Keyshon all right. Keyshon was a little bit afraid of him, though. I think he wanted to get married, but Mom told him no."

Keith and Elisabeth started dating and seemed to be getting serious about each other. This didn't seem to phase Mace or Keyshon, but Annie was concerned. Everything seemed to be happening too quickly for her. Especially on Thursday after her father told her about their plans for the weekend.

"Sweetie, I need to talk to you."

"What's up, Daddy?"

"Come and sit by me."

"Uh-oh! Is this another sex talk? I haven't kissed any boys yet, Daddy."

"What about Derrick Keasling? You told me you kissed him once."

"I was twelve. That doesn't count."

Keith looked at Annie and wondered how she would react to his news. He decided there was no easy way to tell her, so he simply spilled the beans.

"Elisabeth and I have some time off this weekend, so we're going to go into the city."

"Are you going Saturday and spending the day there?"

"Actually, honey, we are leaving Friday night and coming back Sunday evening."

Annie was quiet for a moment as she thought about this news.

"You can stay out at the farm with Grandpa if you want. He would like for you to stay. He doesn't get to see you much and would enjoy the company."

"Does Grandpa know where you are going?"

"Yes, he knows where, and who I'm going with. It's not like I need his permission, Annie."

"Would it be all right if I spend the weekend with my boyfriend instead of at Grandpa's? He's been wanting to sleep with me, and I've been putting him off. I really think it's time I let him ravage my body."

"Annie Mercer O'Dell! That's not the same thing, and you know it. I am an adult and you are not."

"Oh! So I'm still a child, huh?"

"Annie, I realize this is difficult for you, but please try to understand. Elisabeth and I like each other very much, and we want to spend time away from the pressures of our daily routine."

"So I'm a routine now. I thought you loved me!"

Annie stormed off to her room and locked the door. Keith sat on the couch for a time, thinking about his plans. He decided to go ahead and spend the weekend with Elisabeth. He knocked on Annie's door.

"Go away! I don't want to talk to you. You're a hypocrite."

"Just listen then. I am going to spend the weekend with Elisabeth. You can either accept that as an adult, or else be miserable as a spoiled child—your choice. I would like you to spend the weekend with Grandpa."

"Maybe I should just move in with Grandpa. At least he doesn't sleep around."

As soon as Annie said the words, she regretted it. Her father went back to the living room and sat on the couch to watch

TV. A few minutes later Annie opened her bedroom door and came out to the living room. She sat next to her father.

"I'm sorry, Daddy. I was acting like a spoiled brat, wasn't I?"

"In a way."

"I know you don't sleep around. I didn't mean that, and I never should have said it."

"I know you didn't mean it. You were angry and surprised. You do like Elisabeth, don't you?"

"Yes, I've always liked her, but I never thought of her as a replacement for Mom."

"Annie! She's not a replacement for your mother. No one will ever replace her."

Annie started to cry, and Dad put his arm around her and held her close. She stopped after a couple of minutes.

"Sometimes I forget what Mommy even looked like, and it's hard to remember what she sounded like."

"It's okay, Annie. You were so young when she passed away. She has been gone so much longer than she was here with you."

"Why didn't you get remarried when I was a little girl?"

"I never met anyone I wanted to share my life with. I knew you needed a mother, but I didn't love anyone enough to marry them."

"Do you think you might love Elisabeth?"

"I don't know. We are very fond of each other. It's different now. You and Mace will be going to college and Elisabeth could use some help with Keyshon. Keyshon doesn't remember his father at all."

"I love you, Daddy. You and Mrs. Franklin have a good time. I will stay with Grandpa."

"Thank you, sweetie. I wasn't going to leave until we talked this out."

"You should go then. You need time to chill. I'm fine now, and I'll go out to Grandpa's this weekend. I'll have to clean up the house before you get back and I've got laundry to do, too."

Chapter Fifteen

Annie ran down the first floor hallway at Roosevelt High on Friday morning hoping to catch Elaine at her locker. "Hey, Lainey!" Annie waved as she dodged a bunch of kids heading toward her.

Elaine grabbed her books and closed her locker with a bang. "Hi, Annie. How are you?"

"I'm okay. Have you seen Mace this morning?"

"Not yet. He's probably in the gym shooting baskets."

"Shoot! I need to talk to him. If you see him, will you tell him, please?"

"Sure, Annie. Is everything all right?"

"Yeah, I'm fine." Annie leaned back against the lockers.

Elaine leaned in close so no one could overhear. She whispered, "Cindy and I know about your father dating Mace's mom. Mace told us."

"What else did he say? Did he say if he liked it or not?" Annie asked as she glanced at some students walking past.

"He said it didn't really bother him. Are you upset about it, Annie?"

"Not really upset, but it would be weird if they got married, or moved in together. Mace and I would be brother and sister."

Elaine shrugged and said, "That wouldn't be much different than the way you guys are already. At least you and Mace and Keyshon like each other. Just think about some of the other kids who are in blended families. I heard that Laura Russell and Adam Wozniak can't stand each other, or their stepparents. You should be thankful."

Annie stared at the floor as she said, "I suppose you're right, but it would change a lot of things."

"I'll talk to you later. I need to get to class."

Annie didn't see Mace until lunch when she saw him sitting at a table with some of his basketball teammates. She walked over, stood behind Mace and put her hands on his shoulders.

He looked over his shoulder. "Hey, Annie. What's new?"

"Nothing, how are you doing?"

"Okay."

"Did you see the game Tuesday night, Annie?" Marcus Bell asked.

"No, I couldn't go. I had too much homework, and since it was in Aurora, I stayed home. I heard you made the winning shot, Marcus."

"It was sweet!" He had a much higher pitched voice than one would expect of a guy six and a half feet tall and built like a football lineman. "Your bro faked this guy out of his shorts, and hit me with a pass in the lane and I jammed it home."

Annie high-fived Marcus. "You're my hero, Marcus."

Annie needed to talk to Mace but didn't want to in front of his friends. Mace sensed it.

"Hey, would you guys mind. I need to talk to Annie alone."

"Oooh! Do you need a grade changed again, Mace?" Marcus asked.

"No, he probably wants Annie to fix a parking ticket or something."

"You guys are so wrong. Mace wants Annie to pull his permanent record."

Annie smiled at the guys. "You guys know I would never do anything mischievous like that, right? I am an angel."

"Right! You were just being angelic that day you unlocked the coaches locker room for LeVertis, so he could get those magazines back he swiped from his brother. Do you still have keys to all the locks in the building?"

"I don't know what you are talking about," she said as she grinned. "I don't have any keys except my house key, and I opened the locker room so LeVertis wouldn't get trashed by his brother for stealing those magazines with the, how should I put this, the tasteful art photographs." She batted her eyes and moved her hips trying to look seductive.

The guys laughed.

"He said you looked at them, too!"

"Just saw an interesting article I wanted to read."

Marcus' laugh sounded like a twitter as he said, "Yeah, I saw that article, too. Something about reproduction, wasn't it?"

The guys laughed like kids and low-fived each other.

"If you're trying to embarrass me, just forget it. I've had sex ed already."

LeVertis shook a finger at her and said, "You can't fool us, Annie O'Dell. We know you're really an innocent virgin, despite you trying to act all naughty and vulgar."

She put her the back of her hand to her forehead, sighed and said, "That's my curse. I'm destined to be an innocent virgin all my life."

"Come see us when you turn eighteen. Maybe we can help you with that little situation," Marcus said.

"Yeah! I've had lots of experience," another player added.

Annie grinned. "Oooh! An offer I can't possibly refuse."

The guys left after a couple more minutes of teasing her, giving Annie and Mace their privacy. She sat on the table facing Mace. She put her hands on his shoulders and leaned in close. For a second Mace thought she was going to kiss him.

"What's up?" Mace asked.

"Do you know about this weekend?" Annie asked very seriously.

"Yeah, I know about it. Why?"

"Does it bother you at all?"

"Not really. You do realize that even when you get to be our parents age, you still have sex."

She pushed him away and said sarcastically, "Thanks for that info. I really needed to hear that."

"Hey, I like your Dad and he makes Mom happy. She seems happier now than she's been for a long time. If they want to spend time together, it's their decision. You should be happy for your father."

"What if they have a baby?"

"I don't think you need to worry about that. They will be careful, I'm sure."

"How's Trish?"

"I know you're just changing the subject, but Trish is fine."

"Have you and Trish...?"

"None of your business, my little friend."

"You better be careful when you do."

"Believe me, I will. I certainly don't want to get Judge Eiffert's daughter pregnant."

"You're a creep, but I suppose you'd be a better stepbrother than Adam Wozniak. He's a total jerk."

"Hey! Hold on a sec," Mace said as he stood up. "They're just spending the weekend together. No one is talking about getting hitched except for you."

"Daddy and I had a fight about it."

"Did you pull the old 'what if I did that with my boyfriend' trick?"

"Yeah." She hopped up onto the table.

"Has that routine ever worked?" Mace teased.

"Oh, shut up. One of these days I'll have a real boyfriend and then you won't be laughing." She punched him in the shoulder. "Stop laughing at me, creep. I could get a boyfriend if I want. I'm not totally ugly."

Mace stared at her for a moment. "No, you're actually pretty cute if you squint your eyes just right."

Chapter Sixteen

After school on Friday Annie carried her overnight case into Principal O'Dell's office. He was talking on the phone so she sat in a chair and waited for him to finish. He finished the call and then looked at her with a stern expression.

"Now then, young lady, what did you do today that has you in my office. Don't bother trying to proclaim your innocence, I know better." He waved a hand at her.

"I'm sorry, sir, but I didn't know it was against school policy to sell drugs to freshman boys. And that half-full bottle of Scotch in my locker belongs to my Daddy." Annie rubbed her eyes and pretended to start crying. "He's an alcoholic and he beats me when he's drunk. I stole his booze because I was afraid for my life. I'm pregnant and don't want to lose my baby again."

"Well! Well! Well! It certainly doesn't sound like a very good excuse to me. I will have to punish you, young lady. I sentence you to a weekend with your grandfather."

Annie smiled and went around behind the desk to hug her Grandpa. He swiveled his chair, and she sat on his lap as if she were still his little granddaughter.

"Can I stay for the game tonight?"

"Of course. I was planning to stay. We could get something to eat first and then come back. Is that all right? Did you want to bring any of your friends?"

"No, I just want to be with you. I see my friends all the time, but I don't get many chances to spend quality time alone with my favorite Grandpa."

Grandpa didn't mention he was her only living grandfather, or grandmother for that matter.

They ran out to Darby's for a quick bite to eat. It was crowded with high school kids, but they managed to find a place to sit and eat.

Back at the school for the game, Annie asked Grandpa, "Do you want me to sit with you?"

"You should sit with your friends, Annie. I need to talk to Mr. Kemmerick, so I'll sit with him."

"Don't believe anything he says about me. He doesn't have any proof at all, and if he does have any evidence, it's probably all circumstantial."

"What have you been doing, Annie? No, don't tell me. I want to have plausible deniability."

"I'll meet you after the game, Grandpa. Love you!"

Annie joined her friends for the game, but she was unusually quiet and reserved. She did not even get excited when Mace stole the ball and raced down the court for a slam dunk.

Elaine and Cindy looked at her and Elaine asked, "Annie, what's wrong? You're not yourself tonight."

"It's nothing, Lainey."

"Nothing my foot. Something is bothering you."

"I just don't want to talk about it, okay?"

"It's not about a boy, is it?"

"What? Me with boy trouble. Get real!"

Annie didn't say anything more to her friends about what was troubling her. She met her grandfather outside the door to the gym after the game. He was still talking to vice-principal Kemmerick. Annie looked at Mr. Kemmerick wondering if he told Grandpa anything.

"I'll be back in a minute, Annie. I need to check something."

"I'll wait right here, Grandpa."

Annie turned to look at Mr. Kemmerick.

"Miss O'Dell, it's nice to see you here and not in my office. Have you been behaving yourself and not causing any harm?"

"I always behave, Mr. Kemmerick," Annie said as she smiled angelically.

"Yeah, right."

Principal O'Dell returned and asked, "Are you ready to go, Annie?"

"Whenever you are." She waved goodbye to Mr. Kemmerick and he smiled.

Annie walked arm in arm with Grandpa out to the car and they headed to Grandpa's house out in the country. Grandpa lived about ten miles out of town on a fifty acre farm he purchased twenty years ago. As he drove, they talked about the game and a little about school. They were quiet for a moment.

"Grandpa, can I ask you something?"

"Of course, what's on your mind, sugar?"

"Do you still miss Grandma?"

"Every day. Not a day passes that I don't think of her."

"Did you ever think about getting remarried?"

Grandpa knew where this was coming from.

"You know it's different for me. I was a lot older than your father when Grandma passed away. I had a lifetime to spend with her. I'm too old to even think about remarrying. I don't even want to date anyone."

"You know where Daddy is this weekend, right?"

"I do."

"Does it bother you at all?"

"Nope. Not a bit. He and Elisabeth are old enough to make their own decisions. In case you haven't noticed, they are just normal people with normal needs and wants. Would it bother you so much if Elisabeth was white?"

"That's not it at all. I never gave that a second thought. What bothers me is that Mace and I have been friends for so long, and Daddy has known Mrs. Franklin just as long. Why all of a sudden are they so hot and heavy to become lovers?"

"It happens sometimes, Annie. Two people can know each other a long time and then one day it changes somehow. They see each other differently. You do want your father to be happy, don't you?"

"Of course I do. I came home the other day, and they were on the couch kissing. What if I come home and they are in bed together? What if she moves in with us?"

He patted her knee. "Don't go getting all ahead of everything. I'm sure your father is not going to make any rash decisions without talking to you first. You are still the most important person in his life. Don't forget that."

On Saturday Annie and Grandpa went hiking through the woods and checked out an auction. Grandpa bought an old antique dresser for Annie to have when she was older. They made lunch and watched TV together. Grandpa was a big football fan so that's what they watched—two NFL games in the afternoon.

During halftime of the first game Grandpa asked, "Will you grab me a beer, please, Annie?"

"Sure, Grandpa."

Annie got up from the couch and went into the kitchen. Grandpa didn't bat an eye when Annie brought two beers back from the kitchen. That evening after a light dinner, they watched a movie together.

Sunday afternoon was time for more football. Grandpa didn't say anything when Annie brought two beers out to the family room.

She was going to get a second one when he told her, "I think one beer a day is enough for you."

"All right. I guess I was thinking about Daddy and wanted to have another one."

"Have you ever had more than one beer in a day?" Grandpa asked and as soon as he did, he realized he knew the answer.

"I've had three in one day, but I've never gotten drunk. If I ever decide to get drunk, can I do it with you here at the farm?"

Grandpa looked at her and smiled. "I suppose that would be better than getting drunk while you were out with your friends, or with a boy."

"I might not ever want to get drunk, but who knows? And I know better than to get drunk with a boy and let him use me."

"Please don't talk like that, Annie. I couldn't bear the thought of any boy ever 'using' you." He hugged her close. "I know you are worried about your father. If you want another beer, it's okay."

"Maybe later. Thanks for understanding, Grandpa."

Grandpa kissed the top of her head. "You can always talk to me about anything, Annie Mercer."

"Anything?" she grinned as she asked.

"Okay, maybe not about boys in detail."

"You don't have to worry about that yet," she whispered.

Annie stayed over on Sunday night and rode to school with Grandpa on Monday morning. She saw Mace with Elaine and Cindy by their lockers.

"Hey, guys! How was your weekend?" Annie asked.

"It was all right. Are you okay now, Annie?" Cindy asked.

"Yeah, I'm back to normal I suppose."

"Did you see your father yet, Annie?" Elaine asked.

"No, I stayed at Grandpa's and rode in with him this morning. What time did your mother get home, Mace?"

"Around nine last night. She said they had a great time."

"Yeah, I bet."

"She didn't mean that, Annie. She meant being in the city. They went out to dinner and even to a play. It was good for her to get away and if they had a good time in bed, so what." He shrugged. "I've always liked your father, and he's treated my Mom with respect over the years."

"I guess I should cut him some slack."

When Annie got home after school, she saw a note from Dad on the kitchen island.

"Hi, honey. I missed you this weekend. Elisabeth and I had a great time. We might do it again sometime. Hope you are okay with that."

Annie made dinner and waited for her father to get home. He arrived a little after six, and she greeted him at the door. She jumped into his arms and hugged him.

"I missed you too, and I'm sorry I was such a spoiled brat. I made meat loaf for dinner."

"I love you, Annie. More than anything or anyone in the whole world." He looked at the oven. "I hope you didn't burn the meat loaf."

"Oh, Daddy," She jumped down and took the meat loaf out. "Crap! The edges are burnt."

"Have I ever told you about the first time your mother made meat loaf?" He grinned. "It was like eating cinders, but I didn't complain."

Chapter Seventeen

The Christmas holiday arrived and Annie and her father drove out to Grandpa's farm to chop down a tree. They walked through the woods inspecting several candidates.

"What about this one, Annie?"

She gave it the once-over. "It's better than the last one, but this side looks a little weird."

They kept walking until Annie spotted one she thought might pass inspection.

"I like this one, Daddy. It looks perfect!"

Dad smiled as he watched her eyes light up. "Are you sure that's the one?"

"Yes, I'm positive."

Ten minutes later, he was dragging the tree back to the car.

"Do you remember the first time the three of us did this?" He paused for a moment to catch his breath.

"I know I was three because you've told me the story before, but I'm not sure if I actually remember the first time. That was almost fourteen years ago."

"Do you still like picking out our tree?"

"You know I do," Annie said.

"Well, could you help out a little? This thing isn't light, you know."

Christmas was a little different at the O'Dell home this year. Grandpa was with Annie and her father, but there were other people as well—the Franklins. Keith and Elisabeth were still dating so she was at the house with Mace and Keyshon. There were gifts for everyone under the tree. Annie had bought presents for Mace and Keyshon, but not Mrs. Franklin. Her father did not think she needed to buy for her. After all Mace and Keyshon didn't buy gifts for Detective O'Dell.

The phone rang and Annie grabbed it without checking the caller ID.

"Hello."

"Merry Christmas! Is this my favorite niece?"

"Uncle Robert! How are you? Merry Christmas. How's

everyone doing? Do you guys have any snow?" Annie joked.

"No, it's been a bit too warm for snow."

"Daddy! It's Uncle Robert. Grab the other phone."

Robert Mercer, Amy Catherine's older brother, worked for an American medical supply company in Kenya which was why Annie joked about having snow for Christmas.

"Hello, Robert. How are things in your part of the world?"

"Kinda cool today. I don't think it's above ninety-five in the shade."

They talked for thirty minutes and then Annie asked about her other uncle.

"Have you seen or heard from Uncle James lately?"

The oldest brother, James, lived in Peru, South America. He had served as a missionary in that country for over twenty years.

"We exchange letters about once a month, or two months. He did say he would be back in the states next year for three months."

"I hope he remembers to come and see me. I haven't seen him since I was a little girl."

Uncle Robert laughed and Annie could almost see his large belly jiggling. "I'm pretty sure he will want to see his favorite niece."

"You're silly. I'm his only niece. I wonder if I'll ever see my cousins again. They must both be close to thirty by now."

"They are over thirty if I remember correctly. They're both married and each have two kids," Uncle Robert said.

"When you talk to him again, tell him he needs to send me some photos. I want to see what my relatives look like."

"I'll do that, sweetie. You have a good holiday."

"You, too. I love you."

After Uncle Robert hung up, he looked at two photos in his hand through tear-filled eyes. One was a photo of the two brothers flanking their younger sister on the day she graduated from high school. Then he looked at the other one—a photo of Annie. *Your father wrote and told me you are looking more and more like your mother. I'm glad he included a picture. He's right. You do like so much like Amy Catherine.*

As they were eating Christmas brunch, Keyshon got a bit impatient. He was ready to open presents. After they finished eating, Annie pulled Mace into her room, closed the door and locked it. Keyshon tried to open the door.

"Annie, I want to come in. Let me in, please."

"Go away, Keyshon. Annie and I are busy right now," Mace told him.

Keyshon heard a noise that sounded like the bed squeaking.

"I know what you're doing in there and I'm telling Mom." Keyshon walked out the the living room and informed Mom. "Mace and Annie are in the bedroom. They are having sex because they won't let me in. Make them stop. I want to marry Annie and make babies. Mace already has a girlfriend."

"I don't think they are misbehaving, Keyshon, but I'll check for you."

"Thanks, Mr. O'Dell."

Keyshon sat next to his mother and Keith knocked on Annie's door.

"Go away! I told you we're busy, Keyshon."

"Annie, it's Dad. Can I come in?"

"Daddy! Just give us a minute okay?"

He listened at the door. He heard the bed squeak and then Annie opened the door. She stuck her head out but hid behind the door.

"Can I come in?"

"Is Keyshon with you? I don't want him to see what we're doing."

For just a second Dad wondered if they were doing something they shouldn't. He came in the room and Annie closed the door and locked it.

"What don't you want Keyshon to see? He walked up to Elisabeth and told her you and Mace were having sex."

"How does he know about that?" Mace wondered. "I never told him."

Detective O'Dell and Mace looked at Annie.

"Hey! He asked me about babies a while back. What was I

supposed to do? I'm not gonna lie to him." She held out her hands, palms up. "Are you gonna arrest me."

"We'll talk about that later, young lady." He didn't know whether to be mad at her, or proud of her. "What are you guys doing that is so secretive?"

"We bought Keyshon a present, and we are trying to wrap it without him seeing it."

"So you weren't having sex?" Mr. O'Dell joked.

"No, sir! I would never do that with Annie, even if she's not my sister yet."

"Good to know, Mace," Dad said as he left the room.

Annie and Mace finished wrapping the gift but left it in the room. They joined everyone else in the living room. They spent an hour opening presents before Mace brought out Keyshon's special gift.

"This one's for you, Keyshon. Annie and I bought it with our own money."

"You mean Santa Claus didn't deliver it?"

"Yeah, he delivered it, but we had to pay him," Mace said.

"Sounds like a racket to me," Keyshon said.

"Just open the present before I send it back," Mace told him but didn't mean it.

Keyshon opened it and inside was a new slot car race track. He wanted to set it up right away.

"We have to wait until we get home, little buddy. Annie doesn't have room here," Mace said.

"Thanks for getting that for me, Mace. I love you!"

"You're welcome. Annie bought it, too."

Keyshon hugged Annie and she kissed his cheek.

"Thanks, Annie. I love you, too, even if we can't make babies."

"I love you, too, Keyshon."

They were both crying as she held Keyshon tightly. She had a special place in her heart for Mace's little brother—and not just because he was born with Down Syndrome.

Chapter Eighteen

Damon Barclay hosted a New Year's Eve ball at his parents huge, over ten-thousand square foot, home and invited a hundred friends to the affair. His parents were in the house, but their rooms were upstairs in a private wing. The party guests stayed on the first floor or in the finished basement. The crowd soon divided into two groups. One group caroused in the pool area while the other group mingled in the ballroom waiting for the dancing to start. Diana Ahronson acted as Damon's party co-host.

Elaine arrived at the party with a new boyfriend, Adrien Coyle. She started dating him after breaking up with Randy Braun. Adrien was a junior at North Park College and Elaine had known him for several years. They attended the same church. Cindy came to the party with Rachel Lowery, since neither of them had boyfriends at the moment. Derrick Keasling arrived at the party with Clarissa Morgan, while his sister Kristen came alone. The Keasling home was in the Barclay Estates, only a few blocks away. It was huge, but paled in comparison to the Barclay mansion.

The party started at nine but most guests didn't arrive until later. It was fashionable, and expected, to be late. At ten o'clock a DJ began playing big band music in the ballroom.

"Kristen, would you like to dance with me?" Derrick asked his sister a short time later.

"Where is Clarissa?"

"She's taking a break. Do you want to dance or not?"

"Sure, what girl wouldn't want to dance with her handsome older brother?" Kristen said. She noticed the waiters and service staff and asked, "Are some of the staff really security guards?"

"That's what Damon said. He said they took down some of the art collection as a precaution."

"Did they think someone from high school would be bold enough to walk out with a Picasso?" Kristen laughed as she asked.

The undercover security guards were charged with maintaining the no-alcohol-for-underage-kids policy. Even the few guests of drinking age followed the no alcohol policy without complaint. Just to be invited to the party was an honor. To be tossed out would be a major embarrassment and social suicide.

"I thought you were going to bring Tony to the party so he could keep you company?" Derrick asked.

"I asked him, but he didn't want to come. He was afraid he would not fit in with the 'rich kids,' as he put it."

"Damon and Diana are not like that."

"I know. Damon asked me to dance earlier. Diana is so lucky to have him for a boyfriend."

"I think any guy here would be lucky to have you for a girlfriend, Kristen."

"That's very nice of you. I could say the same about you."

Derrick and Kristen were just over a year apart in age and many people even thought they were fraternal twins.

"I thought you were going to ask Emmy to come to the party. Why did you bring Clarissa instead?" Kristen asked.

"Emmy said she would be so uncomfortable coming to the party. I think she meant because her family doesn't have much in the way of material wealth."

Kristen picked a piece of lint from Derrick's sport coat. "I don't care how poor Emmy's family is, she is my best friend."

Elaine and Cindy had almost decided not to come to the party because Annie and Mace were not invited. Earlier that day Mace talked them into going, though.

"Annie and I aren't interested in going to a fancy party. We're going to spend the night at her grandfather's house."

"What do you mean you're spending the night with Annie?" Elaine frowned.

"Not just with Annie. Her father and my mom and Keyshon will be there. Principal O'Dell builds this big bonfire, and we're gonna roast hot dogs and marshmallows. All kinds of stuff that white people do."

"Don't forget you are half white, Mace," Cindy said.

Mace laughed. "Yeah, I know, but I'm trying to be more black this year."

"You're a real dork at times." Elaine jabbed him in the side. "Sometimes I wonder why I ever decided to let you be my friend."

"I think you have that turned around, Ms. Novicki."

"Annie really loves Keyshon, doesn't she? She may not say anything about it, but she does." Cindy blew her bangs out of her eyes. "I really don't like this new hairstyle. It makes me look like that character from Robin Hood."

"Yeah, and Keyshon loves her like a sister. He's always asking, 'Where is Annie?'" Mace shrugged. "I think he cares more about her than he does me, and I'm his only brother."

"I can understand that. Can't you, Cin?" Elaine teased.

"Definitely." Cindy nodded and then blew her bangs out of her eyes again.

Mace put his arms around his friends' shoulders and said, "Have fun at your fancy party. I'll see you next year."

At the Barclay house the DJ did his countdown precisely at midnight. A fireworks display lit up the night sky to help celebrate the new year. Derrick kissed Clarissa and then turned to Kristen.

She put a hand to his chest. "I love you, but don't you dare kiss me like that."

"I wasn't going to, Krissy."

Derrick kissed Kristen's cheek quickly and briefly before he hugged her. The party continued until three in the morning before all the guests were gone. The service staff worked overnight to clean up, and when Mrs. Barclay arrived downstairs in the morning, the house appeared exactly the same as when she retired to her suite the night before.

Out at the O'Dell farm everyone was sitting around the bonfire at midnight. Even Keyshon had stayed awake. They didn't set off any fireworks, but they did hear some off in the distance. Keith kissed Elisabeth and Mace looked at Annie. She saw him looking and put her hand on his shoulder to keep him away.

"Don't you even think about it, buster!"

"What? I wasn't going to kiss you."

"It's a good thing. I would have to smack you if you tried." She did lean against his shoulder and look into his eyes. *What would it be like if I did let you kiss me? Would it excite me, or would it be yucky and weird? I guess I'll never know because it's never going to happen.*

Chapter Nineteen

"Hey, Annie!" Mace shouted as he approached her in the hallway by her locker. "Can you give me a lift to the Valentine party tonight?"

"I suppose. How is the rest of the team getting there?" Annie asked as she slammed her locker closed.

Mace shrugged and said, "I don't think too many of them are going."

"Lainey told me that Tom Sharkey, Joe Oates and Alex Ravella were going."

"Do you notice any pattern in that?" Mace asked with just a trace of bitterness.

Annie thought for a moment before she replied, "They are the white guys on the team."

"Yeah! You got that right."

"Mace, all the guys were invited."

"Maybe so, but..."

"I'm not going to feel guilty because your friends on the team won't come to the party. We decided to have the party at the youth center over on Douglas so everyone would be welcome. You guys don't have a game tonight. You're playing tomorrow."

Mace put his hands on Annie's shoulders as he stared into her eyes. "I'll talk to the guys and see if they want to make an appearance."

"There is going to be a band playing from eight until ten-thirty. It will be fun," Annie said as she stared up at him.

"I know it, but some of the guys are a little..."

"Prejudiced?" Annie interrupted. "Black guys can be prejudiced too, you know. I know there are tensions between different groups in school."

"Will you give me a ride or not?" Mace asked again.

"Not if you are going to have an attitude." She turned to walk away.

He grabbed her arm. "I'm sorry, I didn't mean to take it out on you, Annie. I know you're friends with the guys on the team. I've never known you to judge anyone by their color."

"Apology accepted. I'll pick you up at seven-thirty."

"What's the name of the band again?"

"The Notable Exceptions. They are fairly new, but they are really good. They played at the Sweetheart Ball, remember? They play all kinds of cover songs." Annie added, "It might not make any difference, it shouldn't, but it might, but they have a black bass player in the band."

"They do! Why didn't you say so before? That makes all the difference..."

"Stuff a sock in it, Mace," she said as she used her hip to bump him away.

"Sorry, I'll talk to the guys. I know this thing is important to you."

Mace talked to his teammates after practice, and they agreed to stop by the youth center as a favor to him and Annie O'Dell. She had always stood up for them, and they respected her for that.

Annie picked Mace up at his house, and they arrived at the youth center thirty minutes after the doors opened. Although not technically a Roosevelt High sponsored event, many of the students were planning to attend. The youth center held about five hundred people and looked to be two-thirds full. Annie and Mace spotted a bunch of friends and walked over to talk to them. She and Mace danced and listened to the band. Around nine, the rest of the basketball team arrived. Annie welcomed the guys and danced with all of them who asked.

"Are you having fun, Marcus?" Annie asked Marcus Bell, one of the better players on the team.

"I admit it. I'm having a good time, Annie. You are a pretty good dancer."

"For a white girl?" Annie teased.

"I didn't mean it like that. You are a good dancer, period." Marcus looked around and noticed that no one seemed to care who he was dancing with. All the kids were simply having fun.

"I need to take a break. I've been dancing with everyone," Annie said to Marcus.

"You haven't danced with me yet."

Annie turned around to see Matt Sullivan.

"Matty, I didn't know you were here."

He took a deep bow, chuckled, held out a hand and asked, "May I have this dance?"

"Okay, but then I need to take a break."

"Fair enough."

Annie danced with Matt as the band played an uptempo Fridays At Five song designed to get the crowd energized.

"That was pretty good, but I like the original version better," Annie said.

"I would agree with you there, Annie," Matt said as she stared into her brown eyes and then smiled.

The band leader motioned for everyone to settle down and the crowd gave him their attention.

"I want to thank everyone for coming out to celebrate Valentine's Day with us. Is everyone having a good time?" the leader of the band asked.

The crowd hollered and he continued, "I want to introduce the guys in the band now. On drums is Alan Vicini." The crowd applauded as each guy was introduced. "On keyboards is Sammy Demont. On lead guitar is Elijah Sydney. Playing the bass and hailing from right here in SoHam and graduating from Roosevelt High is Calbert Devondre!" The crowd roared as Calbert was introduced. Most of the kids knew him. "My name is Paul James Joseph, and we are The Notable Exceptions. We're going to play one more song before we take a quick break. We'll be back so don't go away."

"Got enough energy for one more?" Matt asked.

Annie looked up at him, grinned and said, "I think I just might be able to survive one more dance with you, Matty Sullivan."

He pulled her close as the band played a very danceable tune. By the end of the song Annie could feel her heart racing.

"Could I ask for another dance later?" Matt asked.

Annie nodded and then turned around to find her friends.

The band took a break and came back fifteen minutes later. They played until ten-thirty and would have played longer, but that was as late as they were allowed to play.

"Did you have a good time?" Matt asked Annie as they caught their breath after dancing to the last song.

"It was fun, and I'm glad the guys from the team seemed to be enjoying it, too."

"Yeah, this is a pretty cool place to come to hear a band. They don't serve, or allow, any alcohol, so the crowd is usually better behaved than some other places in town."

Annie looked up at him. "I wouldn't have expected you to say that since your father owns a few bars."

"Just because my old man makes a living off of booze doesn't mean I'm going to, or that I'm an alcoholic like some of my uncles," Matt said.

"I'm sorry. I didn't mean it like that," Annie apologized. "Did you like the band?"

"Yeah, I've heard them before. They're good."

Annie looked around the large room, waved her hands and asked, "Did you know this was the first place Fridays At Five ever played a gig?"

"No, I didn't know that. How did you know?"

"I was talking to Emmy Colasanti and she told me," Annie answered.

"I didn't see her here tonight. Is she still here?"

"No, she left about thirty minutes ago. She has an early curfew."

"Even on a Friday night?" Matt asked incredulously.

"That's what she said. Her parents are real strict with her."

"Too bad. I don't know her. I've seen her around, but I've never talked to her, or been introduced to her. I hear she's a good kid."

"She is a good kid unlike her sister who is kinda wild. Did you ever go out with her?"

"No, so you can forget about any rumors you might have heard about me and Diane Colasanti. I've heard stories about her though."

"She's just your type!"

"That was a low blow, Annie."

"Yeah, I know, sorry," Annie said but with a grin. "I wonder why Victoria wasn't here. Do you know?"

Matt shook his head. "No clue and not curious in the least. She's history. Do you need a ride home?"

"Thanks, but I've got Daddy's car. I have to take Mace home. It was good to see you, Matty. Are you coming to the game tomorrow night?"

"Can't, gotta work. See you around, Annie."

"Stay out of trouble, Matty."

He looked at her, grinned and said, "I will if you will."

Annie went to the game the next night and spotted Emmy Colasanti with Derrick and Kristen Keasling. She thought it was rather odd that Emmy would be friends with the Keasling kids who lived in one of the wealthiest sections of SoHam. Emmy's family lived in Raynor Park, which had once been one of the best neighborhoods in SoHam, but now was a neighborhood in decline. Annie knew Kenny Colwell came from Raynor Park and his family had been one of the wealthier families in town in the early days. They still lived in the large family home that had been built over a hundred years ago.

"Hey, Annie, what are you thinking about?" Elaine poked her in the side. "I've been trying to talk to you, but you seem to be a thousand miles away."

"Sorry, Lainey, I was thinking about something."

"Did you hear that the youth center was robbed last night?" Elaine asked.

"No, what happened?"

"I guess some kids broke in the office and ripped off some cash. They will get caught because there is a surveillance camera. Your father might know about it."

"I'll ask Daddy when I see him. It wasn't anyone we know was it?"

Elaine shrugged. "Haven't heard."

Annie hurried home after the game and her father was home.

"Daddy, do you know anything about the youth center

getting ripped off?"

He laughed and then answered, "A couple of the dumbest thieves in history. They broke into the office and stared right at the camera. Then they broke open a desk drawer and took about fifty bucks. Didn't even wear gloves. Left fingerprints everywhere. I wish all my cases were as easy."

"Did they get arrested?"

"Yeah, they got picked up."

"Who were they? Please tell me they weren't from Roosevelt."

He shook his head. "No, they were from Lincoln High. I can't tell you their names because they are juveniles, but I can tell you they were white."

"Good! I would feel terrible it they were kids from my school."

"Did you have a good time at the dance, or party, or whatever you call it? You made it home before your curfew. Wasn't there an after-party anywhere where the kids could go to get hammered?"

"Daddy! I don't get hammered and the dance was fun," she said and then thought about the times she danced with Matt Sullivan. "I think all the guys from the team made an appearance and I even saw Coach Powell there. He was dancing with his wife and he had some smooth moves."

"Are you hungry? There's some leftover spaghetti in the fridge."

"Yeah, I'm starvin'."

"There's salad in that green Tupperware bowl. You need to eat some veggies along with the spaghetti."

Annie heated up a plate of spaghetti in the microwave, fixed herself a bowl of salad and joined her father on the couch.

"Mace had a bit of an attitude yesterday because of the party. He didn't think any of the guys from the team would be welcome."

"You mean the black guys?"

"Yeah, I told him they were just as welcome as anyone else."

"I don't think you have a prejudiced bone in your body, Annie."

"You always taught me to judge a person by their actions and not how they look. I guess that's why I feel the way I do."

"Was there any trouble at the center?"

She sucked a long strand of spaghetti into her mouth and then answered, "No, everyone seemed to get along and just have fun. I danced with a lot of guys from the team and no one seemed to think anything about it."

"You don't see it as much as I do, but there is still racial tension in parts of the city. There are places in SoHam where I wouldn't want you to be, even during the day."

Annie laughed and replied, "I know about some of those areas. Marcus Bell told me there are places he is afraid to go and he's so big and strong."

"Being big and strong is not much protection against a handgun."

"I remember that player who was shot and killed a few years ago. He would have probably made it to the NBA."

"That was sad. He was in the wrong place at the wrong time."

"I hope you're never in the wrong place at the wrong time, Daddy," she said as she snuggled closer to him.

Chapter Twenty

The Roosevelt High basketball team entered the IHSA tournament with a record of 24-2. The best record in school history. They ended the regular season undefeated in the conference and rated number five in the final state class AA poll. Mace had been named to the all-state team and became the school's all-time leading scorer. The Rough Riders breezed through the regional with easy wins. They faced tougher competition in the sectional, but Mace took over the championship game in the fourth quarter, and they defeated Aurora Manual for the sectional championship.

The next game was on Tuesday, March eleventh—the supersectional against top ranked Proviso Township in the fieldhouse of North Park College. Not exactly a home game, but close. The gym was sold out, and they were allowed to sell some standing-room tickets. Annie and the whole gang arrived early for the biggest game in school history. Annie even had a ticket for Keyshon. It was a rare treat for Keyshon to see his brother play. Keyshon had no idea of the importance of the game, but was thrilled to see Mace in his uniform on the court. As the team was warming up, Annie brought Keyshon down to the court. The whole team came over to high-five him.

"We're going to win this game for you, Keyshon. I promise!" Mace exclaimed.

"Okay, but can we go to Burger Bob's after the game? I want a milkshake."

"Sure we can go."

"I want Annie to go, too. Can we take Annie?" He clung to her hand until it hurt her.

"If you ask her nicely, maybe she will come with us."

Keyshon turned to Annie and asked, "Will you come with us to Burger Bob's? I'll buy you a milkshake, and I'll sit with you."

"That would be very nice of you, Keyshon. We need to sit down so Mace can play his game."

"Bye, Mace. I'll see you after the game. Do a good job!"

The game was tied with ten seconds left. Proviso had the

ball and their coach wanted a timeout, but the players didn't hear him, as the crowd screamed louder than ever. Mace tapped the ball away, and it was recovered by LeVertis Thompson who passed it back to Mace. Mace glanced at the clock and made a move that froze his defender to the floor like a tree. Marcus Bell set a screen and Mace went up for a jumper. It swished through the net as the buzzer sounded. The students rushed out onto the court as the Rough Riders had upset the mighty Buccaneers of Proviso. Mace was held aloft on his teammates shoulders.

In the stands Keyshon held onto Annie's hand and asked, "Is the game over, Annie?"

"It's over, Keyshon. We won!"

"That's good. Can we go to Burger Bob's now? I want a milkshake."

"We'll go as soon as Mace can get away."

Annie held onto his hand as they walked carefully down the quickly emptying bleachers.

"Where is Mace?"

"I can't see him right now. Let's sit here and wait for him okay."

Annie and Keyshon sat patiently on the first row as the celebration continued.

"Do you want a cheeseburger, Annie? I think I might need a cheeseburger with my milkshake."

"I'm sure you can have a cheeseburger. You might even be hungry enough for two." Annie grinned.

His whole face shone as he grinned and said, "I know I can eat two of them."

Eventually, Mace saw them and ran over. He hugged Keyshon and then grabbed Annie.

"Let me go! You're all sweaty. You can hug me after you shower."

"We won, Keyshon! We won the game! Did you see my shot?"

"Did the other team win, too?" Keyshon asked with a smile.

"Yeah, little bro, they won, too."

"Good! Can we go to Burger Bob's now. I want a chocolate milkshake and two cheeseburgers and so does Annie!"

"I have to shower and change clothes, Keyshon. You wait here with Annie, okay."

"Hurry!"

The whole team went to Burger Bob's, and Coach Powell bought milkshakes for everyone, including Keyshon and Annie O'Dell.

On Friday the Rough Riders used a Greyhound charter bus to travel to Peoria for the final games of the year. They would play Friday night against Chicago Simmons, the defending state champions. If they won they would play Saturday night for the championship. If they lost they would play for third place in the early game Saturday evening. The team would be staying overnight in a hotel downtown. Some of the fans were lucky enough to book hotel rooms in Peoria. Others settled for rooms in nearby towns. Some fans would travel back and forth from SoHam to the games. Detective O'Dell had planned ahead and back in November had booked two rooms in the Peoria Holiday Inn. There were two queen-size beds in each room. Annie and her friends would be staying in Peoria overnight. All Annie had to do was choose who got to stay, so she made a list. Elaine Novicki and Cindy Mackens were obvious choices. She talked to Mrs. Franklin about taking Keyshon, but Mrs. Franklin had to work Saturday morning so Keyshon couldn't stay overnight. Keith, Elisabeth and Keyshon would come down Saturday afternoon and be there for Saturday's game, whichever one it turned out to be. Annie asked Trish to stay with her. Now she had to find four other friends for the other room. She asked Maris Miller if she could go but she already had a room with her parents.

"Grady doesn't have a room, Annie. Do you think it would be okay with your father if you ask four boys to go?"

"I'll ask him."

Dad didn't mind if she asked some boys to use the other room.

Annie called Grady Harris. "My father reserved two rooms,

and I can't find any other girls I trust to use the extra room. Would you like to use it?"

"Sure! I need a place to crash, or else I will have to drive home. Have you asked any other guys?"

"No, do you have a couple friends who are going and would share a room with you?"

"I know Derrick Keasling is going, and Tony Bertucci might be able to stay."

"I know of one guy who is looking for a place to crash," Annie mentioned.

"Who?"

"Matt Sullivan is going. He told me he would sleep outside somewhere, if he couldn't find a room. Would you be okay with him sharing the room?"

"I don't mind," Grady said.

"Then it's all settled. It's going to be a great weekend. I just know it," Annie beamed.

The school arranged for buses to transport students to and from Peoria. School dismissed at noon and the buses were loaded for the trip. Annie and Trish sat together right behind Elaine and Cindy. Annie noticed Matty Sullivan sitting by himself. She moved and Rachel Lowery sat beside Trish.

"Are you coming back, Annie?"

"Probably not. That's okay you can sit with Trish. I'll find another seat."

Annie asked Matt, "Do you mind if I sit with you?"

"I don't care. Nobody else wants to have anything to do with me, I guess."

"What? None of your hoodlum friends are going?"

"No, they're all in jail. Your father busted them all, remember?" he joked.

"That's right. How could I forget? It was that armored truck robbery, wasn't it?"

"Are you sure you want to sit with me? Aren't you worried about what could happen to your reputation if you are seen with me?"

"Everyone thinks I'm either a snitch for my Grandpa, or Daddy, or else they think I'm a slut."

Matt shook his head and said, "No one who knows you thinks you're a slut, Annie."

"That's a relief. I heard last week that I was pregnant, and didn't know who the father was because I had let the entire basketball team use me after a game."

"The whole team?"

"Well, just the starters actually. I do have some standards, you know."

"You can be a riot sometimes, Annie. Will your father be upset if you sit with me?"

"I don't tell Daddy everything I do," Annie told Matt with a devilish grin.

She and Matt sat together for most of the trip and then Annie saw Kristen Keasling sitting with her brother."

"Hey, Derrick, can we switch seats?" Annie asked. "I need to ask Kristen something."

"Sure, Annie. I need to stretch my legs."

Annie sat next to Kristen and asked, "Are you staying in Peoria tonight? You probably are since Derrick is staying."

Kristen shrugged and said, "I doubt it. I don't have a room, and the hotels are probably all full."

"Would you want to share a room with Lainey, Cindy, Trish and I? I'm sure we could squeeze in one more."

"Are you sure? I did bring my overnight bag, just in case."

"I hope you don't mind sharing a bed with Trish Eiffert."

"Trish and I are friends."

"I'll let her know."

"Where are you sleeping, Annie?"

"There is supposed to be a love seat in the room. That will be big enough for me."

"Oh, I shouldn't take your bed, Annie. I can sleep on the love seat."

"Don't be silly. I'm short, like your friend Emmy. It will be easier for me. By the way, did Emmy come with you?"

"No, she didn't. Don't say anything, but I don't think she

106

had the money, or else her parents just wouldn't let her. She has very protective parents."

"Too bad she couldn't come. I don't know her all that well, but she seems really sweet. Real quiet and shy, but nice. She's so pretty, too. Does she have a boyfriend?"

"Not really. She and Derrick dated a little. Actually, I'm not sure 'dated' is the right term." Kristen used air quotes. "She and Derrick are good friends, so it wasn't like romantic dates. She is good friends with Kenny Colwell, and sometimes I think there is more to their relationship than just being good friends. It wouldn't surprise me if they start dating when she is older."

"I heard they were close friends, but I didn't know about the other part. They are neighbors or something, right?"

"Kenny lives a couple of houses away, and they have been friends for years." Kristen looked around to see if anyone had overheard their conversation. "Please don't tell anyone about Emmy and Kenny. They try to keep it a secret."

"My lips are sealed," Annie said.

Annie sat with Kristen until they arrived in Peoria. Derrick sat with Matt Sullivan. They knew each other, but were not exactly friends. Derrick always made friends easily, though, and by the time the bus pulled into Peoria, he and Matthew were better acquainted.

Chapter Twenty-One

"Welcome to Karner Arena for tonight's edition of the original March Madness."

The PA announcer's voice boomed across the gym as he introduced the schools and players. The Roosevelt Rough Riders faced the Wolverines of Chicago Simmons High in the first game of the night. The second game pitted the Wesclin County Tigers against the Lions of Decatur Lincoln.

Annie stood up and screamed at Mace. He turned around and shook his head as he waved.

Cindy covered her ears and said, "Will you warn me if you decide to do that again?"

"Sorry, Cindy, but I wanted to make sure Mace heard me."

Randy Braun tapped Annie's shoulder and yelled in her ear, "I think everyone back in SoHam heard you, Annie."

Coach Powell had scouted the Simmons team several times. This was the first time all season that Roosevelt would be facing a taller team. The frontline of Simmons averaged six-eight. Led by their all-state player, Javarius Mays, the Wolverines had lost only once during the year and that was to Proviso Township. Coach Powell was counting on two factors that seemed to favor his guys. Team quickness and Mace Franklin. If Mace could have a good game and not turn the ball over too many times, Coach felt they would win.

Two minutes into the game Coach Powell called a timeout. He looked up at the scoreboard. His worst nightmare had happened. He knew Simmons would count on their experience in big games to get off to a fast start and they had. Simmons was up by twelve points, and the game was on the verge of becoming a blowout. The players trudged over to the bench, plopped down and stared at the floor.

Coach Powell knelt in front of the starters, smiled and said, "Well, we got 'em right where we want 'em!"

Marcus looked up at Coach Powell and replied as soon as he caught his breath. "Coach, you okay? We're getting our butts kicked. We're down by twelve."

"What? You gotta be kidding!"

Mace wiped the sweat from his face with a towel and then said, "We weren't ready, Coach. We all felt a little intimidated."

"Are you guys sure about the score? I can't read that scoreboard without my glasses. I thought we were ahead by ten." He looked over his shoulder at the scoreboard. "Well, never mind, I just needed a break to grab a Coke and a burger, so I called timeout. Are we really that far behind?"

The guys realized Coach Powell was just trying to loosen them up so they could relax and play ball.

"Okay, we need to switch a couple things around..."

Coach Powell made two changes and sent the guys back on the court feeling they were still in the game. By the end of the first quarter, the Rough Riders had cut the deficit to six. Mace took over in the second quarter, and dominated the slower Simmons' players. He stole the ball and his slam dunk ignited the team and energized the crowd.

Annie high-fived Cindy and pounded on Elaine's back. "Did you see that?"

"I could see it perfectly, Annie. I'm glad I wore my contacts today."

By halftime Roosevelt was up by eight points. Now it was the Simmons players who were feeling the pressure.

The second half opened with Simmons in a two-three zone. They wanted to force Roosevelt to hit outside shots. The Rough Riders missed their first three shots of the half, and Simmons began to claw their way back into the game. Now up by only two points the Rough Riders were beginning to feel the heat. That is everyone except Mace Franklin. He hit three threes in a row and took the steam out of the Simmons team. Simmons started to press Roosevelt all over the court, but Mace handled the pressure and the Rough Riders used their quickness to blow the game apart. When the final horn sounded, Mace looked up at the scoreboard. They had won by a score of 78-63.

Mace pumped his fist and ran over to ask Coach Powell, "Hey, Coach! Can you see the score all right now?"

"I can see much better now, Mace, thanks to you!" Coach

Powell wrapped his arms around Mace.

Later, Coach Powell was already thinking about tomorrow's game, as he sat next to his assistants Art Trout and Tom Eddleman to watch the second game. He would savor the fifteen point victory later.

Coach Powell leaned over to talk to Art. "I know Wesclin is up by four right now, but surely they can't keep this pressure up for the whole game. They haven't used a single sub yet."

Coach Trout shrugged and said, "I don't know. Those kids look like they're in great shape and could probably run all day."

"Jeff, do you even know where Wesclin County is?" Coach Eddleman asked and then grinned as the shortest player on the court ripped the ball away from the tall center from Decatur.

"I'm pretty sure it's down somewhere close to Centralia, but I don't think I've ever been there."

"I've heard of Centralia, but, yeah, I couldn't tell you where it is," Coach Eddleman said.

Coach Trout smiled and said, "I've been in the gym at Centralia a few times. It's a nice place."

Right now Coach Powell was still wondering who would win game two. He knew a little about Decatur, but he had never seen the Wesclin team play.

"Their record isn't all that impressive. They've lost nine games this year."

"Coach, at this point I don't think that matters much," Art said. "They got hot during the tournament and pulled a couple of upsets."

"You're right, Art." Coach Powell shook his head as he watched his team having fun.

The guys were celebrating their win and having a good time. Coach reminded himself they were just kids despite their size.

As the game progressed it become clear that Wesclin was going to be their opponent tomorrow. They were small, but really quick. They played a pressure defense and never seemed to tire.

"I see what you mean about running all day," Coach Powell shouted to Coach Trout. "The crowd is really urging them on."

Coach Eddleman added, "They're only seven players deep if today is any indication."

"I think you might be right. Have you guys noticed anything else?"

"You mean the fact that only two players are scoring?" Coach Trout smiled.

"Right you are."

"The other kids are reluctant to take a shot unless they're wide open."

"And even then, they're tentative. We will have to find a way to shut down one of those two kids."

Both coaches watched the game without talking for most of the fourth quarter.

Coach Powell stood up and got his players' attention. "Mace! Come here for a minute. I need to talk to you."

Mace hustled over as his teammates jeered.

"What's up, Coach?"

"Have you noticed anything about this Wesclin team?"

"Yeah! It seems like there are ten of them on the court. They are all over the ball." Mace grinned and then added, "They look like midgets, though."

"Midgets, huh?" Coach thought he knew how to negate the swarming pressure of the feisty Wesclin County team.

Chapter Twenty-Two

After watching the two games, Annie and her friends were ready to head to the hotel. There caught a ride on the shuttle bus and checked into their rooms.

"Anyone want to go swimming?" Derrick asked as they stood in the hallway.

"I'll go, Derrick. I brought a suit," Annie answered.

"How late is the pool open?"

Derrick answered, "I called the front desk and asked them. The guy said we could use the pool all night, if we were quiet and didn't disturb anyone."

"Party time!" Annie yelled.

Elaine put her hands on her hips. "Annie, you can't stay in the pool all night. You have to go to bed sometime."

"Says who? I can stay up all night. I've done it before."

"I'll go swimming with you," Kristen said.

"Thanks, Kristen. Come on, Lainey, Cin, it will be fun. I know you brought suits."

"All right. We'll be down there in a few minutes."

Annie and Kristen quickly changed into their suits. They each had bikinis to wear. Annie wore shorts and a t-shirt over her bikini to the pool. Kristen wore a swimdress. When they got to the pool Derrick, Grady Harris and Tony Bertucci were already there. Annie and Kristen slipped off their clothes and jumped into the pool with the guys. A few minutes later Elaine, Cindy and Trish showed up.

"Come on in! The water's not too cold," Annie yelled.

"Then why are you shivering, Annie?" Cindy asked.

"You'll warm up," Kristen told the girls.

"Where is Matty?" Elaine asked as she sat on the edge of the pool and stuck a foot in the water.

"He told me he would be down in a while. He needed to take care of something first," Annie said.

"He's probably placing a bet on tomorrow's game, if I know him."

Maris joined the kids at the pool. She and her parents were

staying in the hotel on the floor below Annie's rooms. The rest of the girls finally got in the pool. Grady and Maris stayed together while the rest of the kids goofed around. Tony teased Kristen and chased her around the pool. Derrick watched as they acted like little kids. Elaine, Cindy and Maris were wearing one piece bathing suits while the other girls had on bikinis. Trish was shy about letting the guys see her, but Kristen and Annie didn't seem to care. Maris had some news for Grady.

"Father said it was okay for you to use the couch in our room. It folds out into a bed. The suite is huge and the couch is in a sitting area so you will have some privacy."

"That sounds better than sharing a bed with one of the guys," Grady said.

"Father trusts you. Mother was a little leery, but father and I convinced her it was all right."

Grady and Maris got out of the pool and sat at one end on deck chairs. They weren't ready to go up to the room yet. Maris knew that once they were in the room he wouldn't kiss her. Matt Sullivan finally made an appearance at the pool. Annie noticed and hollered at him.

"About time you showed up. Take that t-shirt off and get in here with us."

"Are you ordering me around, Annie O'Dell?"

"It wasn't an order, Matty. Just a strong suggestion."

Matt stripped off his t-shirt and dove in the pool. He was not a strong swimmer so he stayed at the shallow end. Annie, Kristen and Derrick were like fish and swam underwater chasing each other.

After about forty-five minutes, Elaine said, "We're going back to the room, guys. We'll see you later."

Annie got out of the pool to talk to her friends. "Is it all right if I stay down here? I'm not ready to go to bed."

"We're not going to bed already. We just want to go back to the room and get ready for bed. We plan on staying up for a while," Elaine told her.

"I'll be up later," Annie said as she jumped back in the pool and splashed Tony and Kristen.

"You gonna get it, Annie!" Kristen promised her. "Tony get her and bring her back to me."

Tony tried to corner Annie, but she was too quick for him. It took the combined efforts of Tony, Derrick and Kristen to corral Annie. Tony finally caught Annie and tossed her over his shoulder. She was laughing and not really trying to get away anymore. Tony held her above his head and tossed her. She landed with a huge splash—especially for such a petite girl. Derrick joined Grady and Maris, and they were soon ready to head upstairs. Tony, Kristen, Annie and Matty Sullivan were still in the pool.

"Matty, do you ever go swimming at home?" Annie asked.

"Not very often. We don't have a pool at our house."

"Neither do I, but I still like to swim."

"Tony and I are going upstairs, Annie. Are you going to stay down here?" Kristen asked.

Kristen was asking because she wasn't sure she should leave Annie alone with Matt Sullivan. Kristen didn't know Matt very well but knew of his reputation.

"I'm gonna stay here, and teach Matty how to swim. I'll be up in a while."

Tony and Kristen left the pool area and headed upstairs. Annie turned to face Matty.

"So, you think you can teach me how to swim, huh? Give it your best shot, Annie."

Annie swam over to Matt and dunked him. He came up sputtering, but with a smile.

"First basic rule, Matty Sullivan. Don't open your mouth under water. Water in the lungs is not a good thing."

"What's rule number two?"

"Don't forget rule number one!"

"You are such a comedian, Annie."

"Thank you. I try."

"I didn't want to say anything in front of the other kids, but you look really good in that bikini. I was a little surprised."

She looked down at her top. "You mean you were surprised I have breasts or what?"

"Well, that's one thing. The other is that you look really

114

pretty under water."

Matty dunked Annie underwater and then released her. She popped up and grinned. Matt moved closer and Annie swam away as Matt watched and smiled. As Annie got out of the water, Matt watched closely. She sat on the edge of the pool, and Matt moved in front of her.

"What would your father say if he knew you were alone with me in that skimpy bikini?"

She checked her bikini. "It's not all that skimpy. The important parts are covered."

Matt looked at Annie.

She looked back at him and closed her eyes for a second before asking, "Are you and Victoria still seeing each other?"

"No, she has moved on to greener pastures—college guys."

"Do you miss her?"

"No, not at all. There are other fish in the sea, or should I say, other girls in the pool."

"Why, Matty Sullivan! I do believe you just used a line on me. Are you trying to seduce me by any chance?"

"Not yet, Annie. You aren't eighteen."

"I'm not even seventeen yet. Not until May."

"You look very good for a sixteen year old, Annie O'Dell."

Annie and Matt stayed in the pool for another half hour. Annie flirted with Matt because she knew he couldn't try anything. He did put his arms around her waist one time and held her close— too close!

"Matty, we should go upstairs. I'm getting cold."

"If you let me hold you, I will warm you up."

"Yeah, I know you would, but we better not. Daddy might have spies in the place. Let's go upstairs. I'm not ready to go to sleep, but I want to change out of my bikini."

"I'm ready to go if you are."

"Will you stay in the pool for a minute and turn around."

"Okay, why?"

"I want to take off this bikini and put my dry clothes on."

Matt turned around as Annie got out of the pool. She picked up her t-shirt and shorts off the chair. She made sure Matt was not looking as she dried off as best she could. She wrapped the towel around her waistband then slipped her bikini bottoms off. She quickly put on her shorts and finished drying off.

"Make sure you stay facing that direction and close your eyes, please."

"If I'm not looking at you, why do I have to close my eyes? How will you know if I have my eyes closed, anyway?"

"Because I trust you."

"All right, my eyes are closed."

Annie faced Matty and slipped off her bikini top and slipped on her t-shirt in a flash.

"You can open your eyes and turn around now, Matty. Thank you for being a gentleman. I owe you."

"Are you going to close your eyes if I change clothes?"

"Nope! I'm gonna watch."

"You are something else, Annie. Actually I don't have anything to change into except for putting my shirt on."

"Too bad!"

Matt climbed out of the pool and dried off. He grabbed his shirt, and he and Annie headed upstairs. When they got to their rooms they could hear some laughter and talking in the boys room.

"Are they having a party in there?"

"Sounds like it, Matty. Open the door so we can see."

Matt opened the door and they stepped inside. All the kids were in the room, except for Grady and Maris. The guys were on one bed, and the girls were on the other one.

"Now I see why your father requested these rooms, Annie. We are at the end of the hall, so we won't disturb any of the other guests. He's pretty smart."

"That's my father!"

Matt sat in the chair in the corner of the room. Annie sat on the bed with the girls facing the guys. Soon the guys were staring at Annie.

"Why are you guys staring at me? What are you looking at?"

The girls looked at Annie and Cindy noticed.

"Annie, did you take off your bikini?"

"Yeah, I didn't want to put my dry clothes on over my wet bikini. Why?"

"The guys are just looking at you because you are braless and…"

"You're sticking out a little bit, Annie, and these freshman have never seen that before," Elaine told her.

Annie put her arms over her chest and rolled her eyes. "Like you guys have never seen…"

"Where did you change, Annie?" Kristen interrupted. "There isn't a changing room in the pool area."

"I changed after I dried off by the deck chairs."

"Right in front of Matthew?" Cindy screamed.

"No, I didn't let Matt watch."

Elaine got off of the bed and motioned. "Come on, Annie. I'll let you in our room and you can get dressed."

Elaine and Annie left so Annie could change.

"Why did you change in front of Matt Sullivan? Are you nuts?" Elaine asked.

"He didn't see anything, Lainey. He had his back to me the whole time."

"Why did you stay in the pool with him for so long? What were you guys doing?"

"We were just having fun. We didn't 'do' anything. He didn't kiss me."

"You need to be careful, Annie. Matthew can be a little…"

"He's never done anything to me. He's always treated me with respect."

They returned to the other room, and Annie surprised the guys. She lifted up her t-shirt to show them her navy blue sports bra.

"There! Now you don't have to stare at me."

All the guys laughed except for Matt Sullivan. The girls stayed in the boys room for another hour before Elaine, Cindy and Trish wanted to go to bed. Tony and Kristen were sitting on one bed talking about school, and Derrick and Annie were on the other bed. Matt was about to fall asleep in the chair. Annie kept looking at Matt and then at Tony and Kristen. She smiled. *If I didn't know better I would think you guys are brother and sister instead of cousins.*

A half hour later Derrick told his sister, "Kristen, you need to get out of here. I want to go to bed and you're in it."

Kristen got off of the bed. "Fine! If you want to spoil the party. Be that way."

Derrick moved onto the bed he was sharing with Tony.

Matt opened his eyes, stood up and moved onto the bed Derrick just left. "I guess that means I have this one to myself."

"Why do you get to sleep in a bed by yourself?" Annie asked. "Everyone else is sharing a bed, and I have to sleep in a chair or on the floor."

Matt looked at Annie and she looked at him. Everyone else looked at Annie.

"Dream on, Matthew Sullivan!"

"You know I wasn't making a move on you, Annie."

"Are you going to sleep in your clothes?"

"Maybe. Why?"

"If you sleep in your clothes and stay on top of the covers, I could get under the covers and sleep in my clothes and nothing could happen."

"Annie, I don't think you should do that. I'll sleep in the chair and you can have the bed," Kristen volunteered.

"Don't be silly, Kristen. I'll be okay in the chair."

Kristen smiled at Tony and Derrick. "See you guys in the morning. Don't stay up too late."

Kristen and Annie went to the girls room. The other girls were sound asleep. Kristen changed into her pajamas, but Annie stayed in her clothes.

"Aren't you going to change, Annie?"

"I would, but I forgot to pack pajamas. I totally forgot. I usually sleep in a t-shirt and old gym shorts anyway. I'll be fine."

Kristen fell asleep in five minutes, but Annie couldn't get comfortable in the chair. She tried the floor, but that was no better. She lay there and thought about Matt and the empty spot on his bed. She stood up and made a decision. Annie touched Kristen on the shoulder and Kristen opened her eyes and sat up.

118

"What is it, Annie? Are you all right?"

"I can't get comfortable in the chair, or on the floor."

"You can slip in next to me. I can scoot over a little."

"Thanks, but I'm going to see if the guys are still awake. I might just stay up all night if they are going to."

"Are you sure, Annie? I could go since they are family."

"I'll be fine with them. Derrick is really nice and Tony is so shy. Matty won't try anything. People think he's such a wild kid, but he isn't really all that bad."

"Be careful, Annie," Kristen said, yawned, lay back down and closed her eyes.

Annie quietly left the room and knocked on the boys room. Matt opened it after a few seconds since his bed was closer to the door.

Annie grinned shyly at him. "Still got room for one more?"

"Are you sure, Annie? I don't want your father to kill me because his innocent daughter spent the night in a room with me."

"He won't know and besides there are three guys in here."

Matt laughed and said, "Somehow I don't think that will make it any better."

"Are you going to let me in or not?"

Matt let her in the room. Tony and Derrick sat on their bed watching TV—still wide awake. They looked at Annie but didn't say anything.

"Are you guys going to stay up all night? If you are and then so am I," Annie said.

"We're going to watch TV until we crash," Matt said.

"What's on?"

"This is *Devil In A Blue Dress* with Denzel Washington. Have you ever seen it?"

"No, but I like Denzel. He's hot! Which side of the bed is yours, Matty?"

"I like this side best." He pointed the the right side nearest the phone on the table which separated the two beds.

"Then give me some room so I can see the TV."

Matt gave Annie some room in the middle of the bed so she could see the TV. The movie lasted until three, but Annie didn't.

She fell asleep leaning on Matt's shoulder.

"Hey, guys," Matt whispered.

"What is it, Matt?" Derrick looked over at Matt and Annie.

"She's out like a light. What should I do? I can't sleep with her against me."

"I'll move her. That way you won't get in any trouble," Tony said as he got out of bed and walked over to Matt's bed.

"Thanks, Tony. I appreciate it."

Tony reached over, gently picked up Annie and held her. Matt jumped out of bed and pulled down the covers on the left side. Tony placed Annie on the bed and covered her with the sheet and blanket. She didn't wake up at all. The guys turned off the TV, shut out the lights and were soon asleep also.

During the night Annie got hot and kicked off the blanket and sheet. Matt was on top of the covers and now so was Annie. She moved to the middle of the bed close to Matt and put a hand on him without realizing it. Matt woke up for a moment and could feel Annie close to him as he lay on his back. He couldn't move any farther away from her without falling out of bed. He thought of her father and was grateful they were fully dressed.

Derrick woke up first and went to the bathroom. He noticed Annie on top of the covers and next to Matt. He wondered how close a relationship they really had. Derrick took care of business and went back to sleep.

At eight o'clock the phone rang in the girls' room. Elaine answered it, still half asleep.

"Hello."

"Hi, this is Detective O'Dell. May I speak with Annie, please."

"Sure, I'll get her for you."

Elaine looked for Annie, but she wasn't in the chair. Elaine got out of bed to see if Annie was in the bathroom, but it was empty. Elaine looked on the floor but Annie wasn't there, either. Elaine picked up the phone again.

"She's not here, Mr. O'Dell. She must have gone downstairs to get some breakfast."

"Okay, thanks, Lainey. I'll call later."

"Okay, I'll tell her you called when she gets back."

Cindy and Kristen woke up when they heard Elaine on the phone.

"Who was calling so early, Lainey?" Cindy asked.

"Annie's Dad. Where is she anyway?"

Kristen realized where Annie was. "What did you tell her father, Lainey?"

"I told him she was probably downstairs having breakfast. Isn't that where she is?"

"Most likely." Kristen covered for her.

"Where is she really?" Trish asked.

"I think I know. I'll be right back." Kristen threw on a t-shirt and ran out of the room.

"Please be awake, Derrick."

Kristen knocked softly on the door, and in a few seconds Derrick opened it.

"Why are you up so early, Krissy?"

Kristen slipped past Derrick and stood just inside the door. "Annie's father just called. Is she still in here? Where's the light switch?"

Derrick flipped on a light. "Yeah, everyone else is still asleep. She's with Matt. Not with Matt. Just in bed with him."

Kristen rolled her eyes. "You're making it sound worse. I need to take her back to our room before her father calls again."

Derrick stepped aside, and Kristen ran over to where Annie lay sleeping. She tried to wake Annie up without waking Matt or Tony, but they woke up before Annie. Tony sat on the edge of the bed facing the windows.

"Annie, you need to wake up." Kristen reached across the bed, touched her shoulder and Annie opened her eyes.

"Your father called. He wanted to talk to you."

Annie rubbed her eyes as she yawned. "Okay, sorry I didn't hear the phone."

Annie turned over to grab the phone without realizing Matt was there. She stopped as she realized where she was and who was with her. She looked down to see if she was dressed and then scooted away from Matt. "Oh crap! Is Daddy still on the phone?"

Annie got off of the bed, looked at Kristen and Derrick and then back over her shoulder at Matt.

Kristen shook her head. "No. Lainey answered and told him you must be downstairs already. He's going to call back."

Annie sighed. "I'm going to be grounded for life. Daddy knows I wouldn't be up this early if I didn't have to be."

"What are you going to do, Annie?" Matt asked as he stood up.

She shrugged but then grinned. "I'm going to do what any good daughter would do in this situation. I'm going to tell him the truth. I'll tell him I spent the night with three boys and let them have their way with me."

"I'm dead meat, right?" Matt sounded worried.

"Not at all, Matty. I'll keep you out of this. I promise."

"Come on, Annie. We can tell the girls you were downstairs so they won't have to lie. That way I'll be the only one who has to lie."

"You don't have to lie for me, Kristen."

"Maybe if you run downstairs now, and I go down there and find you and then it won't be a lie."

"That will work. It won't be like I lied to Daddy. It will just be that I didn't tell him the whole truth and if he never asks then he'll never know."

Annie ran downstairs and Kristen waited a minute before she ran downstairs to "find" Annie. They both came back to the room just as the phone rang again. Annie grabbed it.

"Hi, sweetie. Did you have a good time at the game?"

Annie talked to her father for ten minutes and never lied to him once. He didn't ask any questions that she needed to withhold any of the truth, either.

"We'll be there around four. We can have dinner before the game."

"I'll see you then. I love you, Daddy."

"Love you too, sweetie."

Chapter Twenty-Three

It was four thirty when Annie met her father in the lobby of the Holiday Inn. Mrs. Franklin and Keyshon were with him.

"Hi, Daddy! I was wondering if you got lost."

"We got started a little later than we hoped."

"Hello, Mrs. Franklin. Hi, Keyshon."

Keyshon smiled at Annie and said, "Guess what I had for breakfast."

Annie put a finger to her mouth and pretended to be thinking about his question. "I bet you had biscuits and gravy and some hash browns."

"How did you know? You're so smart, Annie."

They had some time to kill before the games began. Keyshon was hungry so they found a place to have dinner. Annie filled them in on how Mace played. She made it sound as if he won the game all by himself. Keyshon liked to listen to stories about his big brother. After dinner they made their way to Karner Arena.

"Where are your seats, Daddy?" Annie asked.

Mr. O'Dell checked their tickets and told Annie the section.

"I think your seats are one section over and a bit higher up," Annie said. "I'll look for you guys when I get to my seat."

"I will need to talk to you after the game, Annie."

"Okay, I'll find you, Daddy."

Annie's friends were already in their seats waiting for her. Annie scooted past some of them and took her seat next to Kristen.

Kristen asked her quietly, "How did everything go with your father?"

"Fine. We had dinner, and he didn't ask about the rooms at all. We talked about last night's game. I'm a little worried because he wants to talk to me after the game. Do any of the girls know where I stayed?"

Kristen shook her head. "No, they just assumed you got up early and had breakfast. Tonight won't be a problem. You can stay in the girls room because Trish wants to go home with Mrs. Franklin and your father."

Annie looked around, located her father, Elisabeth and

Keyshon and waved at them. "Good! I wouldn't want to give Derrick or Tony the wrong idea about me and Matty Sullivan." She spotted Matt two rows behind her and smiled at him.

"We'll catch the train in the morning and my father will pick us up. Somebody will. It might be Mom," Kristen said.

"Okay, that will work," Annie said.

Chicago Simmons defeated Decatur Lincoln for third place in a game no one seemed to care about. Simmons ended up winning by fifteen points. At least all the players had a chance to get on the court and play.

Mace led the Rough Riders onto the court and the Roosevelt crowd stood to their feet to cheer. When the Wesclin Tigers took the court, there was an even louder cheer. It seemed as if everyone would be pulling for the underdog tonight. The Rough Riders controlled the opening tip and as soon as Mace had the ball, he was trapped against the sideline by two Wesclin defenders. He picked up his dribble and held the ball above his head. The whistle sounded and a foul was called on a Wesclin player. Roosevelt inbounded the ball and Mace held it high over his head as he surveyed the court. Mace was as tall as the tallest Wesclin player and his arms were as long as that of a much taller player. The Rough Riders planned to slow the tempo down and control the game. They wanted to force Wesclin to play a slow methodical game. Wesclin wanted to use their pressure defense to force turnovers and speed up the tempo. It would be a battle to see which team was able to control the tempo and momentum.

The first quarter ended in a 6-6 tie. Roosevelt had managed to slow down the game by making the Tiger defense defend the whole court. Mace was the only player who dribbled the ball. They were very patient on offense and scored on three backdoor cuts for layups. Roosevelt took only five shots the whole quarter. The referees called six fouls on Wesclin. Coach Powell knew Wesclin relied almost solely on their starters for offense. On defense Roosevelt employed a two-three zone and packed the lane. Wesclin was unable to penetrate and began to rely on outside shots, which were not falling. They did manage to draw two fouls on Marcus Bell and he went to the bench. Phil McLeish, a six-eight junior, replaced him. While not as quick as Marcus, he took up space in the middle.

The second quarter was more of the same from Roosevelt. The slowdown effectively took the crowd out of the game. They were very patient on offense and only turned the ball over three times. They took more shots this quarter and managed to hit five of them. Wesclin was getting in foul trouble, and the Rough Riders converted on seven of eight at the free throw line. In spite of this, the Rough Riders found themselves on the short end of the score at the half. Wesclin had managed to hit some outside shots and led 29-23.

In the locker room Coach Powell encouraged, "We are still in this game!" He clapped his hands as he paced back and forth in front of the team. "We still need to be careful with the ball. Don't get caught in the corners. Are you tired at all, Mace?"

"No way! I can play the whole game, Coach. Not a problem."

"All right. On defense we need to pay better attention to number twenty-three—the Tockstein kid. He is their best shooter. Know where he is and get up on him. Keep your hands in the air and make him shoot over you. Don't foul!" Coach waved his hands for emphasis. "We don't want to put them on the free throw line. Box out and make sure they don't get any offensive rebounds."

When the third quarter started, Wesclin scored a quick basket to go up by eight. Roosevelt was still patient on offense and they worked the ball around for a whole minute before Mace drove to the basket. He scored and was fouled. It was the fourth foul on Rusk, number thirty, and the Wesclin coach needed to pull him. Coach Breden looked at his bench and sent his son into the game. The small Wesclin team had just gotten even smaller. As the quarter wound down, Mace Franklin hit a pull-up jumper in the lane and was fouled again. It was number four on Tockstein and he left the game. The quarter ended with the score knotted at thirty-nine each. Coach Powell maintained a calm appearance, even though his stomach was nervous enough to churn butter.

Wesclin started the fourth quarter with two starters on the bench. Their offense sputtered and the outside shots were contested by the much taller Rough Riders. The Tigers still didn't have an offensive rebound. Mace started to take control of the game and put Roosevelt up by four. Coach Breden called timeout and was forced to send Rusk and Tockstein back in the game. One other starter picked up his fourth foul but stayed in the game. Tockstein hit a three pointer to pull the Tigers closer. Mace drove the lane, and when he was tripled teamed he passed off to Marcus Bell for a slam dunk and a foul. Rusk had fouled out. The Tigers didn't give up. They increased their pressure and forced two turnovers and made two easy baskets to pull within three. Coach Powell called a timeout to settle his team.

"We have to take better care of the ball! Make sure you meet the pass. Don't let them beat you to the spot. Mace, don't get caught in the corner, but if you do, we have two timeouts left. Spread them out and make them cover the whole floor. No shots unless you're in the lane." Coach turned and yelled, "McLeish!"

"Yes, Coach!" McLeish jumped up.

"Go in for Marcus and give him a break. I don't want him to pick up his fifth foul."

The Rough Riders broke the huddle and worked the ball patiently around the floor. Time was on their side with the clock under a minute. The whistle blew and Wesclin was called for a foul. Another player had fouled out. Wesclin called a timeout. They only had one left now. Coach Powell planned a surprise for Wesclin. Roosevelt hit two free throws to go up by five. They immediately went into a full court press with McLeish guarding the much smaller Tiger trying desperately to inbound the ball. Afraid of a five-count violation, he called the final time out for Wesclin. That had been Coach Powell's only reason for the pressure and it had worked.

When play resumed, the Rough Riders fell back into their zone, but applied more pressure to the three point line. Wesclin tried to move the ball for an open shot, but time was ticking away. Finally they got the shot they wanted. Tockstein was open for a three point shot and hit it. The Tigers were down by two now. The Tigers applied full-court pressure, but Mace got the ball across the ten second line with one second to spare. The Tigers were

126

desperate and their coach was screaming for them to foul. They had to foul Mace Franklin because he had the ball. Mace looked up at the clock. Ten seconds to go! He looked up into the stands and spotted Keyshon waving his arms.

"These are for you, little man," Mace said even though no one could hear him.

Mace calmly dropped two free throws in the basket and the Rough Riders fell back on defense. Wesclin hurried up the court and Tockstein put up a desperation three point shot from the corner. It went in! The Tigers trailed by only a single point. If they could somehow get the ball back... Mace grabbed the ball and looked at the clock. Four seconds to go! He held the ball in his hands and watched the seconds tick away. Wesclin could not stop the clock. When the horn sounded, Mace smiled and calmly tossed the ball to the referee and then his teammates tackled him. The two coaches met and shook hands. It had been an unbelievable finish.

Keyshon asked his mother, "Is it over? Did Mace win?"

"Yes, he did, baby. They won the game."

"Are we going to Burger Bob's? I want a milkshake and a root beer. Can I have both tonight?"

"Tonight you can have whatever you want!"

Keyshon wondered why Mom was crying.

As soon as the final horn had sounded, the student section for Roosevelt went nuts! The kids were yelling and screaming at the top of their lungs. Annie hugged Elaine and Cindy. Kristen hugged Tony and Derrick. Trish rushed down to the court to try to get close to Mace. Even Matthew Sullivan was excited and celebrated. He moved down to Annie's row, slipped around Elaine and Cindy to stand next to Annie. She saw him and opened her arms. He hugged her and picked her up off her feet. She looked into his eyes and he kissed her quickly. She kissed him back and he set her down. Detective O'Dell, Elisabeth and Keyshon slowly made their way over to where Annie and her friends were standing, still celebrating.

"Daddy, they won! Can you believe it? Mrs. Franklin, Mace did it!"

"Yes, I'm so proud of him."

127

"Annie! Annie! We're going to Burger Bob's. I'm getting a milkshake and a root beer! Are you coming with us?" Keyshon was excited, too.

"I can't tonight, but I will come and see you tomorrow. I promise. Mace and I will take you out and you can have another milkshake and maybe even a hot dog."

Annie hugged Keyshon and then her father. Matt Sullivan stood behind her listening and watching as she talked to Keyshon. Detective O'Dell noticed Matt.

"Hello, Matthew. Did you enjoy the game?"

"Yes, sir. I'm not much of a fan, but this was special."

"I'll see you around, Matt. Say hello to your father for me."

"I will, sir."

After thirty minutes of having pictures taken, medallions presented and trophies awarded, the awards ceremony ended. The Rough Riders headed to the locker room to celebrate. Mace hugged Coach Powell as they celebrated. The school had its first state championship in basketball.

It was close to midnight before the kids returned to the Holiday Inn. Elaine and Cindy were wiped out and hit the sack immediately. Derrick, Tony and Matt Sullivan were still wound up from the game and not ready to fall asleep. Kristen and Annie stayed in the boys room to let the other girls sleep. Shortly after one thirty Kristen was ready to call it a night.

"I'm going to bed. See you guys in the morning. Make sure they get up on time, Tony. We can't afford to miss the train."

"See you in the morning, Kristen. I'll set an alarm to make sure Derrick gets up."

"Are you coming, Annie?"

"Go ahead. I'll be there in a couple minutes, Kristen."

Kristen left and went into her room. Annie talked to Matt in the hallway outside the girl's room. She had her back to the wall as Matt stood in front of her.

"Are you mad that I kissed you, Annie?" he asked.

Annie looked up at him and tilted her head back and forth as if trying to decide. Then she grinned. "I'm not mad. It was just the excitement of winning the game that caused you to kiss me."

128

"If you want to believe that, you can," Matt said as he moved closer to her.

"Are you telling me that you kissed me on purpose, and winning the game was just an excuse?" Annie asked.

Matt nodded. "Yep! You got it. I have wanted to kiss you for a long time, Annie O'Dell."

"You are so wicked, Matthew Sullivan. First you tricked me into your bed and now you kissed me."

Annie was teasing Matt because she enjoyed his kiss.

Matt put his hands on the wall to block Annie from moving. "Haven't you ever kissed a boy before?"

"Of course I have! Lots of boys."

"Name one. Name one boy you have kissed." Matt grinned as he moved his head closer to Annie's.

"I kissed Derrick Keasling before."

"I've heard that story. You were like twelve or something."

"It was still a kiss."

"Does he even remember kissing you?"

"It doesn't matter. I remember it."

"Do you think you will remember my kiss?" He moved his lips very close to Annie's.

"For a few days perhaps," Annie teased. She could feel Matt's breath on her mouth.

"Maybe I should kiss you again, so you will be more likely to remember." He let his lips brush against her lips.

She put a hand to his chest and moved him back just a little. "If you think I'm going to let you kiss me whenever you want, Matthew Sullivan, you are sadly mistaken."

It didn't matter. Matt moved Annie's hands to his shoulders, wrapped his arms around her waist, took Annie in his arms and kissed her again. She looked at him not sure if she should slap him or kiss him back. She decided to kiss him. This time Matt held her tightly against his body, and they kissed for a much longer time.

"Will you remember that kiss, Annie?"

She looked into his eyes and nodded.

"I will remember it, too," he whispered.

Annie was blushing because she enjoyed being held tightly

in his arms, and feeling his lips on hers. Her heart raced and she felt a warm tingling sensation throughout her body.

"I need to go in the room. I'll see you in the morning."

Matt let go of her. "I'm looking forward to it."

Annie slipped into her room and walked over to the bed. Kristen was already in bed and Elaine and Cindy were sound asleep. Annie flopped into bed on her back. She looked at Kristen.

"I was worried you might decide to stay with Matt again."

"Kristen, I never would have done that if I could have fallen asleep on the floor in here."

"Did Matt kiss you?"

"You won't tell anyone, will you?"

"No, it will be another secret between the two of us."

"Yes! We kissed again and it was wonderful. Did Derrick or Tony say anything about last night?"

"Tony didn't say anything, but Derrick asked me if you and Matt were more than just acquaintances."

"What did you tell him?"

"I told Derrick that you were just friends." Kristen looked at Annie and asked, "Are you just friends?"

"Yes, but who knows? Maybe we will start dating."

It was customary at Roosevelt High to have a pep assembly to honor teams that won championships. The football team had won six, and the girls softball team had won two. Now the boys basketball team joined that list. Monday afternoon during the last period the whole school gathered in the gym. The band played and the cheerleaders and pom pom girls did their routines. All the members of the team were introduced. Mace got the loudest cheer. Coach Powell gave a speech. Elaine and Randy Braun interviewed the players and coaches for the school newspaper. Cindy took pictures. By the end of the week everything was back to normal. Though it was only March, seniors were counting the number of days until graduation. Freshmen students were counting the days because next year there would a new set of freshmen to harass.

Chapter Twenty-Four

"Matty, come with me. I need you to keep an eye out for anyone coming," Annie said as she grabbed his hand and pulled him along.

"What are you doing, Annie?" Matt asked as he checked the name on the office door. "Please tell me you're not going to break into the guidance office."

"I'm not breaking in. I have a key." She held it up.

"Oh, my bad. That makes it so much better," Matt said sarcastically.

Annie opened the door and turned on the light. "Stay by the door and keep an eye on the hall."

Matt did as ordered. "I have a bad feeling about this, Annie."

"Hush and keep your eyes peeled." She looked around and then walked over to the door leading to the inner office. She quickly unlocked it and moved stealthily to the wall of filing cabinets housing the student records. She pulled another key out of her pocket and opened the cabinet that housed Todd Delaney's file.

"Annie, hurry up! I see Mrs. Shipley coming," Matt whispered as loud as he dared.

"Get out of here, Matty! I don't want you to get caught in the office."

"Annie, I can't let you take the rap for this."

She grabbed the file, closed the filing cabinet and left the inner office. "Get out, Matt! I won't get caught, and if I do I will talk my way out of it."

"I feel like a heel..."

"Please, just go." She shoved him out the door.

Matt took off and wasn't spotted by Mrs Shipley, one of the guidance counselors. Annie looked over her shoulder and froze for a second. "Crap! I left the light on." She raced over to the inner office, quickly opened the door, turned off the light and headed out to the waiting area. She looked out the door and swore again. "Double crap!"

Mrs. Shipley was too close for her to get away without

being seen. Annie thought for a moment and came up with a plan. She took off her coat and sat down in a chair. She used her winter coat to hide the purloined file and started to cry.

Mrs. Shipley was surprised the door was unlocked as she turned the handle after inserting her key. She opened the door and stepped inside. "Annie! What are you doing here? Are you crying? Please, tell me what is the matter."

"Oh, Mrs. Shipley, I'm so worried."

"How did you get in here?"

"I had Mr. Granger, the janitor, unlock the door for me. I hope that's all right. He won't get into any trouble, will he?"

"No, dear, he won't," Mrs. Shipley told her even though she didn't know which of the many janitors was Mr. Granger. "Now you tell me what's bothering you so."

"I know you told me I would be able to graduate this year if I passed all my classes."

"Yes, that's right. Do you still want to graduate early?"

"Oh, yes, Mrs. Shipley. More than ever!" Annie sounded so distressed.

"I can't believe you are not passing all your classes," Mrs. Shipley said as she leaned back against her desk.

"I am! I'm getting A's in all my classes."

"Then what is the matter? I don't understand."

"One of the girls in my English class, I won't tell you who because she threatened me, anyway, she told me I couldn't graduate because of a new state law about requirements for early graduation. She told me I was just wasting my time, and I would have to be here another year," Annie blurted out and then sobbed even harder.

"There! There! You don't need to worry, Annie." Mrs. Shipley patted Annie's shoulder and then handed her a tissue. "Believe me I would know if there was a reason you would not be able to graduate, and I can assure you there is not a new 'law' that would prevent your early graduation."

"Really!?" Annie's tears stopped in a flash. "So I will still be able to graduate this year?"

"Yes, dear, as long as you pass all your classes."

132

"Oh, thank you, Mrs. Shipley. You have set my mind at ease."

"You shouldn't listen to what the other students try to tell you. This girl was obviously just trying to upset you. If you have any more trouble, please come and see me and I will talk to Mr. Kemmerick."

"I will. Thanks again, Mrs. Shipley."

Annie's mind was racing as she wondered if there was any evidence she had been in the inner office. She couldn't think of anything as she walked out into the hall. She forced herself to walk slowly out of the building. She saw Matt waiting by her car.

"Get in! We need to get out of here now." Annie made it seem as if the police were hot on her trail.

"Tell me what happened," Matt asked as they sped away.

Annie told him how she managed to escape.

"The file is in my coat. I need to get it home and take pictures of it. I'm pretty sure I will be able to prove Delaney changed his grades."

"How will you be able to prove it?"

"Remember the day you overheard Delaney talking to his friend?"

"Yeah, so what?"

"Well, I did the same thing that evening that I just did today. I took his file and made a copy. Now I have the file again and if the grades have been changed..."

"Yeah, but how can you prove Delaney is guilty? He will say someone else changed the grades."

Annie cruised through a yellow light and looked at Matt. "I haven't quite figured that out yet, but I'm working on it."

"You could wear a wire and get him to confess," Matt teased.

Annie slammed on the brakes and pulled to the curb.

"You are brilliant! I could kiss you."

"I like that idea. The kissing part, I mean."

"Don't you see? I can get a wire from Daddy's friend and really get Delaney to incriminate himself. It might not stand up in a court of law, but it should be enough to get him suspended again."

After school the next day, Annie visited her father's friend, John Ridgely, who worked as a private investigator.

"Hello, Annie, how have you been? I haven't seen you around since you solved the missing cafeteria money caper. What's the crime this time?"

"I need to borrow a wire so I can get a confession from a kid at school."

"Please tell me you aren't sticking your pretty face where it shouldn't be."

"It's nothing dangerous. Just a case of changing grades..."

Annie told Mr. Ridgely the whole story, and he reluctantly agreed to let her borrow a wire. After she left, he sat in his chair trying to decide if he should call her father. He decided to let Annie handle the "case" for now.

The next day at school Annie had Matt wear the wire. He cornered Todd Delaney in a third floor hallway. She waited twenty feet behind Matt.

"Hey, Delaney, I need to talk to you."

"What's up, Matt? Need help placing a bet?" Delaney joked because Matt's father was reputed to be involved in the local betting racket.

"Aren't you the funny guy." Matt was rather intimidating to Delaney, and he used that to his advantage. "In a way I need to place a bet. I'm betting you don't want to be expelled. Would that be right?"

"I'm not going to be expelled. I haven't done anything," Delaney said but he didn't sound very convincing to Matt.

"I have proof otherwise. I might be willing to get rid of the proof in exchange for... say... two hundred bucks. I'm betting that you are aware of what I'm talking about."

"I don't know anything."

Matt laughed as he replied, "That is so very true, but I'm talking about grades. Does that ring a bell?"

Todd looked for a way to escape, but Matt had him trapped.

"Fine. I'll pay you to keep your mouth shut. I had to change my grades so I wouldn't flunk. How much do you need now?"

"I'll tell you tomorrow when I see you." Matt turned and walked away. "Probably at least half."

Delaney watched him as he left. He saw Annie, swore under his breath and smacked a locker. "You will pay for this, Annie O'Dell. I swear it."

Annie and Matt hurried to her house and listened to the recording. Sure enough, it was clear Delaney had tampered with his grades.

"I'm going to take this to Grandpa in the morning. I don't want you involved, Matty. I'll handle this myself."

"I don't feel right about you sticking your neck out. What if Delaney discovers it was you who caught him? I'm sure he saw you in the hallway."

"Then you will have to protect me. You better get out of here before Daddy gets home. I'll talk to you later."

When Detective O'Dell returned home later that night, Annie was already in bed, sound asleep. He was about to turn off the light when he noticed a suspicious looking folder on top of her dresser. He was familiar with those types of folders and wondered what Annie had in her possession. He opened the folder and began to read. It only took a few seconds for him to realize what he was holding in his hands.

"Annie, what have you done now?" he muttered as he took the file with him.

When Annie woke up the next morning and wandered out to the kitchen, the file was sitting on the island. She noticed it and looked at her father.

"Would you like to explain it here, or do I need to haul you to the station?"

"I can explain."

"Please do. I'm all ears."

Annie spent the next ten minutes explaining everything to her father as he listened patiently.

"Is that everything? You did this all by yourself, huh?"

"Yes! It was all my doing."

"Okay, I know you're covering up for someone, and I know

where you got the wire..."

"Did he..."

"No, he didn't call me, but I know. I know Matt was involved because I recognize his voice. How are you going to explain that to your grandfather? He will recognize Matt's voice, too."

"I don't know yet." Annie looked at her father and sighed. "Any suggestions."

"No! How are you going to return the file without getting caught? You know you will be suspended if you're caught."

"I know. I can handle that part."

"Do I want to hear how?"

Annie shook her head. "No, you don't want to know."

Detective O'Dell sighed as he stared at his daughter. He looked at the ceiling and rubbed his jaw for a moment. "All right, this is what I'm going to do. I assume you have copies of his grades and can return the file to its proper place. You present your evidence to your grandfather, and he will decide what to do with you and Delaney. Regardless of his decision, you are hereby grounded for life without the possibility of parole."

"But, Daddy!"

He lifted his hand to stop her in mid-sentence. "That is my decision."

Todd Delaney clenched his jaw, balled his hands into fists and shook his head as he sat in a booth at Darby's with Stewart Akens.

Stewart took a sip of his root beer and asked, "What's bugging you? You seem pissed off at the world."

"I'm gonna get even with Annie O'Dell if it's the last thing I do," Todd swore to his friend as he pounded his fist on the table.

"Why? What did she do?" Stewart shrugged. "You said it was Matt Sullivan who demanded blackmail money from you."

"I think she took my file from the guidance office. She turned me in to O'Dell."

"You mean Principal O'Dell?" Stewart asked.

Todd rolled his eyes. "Yeah! Who do you think I mean,

dorkbrain? You're about as dense as a rock sometimes. No, make that all the time. Dumb as a rock."

"So what if she took your file. What's the big deal?" Stewart shrugged.

"She has evidence that I changed my grades. That's what, you imbecile," Delaney shouted.

"Do you think you'll get suspended again?"

"I think they're going to try to expel me since this will be my fourth suspension of the year," Todd answered.

"That kinda sucks."

Todd stared at Stewart and then asked, "Why am I friends with you? Please remind me."

"Because we're cousins. Your father is my mother's brother. We're family."

Todd lowered his head to the table. "Why am I being punished like this."

Two days later, Todd Delaney was expelled for the rest of the school year. Annie was not suspended, but given detentions for a week. Her father stuck by his original sentence and Annie was grounded for life.

Chapter Twenty-Five

The last big social event of the school year was the senior class sponsored prom. The site was the Regency Hotel in downtown South Hampshire. The Barclay family donated enough money to cover the cost of the event. Although tickets were free, there were many students who could not afford the cost of a formal dress or tuxedo. Seniors were treated as special guests for the event. Juniors were allowed to attend but freshmen and sophomores were only permitted to attend as guests of juniors or seniors. This year's theme was "A Red Carpet Night," and the ballroom at the Regency was decorated as if it were the opening of a blockbuster movie.

Elaine hoped to go to the prom with her twenty-one-year-old boyfriend, Adrien Coyle. She asked him about going at dinner one evening.

He cut another piece off of his steak and responded, "Lainey, I would feel so out of place going to a high school prom. Besides aren't there rules about how old you can be?"

"You can go as long as you're not over twenty-one," Elaine said and then took another bite of her garden salad.

"What day is prom?" he asked

"Saturday the twenty-fourth. I told you that before," Elaine said.

He shook his head. "I can't go. I have to be in Columbus that weekend."

"Are you still going to that?"

Adrien shrugged. "I can't not go. It's a big event for the church, and I have to be there. I'm sure there are lots of boys who would be thrilled to take you to the prom."

"Boys, huh?" She rolled her eyes.

"Excuse me. There are probably a plethora of 'young men' who would willingly take you to the prom."

"You won't be upset if I go with someone else then?" she asked.

"No, you should go and have a good time."

Word got around school of Elaine's availability for prom

and several young men asked her to go. She and Cindy discussed the merits of each candidate in Elaine's room one evening.

"Let me see the list again," Cindy said.

Elaine handed Cindy the list.

Cindy read the names again. "Who is Gabe Hammond?"

"He's that tall guy in our English class who wears glasses and sweaters all the time."

"No chance," Cindy said as she crossed off his name.

Ten minutes later, Cindy crossed off another name. "That only leaves one. Mark Rizzo is declared the winner by default."

Elaine laughed and said, "He's not that bad."

Cindy rolled her eyes. "I could ask Bryce if any of his friends are available."

"No, I don't think Adrien would like it if I went with a college sophomore," Elaine said.

"Suit yourself, Lainey."

Dawn Matuzak had been telling everyone at school she was going to prom with Bert Hodges. That was news to Bert because he had asked Laura Russell to be his date.

"Dawn, why are you telling everyone you're going to prom with me? I never asked you to go," Bert angrily told her in the hallway outside of her locker.

"I just assumed you would go with me after the weekend we spent together last month," she replied.

He shook his head and slapped the lockers. "Well, I'm not. I asked Laura Russell to go, and she told me yes."

"I always say yes to you, Bert," Dawn said.

"Yeah, and to half the other guys in school. I'm not taking you, and it was a big mistake to spend that weekend with you."

"You'll regret this, Bert Hodges! I'll make you pay. I'll tell everyone that I'm carrying your child."

"How would you even know, Dawn? You would have to get a paternity test from half the school to prove who was the baby's father."

Dawn swore at Bert and vowed to get even.

Mace and Annie were talking by her locker later that day

after the last class.

"Annie, has anyone asked you to the prom yet?"

"Not yet, Mace. I'm not sure I could even go if anyone would ask."

"Are you still grounded because of that stunt you pulled last month?"

"Daddy is still pissed and insists I am grounded for life. I may never have another date in my life."

"At least you didn't get suspended."

"I would have if Grandpa found out I broke into the guidance office again. If I hadn't fallen asleep and left Delaney's file on my dresser, Daddy wouldn't have known either. I should have hidden the file in my underwear drawer. Daddy would have never seen it there."

"The school is better off without him around. In the yearbook he will be elected most likely to end up in prison or murdered, or murdered in prison."

"See ya later. I have to go straight home," Annie said as she waved goodbye.

When Annie got home, her father's unmarked squad car was already there. She gazed at a car parked on the street in the shade of the large maple tree. She turned to look at it as she walked up the front sidewalk.

"I'm home, Daddy! You're home early," she shouted as she dropped her backpack on the bench inside the front door.

"I'm in the living room, sweetie. You have someone here to see you."

Annie walked into the living room.

"Hey, Annie."

"Hey, Matty. I thought that might be your car outside. What brings you to our humble abode?"

"You do."

"What do you mean? We have barely spoken to each other the last couple of months," she said as she stared at Matt.

Annie knew exactly when they last spoke. It was in the guidance office the day she borrowed Delaney's file.

"Yeah, it's been a while," Matt said.

"Matthew came to see me at the station today. He wanted to talk to me about something. At first I flat out refused him, but he managed to convince me."

"What are you talking about, Daddy? Convinced you of what?"

Annie's heart raced as she wondered if Matt spilled the beans about the hotel stay in Peoria.

"Matt would like to ask you something, honey. Go ahead, ask her, Matthew."

"Would you go to the prom with me, Annie?"

"I can't."

"Why not?"

"I'm grounded for life. That's why not."

"Annie, I am willing to place you on probation. Since this is going to be your last year at Roosevelt, I think it's important that you be allowed to do some of the things seniors do—like prom."

"Are you sure, Daddy?"

"Yes. Matthew has convinced me he was partly to blame for what happened. He was going to inform your grandfather what Todd Delaney was planning, but you convinced him to stay out of it. Mind you both, I'm not pleased with what you did. At least how you did it, but the result is what mattered in this case."

Annie looked at Matthew. "If I go with you, you have to promise to behave. No kissing and no... never mind!"

Daddy looked surprised.

"I promise to behave, Annie, but I can't guarantee I won't try to kiss you."

Detective O'Dell looked at Matt and then at Annie as he wondered what was going on. "Well, I guess that's settled. Would you like to stay for dinner, Matt. We have leftover meat loaf and potatoes that Annie made yesterday, and I can put a salad together."

"I can stay if Annie doesn't mind."

Dad and Matt looked at Annie to see her reaction.

"Fine! You can stay, Matt. I have to change."

Annie ran to her room and changed out of her school clothes. Matt helped Detective O'Dell in the kitchen. They talked about Matt's family, but not about his family's businesses. Detective O'Dell didn't want to discuss that with Matt. There were some things about his father and his father's business affairs that were best left secret. Annie returned to the kitchen.

"What do you want to drink, Matty?" Annie asked. "I'm having a Sam Adams."

"A Sam Adams would be fine with me, Annie."

"I'm going to pretend I never heard that. We have Dr Pepper or Coke for you two. I will have a Sam Adams, though," Dad told them.

During dinner Annie was unusually quiet. She listened as her father and Matt talked about school and Matt's plans for the future.

"I never thought this would happen, but I applied to North Park," Matt said. "My grades are actually decent, not that anyone would believe it. My scores on the ACT and SAT were high enough. I haven't heard back yet, but I'm hoping to get in."

Mr. O'Dell poured more ketchup on his meat loaf as he said, "I was surprised when I heard about that, Matt. Annie and her friends have already been accepted. I'm sure you will be, also. My father knows the Dean of Admissions, and he put in a good word for you."

"Principal O'Dell put in a good word for me?" Matt was dumbfounded.

"He can see your potential, Matthew. You may try to be the school 'bad boy,' but some people can see through your disguise."

After dinner, Dad suggested, "Annie, maybe you and Matt should go somewhere and have some fun. I'll take care of the kitchen."

"Does this mean I'm not grounded anymore?"

"Let's say that tonight is a one time deal. A plea bargain of sorts, but if you break your probation, it's back to the slammer for you," he said as he pointed a finger at her.

She hugged him. "Thanks, Daddy."

"Make sure you leave your fake ID at home. Yours too, Matthew."

Matt looked at Detective O'Dell wondering if he was

kidding or not. Annie knew he wasn't kidding.

"We'll be back by ten, Daddy."

"You better be, or else."

Annie kissed her father on the cheek, and she and Matthew ran out the door before her father could change his mind.

"Where do you wanna go, Matty?"

"Wherever you want to go is all right with me."

"Okay, let's go to a fabric store. I need to pick up some fabric to make my prom dress. Then we could go shopping at the mall. I need some makeup and pantyhose."

Matt looked stunned. He never knew this side of Annie existed. "Sure if you want, Annie," he replied weakly.

"Are you nuts? You should know me better than that. I wouldn't have a clue how to make a handkerchief let alone a dress, and I hate the mall. Just FYI, I don't often wear makeup. What you see is what you get."

"You had me going, Annie. I thought you were serious for a minute. Wanna go to Sandusky's and play some miniature golf or something like that?"

"That's more like it. I think the go carts might be running already."

They headed to Sandusky's and played a couple rounds of miniature golf, but the go cart track remained closed.

"Hungry?" Annie asked. "I could use a chili dog, since we're close to Darby's."

"Sounds good to me, Annie."

Matt looked at his watch. They had a little bit of time before Annie had to be home. They grabbed a booth after getting their order from Danny Darby. They were talking and having a good time when Matt looked at his watch again.

"Annie, it's ten till ten."

"Oh crap! I'm gonna get killed."

"Hang on a second, Annie. I have an idea."

"I could use a miracle about now."

Matt walked up to the counter and asked, "Hey, Danny, can Annie use your phone to call home?"

"Sure thing, Matt. You know where it is."

143

"Come on, Annie. At least you can call home and explain."

Annie called her father. "Daddy, I'm sorry, but we're still at Darby's. We lost track of time. We're leaving as soon as I get off the phone."

"Okay, at least you called. Come straight home and we'll call it no harm, no foul."

"Thanks, Daddy. We'll be there in a few minutes."

They hurried home and ten minutes later Annie ran in the front door. Matt followed her inside.

"I'm home, Daddy. I'm sorry I'm late."

Annie looked at the clock on the wall next to the TV. It showed the time as 9:55.

"Is that clock right?"

Dad looked at his watch. "It appears to be right. Why?"

"What's going on? Matt, why did you tell me it was ten till back at Darby's?"

"Sorry, Annie."

"It's not Matthew's fault, sweetie. I made him tell you it was almost ten because I wanted to see what you would do."

"Don't you trust me?" she shouted with her hands on her hips. "That was so mean, and I'm mad at you too, Matthew Sullivan. You can forget about prom. Oh, I am so pissed at both of you."

Annie stormed off to her room and slammed the door shut.

"Matt, I'm sorry. I never expected her to get upset at you, too. Just wait here and I'll talk to her."

Dad walked down the hall and knocked on her door.

"Go away! I'm still mad at both of you."

"I'm coming in, Annie."

Dad entered her room and saw Annie sitting cross-legged on her bed. She threw a pillow at him.

"How could you do this to me? Now Matt will think I'm a child."

"I'm sorry, honey. This was all my fault. I made Matt go along with my plan. Please don't be mad at him. You can be upset with me, but Matt deserves better."

"That was a crappy thing to do to me, Daddy."

144

"I confess." He held out his hands, palm up. "I'm not perfect or all knowing."

Annie rolled her eyes and gradually smiled. "Oh, all right. I forgive you. But you need to trust me from now on. And another thing!"

"What, Annie?"

"There better not be any plainclothes detectives at the prom."

Dad laughed and said, "I swear. No undercover operatives at the prom."

Annie got off the bed and hugged her father. Then she walked out to face Matt. He stood up, not sure what to do.

"I'm sorry I blew up like that, Matty. I have a temper and sometimes it gets the best of me."

"It's okay. I like it when you get mad. Not mad at me, but when you get riled up about something. Your eyes seem to sparkle and you look so pretty."

"I'll be in my room if you need anything, sweetie. Don't stay up too late," Dad told her.

"Night, Daddy. I'll see you later. Matt won't stay too late."

Annie and Matt sat on the couch and talked. They talked about school mostly. Matt told Annie about his father's health and then asked Annie a question.

"Why do some kids call you Annie Mercer?"

"That's my name."

Matt tilted his head. "I thought it was O'Dell. Were you adopted or something?"

"No! How long have we known each other? Mercer is my middle name. It was Mom's maiden name."

"Oh, shoot! I should have known that. I'm such a dork."

"You're a cute dork though, Matty. Do you have a middle name?"

"Michael. All Irish kids have a middle name of Michael. It's a law or something."

They laughed and Matt moved closer to Annie.

"Whoa there, Matthew Michael Sullivan! You are not allowed to kiss me with my father just on the other side of that wall. He's probably listening to us as we speak. This room is bugged, no doubt."

"I'm not listening," Dad hollered from his room.

"Daddy, turn off the recorder. We need some privacy out here, or else we will go to my room. You better not have my room bugged."

"It's not. I swear it's not. I won't listen anymore."

"Your father really loves you a lot, Annie."

"I know. He's the best dad in the world."

"Thanks, honey."

They all laughed. Matt left a few minutes later, and Annie went in to see her father. She sat on his bed as he worked at his desk.

"I meant what I said, Daddy."

He spun around to face her. "I appreciate that. You know I try to do what's best for you. Sometimes I screw up, but my intentions are good."

"I know. You have been the best dad... and mom... a girl could hope for."

"Thank you, but you're still grounded except for the night of the prom."

"Oh, Daddy," she huffed as she marched off to her room.

Chapter Twenty-Six

Candidates were chosen for King and Queen, and the voting took place during school the week prior to prom.

"Did you vote already, Lainey?" Annie asked as they finished their lunch.

"Yeah, I voted this morning, as if it makes any difference. Everyone knows it will be Damon and Diana."

"I voted for Cindy and Derrick Keasling. They have a chance."

"Sure, they have two chances—slim and none!"

"Who's your date for the prom? Did you make a decision yet?" Annie asked as she piled the trash on her tray.

"I weighed all my options and the winner was... drum roll please!"

Annie rolled her eyes and then made a sound like a drum roll.

"Mark Rizzo," Elaine muttered just loud enough for Annie to hear.

"Mark Rizzo! He's a dork! Why did you choose him?" Annie shouted.

"Shush. I don't want everyone to know," Elaine said as she looked around the cafeteria. "He's not a total dork."

Annie rolled her eyes.

"He's smart, he's reliable, he goes to our church, and he won't pressure me for sex."

"So, you made your choice based on how horny he might be?"

"Annie! Just because you aren't going doesn't give you the right to make fun of my choice."

"I have good news. Daddy is putting me on probation for now. I can go to the prom, and I already have a date."

"Who? Are you going with Randy Braun? He told me he likes you."

"No way," Annie said as she shook her head. "He's your old boyfriend. I'm going with Matt Sullivan."

"Come on! Tell me who you're really going with. Are you

just kidding and you're really still grounded?"

"I am going with Matty," Annie said slowly.

Elaine realized Annie was serious. "Why? Talk about someones old boyfriend. Have you forgotten about Victoria Madison and Amy Porter and all the other girls he has been with. Get real, Annie."

"I trust Matt and, yeah, I know he has been with other girls. Doesn't mean he will try to make a move on me."

"Just be careful, Annie. You can be too trusting of people."

"Do you have a dress already?" Annie asked as they stood up to head to their next class.

"Yeah, if you don't have one, you need to start looking or else they will all be gone. I'll go shopping with you if you want."

"Thanks, Lainey. I could use some help choosing."

The next day after school Annie and Elaine visited the dress shop where Elaine bought her dress. Annie tried on several gowns, but didn't really like any of them.

"Lainey! I can't wear this. Daddy would kill me. Look! If I bend over everyone will see me. I need something more modest."

"What about this style, Annie. It's not as revealing."

"That would be perfect! I wonder if they have it in my size?"

The dress shop did have the right size for Annie. After some minor alterations, Annie was all set for the big night.

Finally, it was May twenty-fourth—Prom night. Matthew arranged to have his father's car for the night. He picked Annie up right on time.

"I need to take some pictures before you go, Annie," Dad said as he held his camera.

"All right, but not too many. We need to get going."

"Have I mentioned how pretty you look tonight?"

"You might have mentioned that once or twice, Daddy. Doesn't Matt look handsome?"

"He looks very handsome," Dad said as he ran a finger along Matt's lapel.

"You better not stay out too late tonight and don't do anything I wouldn't do," Annie told her father.

"Elisabeth and I are taking Keyshon with us. I think it's safe to say we will be home early. But just in case I'm not here when you get home, I will be at Elisabeth's."

Annie frowned as she said, "I hope you aren't planning on spending the night."

"Ain't nobody's business if I do," Dad said. He finished taking pictures and sent the kids on their way.

Matt opened the doors for her, and they entered the ballroom of the Regency Hotel.

"Matty, this reminds me of the pictures I have seen of movie theaters from the thirties and forties when famous movie stars would attend gala openings," Annie said as she twirled around. "There's Lainey and Cindy. Come on. I want to talk to them."

She let Matt take her arm as they meandered through the already crowded room.

"You finally made it, girl," Mace said as he held Trish's hand. "Nice dress."

Annie glared at him.

"Hey, I meant that as a compliment," Mace insisted.

Annie glanced around and spotted Derrick Keasling. "Why is he with Clarissa Morgan? Didn't they break up?"

"They did, but this is what I heard," Cindy whispered. "Clarissa threw a fit because she already had her dress. Derrick was going to ask Emmy Colasanti, but didn't. I don't see her here."

Elaine added, "The Keasling and Morgan families are friends. They live in the Barclay Estates, and the Morgans were thrilled their daughter was dating Derrick. To keep peace between the two families, Derrick agreed to take Clarissa."

Trish pointed at Kristen Keasling and whispered, "Kristen came with her cousin."

"I didn't know the Bertucci and Keasling families were related," Mark said as he adjusted the sweater vest under his tuxedo jacket.

"Tony is their cousin," Annie said.

149

"Don't repeat this, but Kristen told me she chose Tony because the other guys who asked had unfair and unrealistic expectations."

"Like what?" Annie asked.

Mace shook his head. "Girl, are you still that naive?"

Annie glared at him. "No, why?"

Trish glanced at the ceiling, then back at Annie and whispered, "The guys expected her to share a room. A hotel room."

"Oh, I get it," Annie said as she looked at Matt.

Annie and Matt had their pictures taken before they started dancing.

"What are you looking at?" Matt asked as they danced.

"I'm trying to figure out how some of those dresses stay up," she said as she grinned. "I'm glad I found this one. Do you like it, Matty?"

"That color is perfect on you," he said. "Lainey told me so."

A few minutes later, Maris Miller and Grady Harris stopped by to show off her engagement ring.

"It's so beautiful," Annie said. "Have you set a date?"

"We have," Maris said as they left to show off her ring to other friends.

Annie danced with some of her friends, as well as Matt. Derrick asked her to dance and even Tony Bertucci danced with her. He was shy and rather quiet, but a very good dancer.

"Matty, there's Victoria," Annie said later. "She's with Jason Agresta. Do you know him?"

"Not really, but I know he was the quarterback last year. He's a jerk if you ask me," Matt said.

Victoria Madison flaunted the fact she was with Jason Agresta, but didn't announce the fact she was pregnant, though.

Annie noticed Dawn Matuzak arrive with Jayson Mathias.

"Matt, I think Dawn Matuzak might be planning to ruin the prom for Bert Hodges somehow. She made threats against him."

"I heard about that. What could she have up her sleeve?"

"I don't know, but I want to find out."

Annie moved closer to Dawn and noticed her reach into her purse. Annie moved quickly as Dawn pulled out a small can of spray paint.

"What have you got there, Dawn?"

Dawn turned and saw Annie. "Get away from me, O'Dell. I'm going to give Bert Hodges just what he deserves for dumping me," Dawn said as she attempted to remove the cap.

Annie grabbed Dawn's arm and held on as Dawn shook her arm vigorously.

"Let me go, O'Dell, before I kick your ass."

Suddenly, Mr. Kemmerick and Mrs. Doolen appeared at Dawn's side.

"Miss Matuzak, I think you and I need to have a little chat," Mr. Kemmerick said.

"I haven't done anything. This is empty. I used it to help decorate the place."

Annie grabbed the can away from Dawn. "It feels pretty full to me." She handed the paint to Mr. Kemmerick.

"It's just paint. It's not like it would really hurt the jerk."

"Let's go before I call the police."

Dawn left quietly. Jayson stood with a blank expression and glassy eyes not quite understanding what had happened. He was stoned, as usual.

Randy Braun grabbed a microphone, tapped it several times to get everyone's attention and said, "It is now time to announce your senior class King and Queen."

To no one's surprise Damon Barclay and Diana Ahronson were announced as the king and queen. Derrick Keasling and Clarissa Morgan were runners-up.

"Go figure," Mace said. "The election was rigged."

Annie smacked his arm. "How can you say that? Everyone likes them."

"I voted for you, Annie."

"Bull!" Annie replied.

"You better not have," Trish said as she frowned at Mace.

Later, Matt checked the time and said, "We should get going, Annie."

"Okay, but let me say good night to my friends first."

Matt brought Annie home by the promised time, but the house was empty.

"Daddy, where are you?" she hollered almost afraid to look in his room for fear of finding him in there with Elisabeth Franklin.

"I don't think he's here, Annie."

"Do you want to stay for awhile, Matty?"

"Will your father be upset if I do?"

"He might not come home tonight. He was out with his girlfriend."

"Detective O'Dell has a girlfriend? Wow!"

"You do realize he was married once. To my mother."

"I'm sorry, Annie. I don't mean any disrespect. I just never think of old guys as having girlfriends."

"I want to change out of this dress. Do you mind?"

"No, would you mind if I changed out of this tux? I brought a change of clothes just in case. They're in the car."

"Just in case of what, Matthew Sullivan? Did you think you might need a change of clothes for the morning or something?"

"It's not like that, Annie. I brought them in case we got home early. Like we just did. If you want me to stay, I want to be comfortable."

"All right. You can change in the bathroom while I change in my bedroom with the door locked."

"That's all right. I'm not going to break down your door."

Annie changed in her room while Matt went out to his car to get his bag. He noticed the counter of the bathroom vanity seemed to be divided into two separate places on either side of the white sink in the middle. He could tell one side belonged to her father. A razor, shaving cream, toothbrush and an old comb with missing teeth took up a small area. The other side of the sink was crowded with bath soap, hairbrushes, bubble bath and other items that could only belong to a teenage girl. Annie was sitting on the couch holding a small pillow to her chest when Matt came back out to the living room. He was wearing jeans and a t-shirt and Annie had on shorts and a ragged, stretched out sweatshirt over a tank top. She was barefoot and Matt laughed at her.

152

"Well now, Daisy Mae, how have you been?" Matt tried his best imitation of a southern drawl.

"I want to be comfortable. I felt silly in that dress."

"You looked very pretty though, Annie."

She looked at him as if to ask, "How do I look now?"

"I mean you always look pretty."

"Yeah, whatever! Do you want something to drink? No beer. Daddy probably counted them."

"Coke is fine, if you have any."

"We have Dr Pepper."

"That's all right."

"I'm going to make some popcorn. We can watch a movie if you want."

"That's okay with me. What movies have you got?"

"They're in the cabinet under the TV. Pick any one you want."

Annie fixed the pop and the popcorn. She came back to the couch with two cans of Dr Pepper and a large orange Tupperware bowl filled with popcorn.

"Did you find a good movie?" she asked as she sat the popcorn on the coffee table.

He held up a copy of *Animal House*. "How about this one?"

"Okay, I like Belushi."

They settled down on the couch to watch the movie and ate the popcorn. Annie tucked her feet under her and Matt looked at her legs.

"Why are you looking at me like that?"

"Like what? I was just looking at your legs."

"Well, stop it!"

"Okay! I won't look at you! I'll keep my eyes closed while I watch the movie."

Annie smacked his arm. "I'm just teasing you, Matty. I don't care if you look at my legs. After all, you saw me in my bikini in Peoria."

"Yeah, and I saw you change out of your bikini, too."

"You did not see me change. You had your back to me."

"Maybe I peeked."

"You didn't because I was watching you, and so what if you did watch me. I don't have anything you haven't seen before."

"All those other girls don't mean anything to me, Annie. They were just meaningless nights of lust," Matty teased Annie now.

"Well, if you're hoping for another night like that you better find another victim," she said though her brown eyes sparkled as she thought about how it would be to kiss him again.

Annie alternated between sitting close to him and at the end of the couch. She even put her feet in his lap at one point. She got warm and took off her sweatshirt as he watched. Matt looked at Annie to see her reaction as John Belushi's ladder scene played. Annie watched and looked at Matt.

"I've seen this movie before. I'm not embarrassed. Are you?" Annie asked.

"It's kinda weird watching scenes like that one with you next to me."

"I do believe you are blushing, Matthew Sullivan!"

"No, I'm not. You were just imagining that."

Annie grabbed the remote and rewound the movie. She paused the movie at a certain point and looked at Matty. He looked at her and she began to giggle.

"Is this why you picked out this movie, Matty. So you could see whoever that is topless."

"You are gonna get it, Annie."

Annie tried to get away, but Matt grabbed her around the waist. They were both laughing as Matt pulled Annie onto his lap. He poked her in the side and she laughed even more.

"Will you push play?"

"Are you through looking at her boobs?"

"I've seen this movie before."

"So you know where all the good spots are, huh?"

"Give me that remote before I spank you."

Annie sat up on her knees and held the remote above her head. "Take it away, if you dare."

Matt looked at her exposed belly button. Then he reached

for the remote, and they both toppled over. Matt ended up on top of Annie for a few seconds. He looked into her eyes. She stared at him with a doe-like expression. He could feel her sweet breath on his face. Her heart raced faster than an out-of-control runaway train. He licked his lips, and she closed her eyes in anticipation... but nothing happened. He got up, and she let him have the remote. The room remained quiet for as moment until he clicked play on the remote and started the movie again.

"Sorry, Annie, I didn't mean to do that."

"Sure you didn't," she said sarcastically. "Did you like it?"

"Annie O'Dell, you had better behave if you want me to stay."

"All right. I'll be good."

They watched the rest of the movie and Annie giggled every time there was anything naughty on screen. Matt poked her in the ribs to make her stop. After *Animal House* was over, Matt looked for another movie.

"I don't know what to choose. You pick out a movie."

Annie looked and pulled one out.

"*Smokey and the Bandit* okay with you?"

"Sure. That one's funny and Sally Field is cute. She reminds me of you. You look like her."

"Yeah, right," Annie said.

They watched the tame, but funny movie, and Annie was starting to fall asleep against Matt's shoulder. When the movie ended she was asleep.

He noticed and grabbed her arm. "Annie! Wake up. You should go to bed."

She opened her eyes, noticed how close she was to Matt, sat up straight, grinned and said, "Are you telling me to wake up and go to sleep?"

"Something like that." He ran a hand through her hair.

"I need to get to bed, Matty. It's so late. Why don't you stay overnight?"

At first he didn't believe he heard her correctly. "I'm not sure I should."

"Don't be silly. Daddy will understand. He wouldn't want

you to be driving this late at night. I'll get you a pillow and there are blankets in that closet. Take what you want."

"All right. I really am more sleepy than I realized."

Annie brought Matt a pillow from her bed.

"This smells like you, Annie. I like it."

"Do you need a night light, Matty?" Annie teased.

"If I get scared, I'll just come into your room."

"Is that a threat or a promise?"

Matt rolled his eyes and shook his head.

"I don't normally lock my door. Should I lock it tonight?"

"Maybe you should. That way if I get up in the night to go to the bathroom, I won't go into your room by mistake."

"Good night, Matty. I had fun tonight. And the prom thing was all right, too." She waited by the couch for a moment.

"I had a good time, Annie. Maybe I'll see you in the morning. I'll probably leave as soon as I wake up."

"You could stay for breakfast," she said.

"Maybe." He lay back down on the couch.

Annie turned off the lights and walked down the hall to her bedroom. As she got into bed, Annie realized Matt hadn't even tried to kiss her tonight. She felt both relieved and a bit disappointed.

Chapter Twenty-Seven

It was nearly nine o'clock in the morning when Keith O'Dell opened the front door, hung his coat on the coat rack in the corner, tossed his keys on the shelf above the bench and walked into the living room. He laughed as he spotted Matt Sullivan sleeping on the couch. Keith tiptoed down the hall to Annie's room. He tried to open the door, but it was locked. He smiled and went to his room. It was noon before anyone woke up.

Annie woke up and stumbled to the bathroom. She came out and looked in her father's room. He was sprawled on the bed, still in his clothes. She wandered out to the living room and saw that Matt was still asleep. She went into the kitchen and started the coffee. The pleasant aroma of coffee reached her father. He got up and walked into the kitchen.

"Morning, Daddy. I'm making coffee."

"It smells good. How was the prom, Annie? Did you have a good time?"

"Prom was all right, but Matty and I left kinda early. We were here by eleven thirty. We watched movies and had popcorn. I had more fun just doing that than I did at the prom." She looked in the fridge for something to eat. "Want a bagel, Daddy?"

"Sure." He scrunched up his shoulders and twisted his head to work out a kink in his neck.

She pulled out the sleeve of bagels, split two in half and popped them in the toaster oven. "Oh! Dawn Matuzak came to the prom with a can of black spray paint. I stopped her from redecorating Bert Hodges and his date. You would have been proud of me."

"That's my girl! Always in the middle of trouble. At least this time you weren't causing the trouble."

They heard Matt stirring on the couch. He used the bathroom and then came out to the kitchen.

"Good afternoon, Matthew. Did you sleep well?"

"Hello, Detective O'Dell. I hope you're not mad because I crashed here last night. We were watching movies and it got to be pretty late."

"Annie explained everything to me. It's probably better that you didn't try to drive after drinking..."

"Daddy, we didn't drink anything but pop. You can count the beer in the fridge if you want."

"I don't have to, Annie. I trust you," he said as he opened the fridge and saw the Sam Adams on the shelf.

The timer on the toaster oven dinged. Annie buttered the bagels and opened the jar of the Huber Family's Apricot Spread.

"Wanna split a bagel with me?" She slathered the spread on her bagel.

Matt stretched his arms over his head. "Do you have any peanut butter?"

"You want peanut butter on a buttered toasted bagel?" Annie asked as she retrieved the Skippy's from the cabinet.

"Is that weird?"

"Sorta, but it's your bagel," Annie teased. "I put bananas on my peanut butter sandwiches."

They drank coffee, ate the bagels, and talked more about the prom.

"Do you kids have plans for today?" Dad asked. "Isn't there always an after-prom-night party somewhere by a lake, or something where the guys compare notes about who slept with who."

"I want to go to that!" Annie's eyes lit up. "Do you know where it's supposed to be, Daddy. I want to hear all the good gossip."

"You better be careful, sweetie, or else they will be gossiping about you."

"They already do that. Remember, I told you the story about me and the basketball team."

"I remember. I was so proud that you only did the starting lineup."

Matt nearly choked on his bagel. Annie laughed at him.

"Daddy knows everything about me, Matty. I don't have too many secrets from him."

For some reason Matt remembered the box of tampons sitting in plain site on the bathroom vanity.

158

"It's funny that you can talk to your father about anything. I hardly talk to my father about even the simplest things."

"Who else can I talk to besides Daddy?" Annie asked as she finished her bagel.

"I'm sorry, Annie. I don't mean to imply anything."

"It's okay, Matt. You don't see your mother much anymore, either."

"I haven't seen her for two years now. She's in Vegas. At least that's where she was the last I knew."

Detective O'Dell refilled his coffee cup. "Your father asked me to see if I could find her a few months ago, Matthew. She's still in Vegas and she got remarried. I gave your father all the info. You can ask him if you want to know more." He held up the coffee pot. "More?"

Matt shook his head and held his hand over his coffee cup. "I don't need to know any more about her. If I never see her again, it will be too soon."

"Matty! She's still your mother," Annie said as she watched her father refill her cup.

"I know, Annie, and I suppose it's better than not having a mother, but in some ways it's not. At least you and your father have good memories of your mom. What I remember most was the drinking and fooling around with anyone who looked at her."

Annie held Matt's hand. He looked at Annie with tears in his eyes.

"Sorry, I just needed to vent a little," he said as he blinked away the tears. "Do you want to do anything this afternoon, Annie?"

"It might be fun to see what Lainey and Cindy are doing. Do you need to run home first?"

"Not really, if I could shower here that is."

"Sure, would you mind if I shower first?"

"No, go ahead. I can wait."

"It won't take me long, Matt. I'm not high maintenance like some girls you know."

Later, while Matt was in the shower, Annie called Elaine and made plans to get together to talk about prom and the upcoming graduation. Matt drove Annie over to the Novicki home. Cindy, Trish and Mace were sitting at the picnic table on the deck in back. Bryce Harper and Mark Rizzo showed up a few minutes later.

"What time did you leave, Annie?" Elaine asked. "I looked around for you and Kristen Keasling told me you were gone."

"It was about eleven fifteen. Matt had me back home by eleven thirty. How late did you stay, Lainey?"

"We left at one. Cindy and I and the guys came back here, and they left at two. Cindy spent the night."

Mace smiled and said, "I guess Trish and I are the winners then. We stayed until they turned out the lights."

"It wasn't a contest, Mace. Where did you and Trish go after you left?" Annie asked.

"Look who's getting nosy. If you must know, I spent the night in the basement at Trish's house. Locked in the basement, I think. At least there was a bathroom down there."

Everyone looked at Annie.

"Spill it! We told you our stories," Cindy said.

"Give it up, girl." Mace poked her in the side.

Annie looked at Matt, and he seemed to find the flowers growing up the lattice next to the deck extremely interesting.

"No! You didn't. Tell me you didn't do what I think you did." Mace was shocked.

"Mace! How can you even think I would do that?" Annie smacked his arm with some authority.

"Well, what did you do?" Elaine asked.

"Matt and I watched movies on the couch."

"Which movies? Tell me the truth."

"We watched *Animal House* and then *Smokey and the Bandit*. I fell asleep before the end of Smokey."

"And!" Cindy grinned.

"And Matt slept on the couch, and I slept in my room. Are you happy now?"

"Does your father know?" Elaine asked.

"Yes, he does. He had coffee with us before we came over here."

Annie didn't mention that her father was not home until morning.

"You are so predictable, Annie O'Dell. I bet you didn't even let Matt kiss you."

"Not that it's any of your business, Mace Franklin, but Matt didn't try to kiss me. I would have let him if he tried, but he didn't. He was a gentleman all night."

Mace looked at Matt, smiled and gave him a high-five. "That's for not taking advantage of Annie."

"I wouldn't do that, Mace. She's different than the other girls I've gone out with."

"How's that?"

"I don't know for sure. I like to look at her because she is pretty and all, but—I don't know." He shrugged. "I just have different feelings about Annie."

The group hung out at the Novicki house until three.

"I am officially bored now," Mace said.

"You could go play basketball with your buddies," Annie said.

"Not today."

Bryce suggested, "Why don't we go to Forbes Bend?"

"Is that the state park along the river at the edge of town?" Cindy asked.

"Yeah, some of my friends are going to meet at four to play Ultimate Frisbee."

"I've played that before! It's fun," Annie mentioned.

"Do you know the rules, Annie?"

"Most of them, I think."

"My friends are pretty good and they play hard," Bryce informed everyone.

"Maybe we could just watch," Cindy suggested.

"We'll see how it goes. They might just want to have fun and not be all macho today."

They got to the park before Bryce's friends and started throwing Bryce's Frisbee around. Mace was a natural athlete, so he caught on really quick. Two of Bryce's friends arrived, and they started tossing Frisbees around.

"I see what you mean, Bryce. These guys know what they're doing." Mace spun a disc on his finger as he watched Bryce's friends.

"They play in a league at North Park and have tournaments and stuff. There are some girls on the team, too," Bryce said.

After warming up for a while, the kids chose up teams and started playing. Ben Barnes and Sam Corry explained the rules to everyone. They played for a time just so everyone got the idea of how to play. David Halligan and Mark Fennelly showed up, and they started playing for real. Elaine, Cindy and Trish stopped playing and sat at a picnic table to watch the guys. Annie was in better shape and could run just as fast as Matt Sullivan. They were guarding each other. Annie teased Matt after she caught a pass for a score. Eventually, it was just the six guys playing. By six o'clock everyone finished playing and sat at the picnic table.

"Annie, I should take you home. I'm supposed to work tonight for my father."

"What time do you have to start?"

"Eight, but I need to get home and shower and all that. I'll grab something to eat at the bar."

"Okay, I'll say goodbye to my friends, and we can go."

Matt drove Annie back to her house and walked her to the front door. They talked for a couple of minutes, but Matt didn't try to kiss her. She wondered why. Matt took off and Annie waited until he was gone before going inside.

"Hi, sweetie. How was your afternoon?"

"It was fun. We were at Lainey's. Then we went to the park and played Ultimate Frisbee with some of Bryce Harper's friends."

"Are you hungry, or did you and Matt eat already?" Dad asked.

"We didn't eat. He has to work tonight."

"You got a taste for anything in particular?"

"I know we've got stuff for a salad we need to use before it goes bad. How about a salad and baked potatoes?"

"Sounds good to me. There's one chicken breast left. We could put that in the salad, or split it in two."

"Okay, let me get the potatoes in the oven and then I'll go

162

clean up and make the salad. I'll put the chicken in the salad."

Annie got the potatoes in the oven. She showered, changed clothes and put the salad together while her father worked in his room.

"Supper's ready, Daddy!"

"I'll be right there, sweetie."

They sat at the island in the kitchen to eat, as usual.

Annie spooned some Marie's Thousand Island dressing on her salad. "What time did you get home this morning?"

"A little after nine. Why?"

"I was just wondering what Keyshon thinks about you spending the night with his mother."

"He went to bed early, and I left before he got up."

"I really like Keyshon. He's so sweet. He doesn't have an ounce of meanness in him."

"I like him, too."

"He's almost like a little brother to me..."

"We're not talking about getting married yet, Annie. It's too soon for that. I'll let you know if we get to that point, okay."

"Thanks. I just want you to be happy."

"I know, but I have your feelings to consider, too."

"If you're happy, then I will be happy."

Chapter Twenty-Eight

The final day of school was Friday, June sixth, although for seniors, classes had really been done for a week. The last week had been just for show, since finals were the previous week.

Graduation was at two o'clock Saturday outside at the football field. The weather cooperated with a bright and sunny day with temperatures in the lower eighties. A slight breeze blew from the south which helped keep everyone a little cooler. Detective O'Dell arrived early to claim a good seat close to the front. Grandpa didn't need a seat because he would be on stage handing out the diplomas. The graduates were supposed to be in the gym no later than one o'clock to get ready. Some of the students were dressed in suits and dresses while others were dressed more informally.

Mace saw Annie running toward him. "Hey, Annie, about time you got here. Where you been, girl?"

"Hey, Mace. I was doing girl stuff. You know, doing my hair, fixing my nails, putting on my makeup. That kind of stuff. It takes a lot of work to look this good."

"Yeah, right. You overslept, huh?"

"Just a little."

"What time did you get up?"

"About fifteen minutes ago. Do I look okay?"

He looked at her attire, shook his head, and laughed. "You look like you always do."

Annie punched his arm.

"I meant that as a compliment. You better go get your cap and gown."

Annie headed over to where Mrs. Etheridge and Mrs. Hart were passing out the cap and gowns for the girls.

"Annie O'Dell! Is this what you're wearing for your graduation? A tank top and shorts and tennis shoes?" Mrs. Etheridge asked as she shook her head. "Totally inappropriate. I am very disappointed in you."

Mrs. Etheridge was shocked, but Mrs. Hart smiled. She knew Annie well enough to know she didn't always follow the rules, or expectations of people in authority.

Annie looked at her attire, shrugged and said, "It's going to be ninety degrees out there and, anyway, no one will see what I'm wearing under my gown."

"You do remember that you have to turn in your gown before you leave today?"

Annie rolled her eyes and said, "Yes, Mrs. Etheridge. I know. You've reminded us a thousand times." She ran back to where Mace and Trish were waiting.

Mrs. Etheridge watched Annie and reminded Mrs. Hart. "She has never had a mother, and her father has tried to raise her by himself. The girl needed a mother. Look at her." The teachers looked at Annie as she stood next to Trish Eiffert. "She is like a tomboy or something. She needs some refinement. See how Judge Eiffert's daughter is dressed?" Mrs. Etheridge pointed.

"Yes, I can see the difference." Mrs. Hart tried to keep the sarcasm out of her voice.

"Trish is a very intelligent and refined young lady. That's the result of good parenting."

"I happen to think Annie O'Dell is a fine young lady, Mrs. Etheridge. She has a good head on her shoulders and doesn't blindly follow the crowd."

"I still think Principal O'Dell would be upset if he knew. Can you imagine, graduating in shorts and a top like that? Disgraceful!"

"Annie, how did you get away with wearing shorts? Does your father know what you're wearing?" Trish Eiffert asked.

"Daddy told me to dress comfortably. He said that was more important than wearing a fancy dress."

"Mom made me wear this shirt and a tie. I hate wearing a tie," Mace complained as he tried to stretch out his collar. "I'm losing it as soon as we toss our caps in the air."

"But you look so handsome, Mace," Annie said as she straightened his tie.

"Yeah! I do, don't I?"

"I think you look very handsome when you dress up." Trish smiled and then kissed him.

Annie punched his arm. "Gag me." She stuck a finger down her throat.

"You just don't recognize my manly qualities because you're still a child," Mace teased.

"Have you seen Lainey and Cindy?" Annie asked.

"Yeah, I saw them a while ago. They had to see Mrs. Hart about something. They should be back soon."

Annie looked around at all the kids. She was surprised by how many she didn't know. Although Annie was graduating a year early, she didn't regret it for a moment. Her best friends were with her. She saw Matthew Sullivan with some of his friends and waved to him.

"Hey, Matt, isn't that Detective O'Dell's daughter waving at you?" Jake Andalayna snickered.

"Yeah, so what?" Matt asked.

"Is she a friend of yours or something?"

"Yeah."

"You better be careful if you're trying to make it with her. Her father will kill you if you touch his precious daughter. He's a cop."

Matt's friends started laughing.

"Shut up, Jake, before I pound you."

"Did I touch a sore spot, old buddy. You got something going on with her?"

"Just shut up. I don't care if this is graduation."

"Hello, Matthew. Anything I can help you boys with today?" Mr. Kemmerick asked as he seemed to appear out of thin air.

"No thanks, Mr. Kemmerick. We got things under control," Matt replied.

"Good! I'd hate to see you blow it when you're so close to getting out of here."

Eventually, the band started playing "Pomp and Circumstance" which signaled it was time for the graduates to march out to the field. They were lined up in alphabetical order. The band played the song over and over as the graduates took their time. Most of the kids were having a good time. Annie O'Dell was

166

in the middle of two tall guys she didn't know except as O'Dale and O'Fallon. They knew each other and were talking back and forth, ignoring Annie, who was at least a foot shorter than either guy. Finally, the graduates were all seated and the ceremony began. Detective O'Dell, Mrs. Franklin and Keyshon sat together. Mr. O'Dell yawned during the speeches.

"Stop that, Keith," Elisabeth said. "You're setting a bad example for Keyshon."

"They should set a timer for some of the speakers."

Justin Chang spoke as the class valedictorian. Annie O'Dell had maintained a 4.0 GPA, but eight students had an even higher GPA because of honors classes, including Elaine Novicki and Cindy Mackens. Mace Franklin had worked hard to get his grades up. He finished with a GPA of 3.05—not bad for a jock.

At last it was time for the diplomas. Mr. Kemmerick read the names, and Principal O'Dell handed out the diplomas along with a few words for the students he knew. Mace accepted his diploma, pumped his fist and got a cheer from the crowd. They remembered the state title the basketball team won. Mr. Kemmerick tried in vain to remind the crowd to hold their applause until all the names were read. Cindy Mackens received her diploma and then Elaine Novicki. Principal O'Dell shook their hands and wished them well. The name Alfred Lawrence O'Dale was read. He marched across the stage.

Mr. Kemmerick looked at the next name on his list and announced, "Annie Mercer O'Dell." Mr. Kemmerick smiled as Annie walked past.

Principal O'Dell handed Annie her diploma, but instead of shaking her hand he hugged her tightly. Mr. Kemmerick waited patiently to read the next name.

"Annie Mercer, what are you wearing under that gown?"

"Just my underwear, Grandpa. It's hot out here."

"I should spank your butt, but that wouldn't look right. Go on with ya!"

"Love you, Grandpa!"

"Timothy Warren O'Fallon," Mr. Kemmerick continued without missing a beat.

167

After the ceremony, Elaine, Cindy and all the gang met to take pictures. For some of them, it could be the last time they would ever see each other. A few of them would be going on to college together. Some of them at North Park College, right there in South Hampshire. Elaine, Cindy, Mace, Trish, Annie and even Matt Sullivan, who finally received word of his acceptance, were among the students who would be enrolling at North Park in the fall.

"Just one more picture, please," Mr. Novicki said as he was taking a shot of Elaine and her friends.

"Now you can go, Lainey. I know there are other parents who want pictures."

Annie and Mace were looking for their parents and finally saw them. Keyshon saw them and ran over to hug Annie and then Mace.

"I saw you, Mace! Did you see me?"

"I did. I waved at you."

"I saw Annie O'Dell, too."

"I saw you, Keyshon. Do you want to wear my cap?"

"Sure! Can I really?"

"Just don't lose it okay."

"I won't, Annie. I promise."

Detective O'Dell shook hands with Mace and then hugged Annie. "I'm very proud of you, Annie. You have grown up so fast the last few years. Your mother would be proud of you, too."

"And her Grandpa is proud of her as well," Liam O'Dell said as he walked up behind Annie.

"Hi, Grandpa! I'm wearing more than what I told you earlier."

Her father was listening. "What are you talking about?"

"When I hugged Annie and gave her the diploma, she told me she was wearing only her underwear under the gown."

Dad shook his head. "That sounds like something she would do."

"Daddy! I have my clothes on. See!"

Annie lifted her gown to let her father and Grandpa see her shorts.

168

"Where's the new dress I bought you?"

"In the closet. I'll wear it tonight when we all go out to eat. You are taking me and Grandpa out to dinner, right?"

"Yes. You don't mind if Elisabeth and her boys come along with us?"

"Of course not. Where are we going?"

"Ciao Bella in The Hill neighborhood. I made reservations for six at six thirty."

"I think Lainey and Cindy are going there, too. I heard them talking about it anyway," Annie said as she waved to some of the guys from the basketball team.

"It will be like a party then."

Matt Sullivan's father made it to the graduation. He had been in the hospital recently, but made it to see his son graduate. Something Cormac Sullivan never accomplished.

"I'm proud of you, son, even if it took an extra year."

"Thanks, Pop. I suppose it's important."

"In another few years I will see you graduate from college. Now that will be an accomplishment. Your uncle Denis is the only Sullivan I know with a college education."

"I gotta go see someone, Pop. I'll be back in a few minutes."

"I'll wait here."

Matt saw Annie with her father and walked over to see her. Detective O'Dell saw Matt first and shook his hand.

"How are you, Matt? I see your father made it after all."

"Yeah, he did. I'm surprised he remembered. Can I talk to Annie for a minute?"

"Sure. Annie! Matt wants to talk to you."

Annie was talking to more of her friends and turned around when she heard her father call.

"Hi, Matty! I saw you earlier with your friends. I waved at you."

"Yeah, I saw you. Can we talk for a minute."

"Sure, what's up?"

"I mean in private."

"Oh, okay. Is everything all right?"

Matt took Annie's arm and led her away. "I just wanted to say goodbye."

Annie stopped suddenly and turned to face Matt. "What do you mean goodbye? Are you leaving?"

"I've leaving in two weeks for New York City. I'm gonna be working for Uncle Denis until college starts. I didn't want to leave without saying goodbye."

"You don't have to leave for two weeks. We can see each other until then."

"I won't be around much."

"Oh, I get it. You don't want to see me."

"That's not true, Annie," he said as he shook his head. "I want to see you, but maybe it's not a good idea for us to be seen together."

"Are you in trouble, Matty?"

"No, nothing I can't handle. I'll see you around, Annie. Take care of yourself and say goodbye to your father for me. I gotta go."

Annie watched as Matt left without a kiss or even a hug. She wondered what kind of trouble Matt had gotten himself into. She knew a detective who might be able to help her find the answer to that question.

Later that day, Grandpa picked everyone up, and they took his van into the "Hill" district. It was one of the older parts of South Hampshire and was now the site of many fine restaurants and shops.

"Can I sit with you, Annie?" Keyshon asked. "I wanna sit with Annie."

"You can sit in the back with me, Keyshon."

Grandpa drove and Mace sat in the front with him. Keith and Elisabeth sat in the middle and held hands. Grandpa found a parking space only three blocks from Ciao Bella.

"Not too bad, Grandpa. Daddy usually parks a mile away, and we have to walk for an hour to get there," Annie teased her father.

Keith took Elisabeth's hand, helped her out of the van and asked, "Do you want me to pay for your dinner tonight or not?"

"Please pay for my dinner, kind sir. My father starves me. I have to beg for food outside the Food King," Annie teased.

Mace walked on one side of Annie while she held Keyshon's hand. Keyshon walked beside her and gawked at all the buildings.

"That is a very pretty frock you are wearing tonight, Miss O'Dell. You look very fetching," Mace whispered.

She elbowed him and said, "Knock it off, Mace, before I send you fetching your head."

"I was just complimenting you on your attire for this evening."

Annie smoothed the front of her dress. "Daddy bought this, and he thinks I look sweet in it."

"You do look very sweet."

Annie punched Mace in his ribs. "I look twelve-years-old in this dress."

"Yeah, but a very pretty twelve-year-old."

Mace took off running before Annie could hit him again. Annie thought about chasing Mace, but decided to act like a more mature young lady. At least for now.

They were seated right away, and Annie saw Elaine and Cindy and their families. As they were walking past, Mace stopped to talk to Cindy and Elaine.

"Mrs. Novicki, doesn't Annie's dress look just perfect for her?" Mace asked knowing it would get a reaction from Annie.

Mrs. Novicki inspected the dress. "She does look very charming in that dress, Mace. More young ladies should wear modest dresses that length and I adore the ruffles. Please tell her I said so."

"I will, Mrs. Novicki. She will be happy to hear that."

Mace told Annie what Elaine's mother said, and she kicked his leg.

"I'm not talking to you, Mace Franklin. Keyshon will be my date tonight."

"Whoa, girl! Who says this is a date? I'm stuck here with you because my mom made me come. I wanted to be with Trish so we could communicate, you know."

171

"I'll communicate my fist in your..."

"Annie, what would you like to order, dear?" Grandpa asked rather seriously. He saved Mace from Annie's wrath.

They ordered and an hour later everyone was stuffed. Even Mace was full. Annie's held Keyshon's hand as they walked back to Grandpa's van.

"Hey look!" Annie shouted. "Grandpa got a parking ticket." Annie sprinted to the van, snatched the ticket from under the windshield wiper, read it and then threw it down. "Oh, it's just a flyer for a new restaurant. I thought it was a ticket."

Grandpa put his hands on her shoulders. "Are you disappointed, Annie."

"Yes, I wanted you to get in trouble like I always do."

"Not my little angel. You never get in trouble."

"No, Grandpa. I never get in trouble. I'll always be your little angel." Annie used her best smile to charm her grandpa.

Detective O'Dell and Mace both suddenly began to cough. They muttered something under their breath that only Annie heard.

"Daddy! How can you say that about me?"

Chapter Twenty-Nine

"I'll get it, Daddy!"

Annie ran to answer the phone.

"Hello."

"Hi, Annie. This is Kristen Keasling."

"Hey, Kristen. How are you?"

"I'm doing fine. I know it's short notice, but we're having a graduation party this Saturday the fourteenth for Derrick. I wanted to invite you. If you're too busy and can't make it, I understand."

"I'm not busy. What time is the party?"

"It's gonna start around three and go until everyone leaves, I guess."

"That sounds like fun," Annie said. "Would it be okay if I bring a friend?"

"Sure. Lainey and Cindy are coming and so are Trish and Mace."

"I was thinking of Matty Sullivan. Would it be all right if I ask him?"

"Sure, Derrick knows him. I'm sorry we didn't invite you earlier, but Derrick didn't know your address. I got your number from Lainey. I hope that's okay."

Annie shrugged and said, "No problem. Do you mind if I write down your number?"

"Please, go ahead. This is my cell phone. You can call me anytime. I'll give you the address."

Kristen gave Annie the address.

"I know where that is, I think. I've been past it with my father."

Annie and Kristen talked for a few minutes about the party.

"Do I need to bring anything, or wear anything special, like a dress, or is it informal?"

"Most girls will probably wear a dress, but you wear whatever you like, Annie. It's just a party not a fancy ball or anything. Mom will make me wear a dress, and Emmy is going to wear a dress."

"I guess if you and Emmy are wearing dresses then I

should, too," Annie said and then asked, "Isn't Emmy kind of a tomboy? That's the impression I have about her."

Kristen chuckled then said, "Yeah, but she's growing out of it."

As soon as Annie got off the phone with Kristen she tried to call Matt Sullivan. No one answered at his house so she left a message.

She waited for a day but no one returned her call.

"Daddy, where do you think Mr. Sullivan would be about now?"

"You mean right this minute?" he asked as he set his newspaper down.

"Yeah."

"Well, if I had to guess, I would say he's probably at his place on Keigher Avenue and Fifteenth Street, or else at The Hungry Lion. Why?"

"I need to talk to Matt, and he told me he was working with his father until he leaves for New York. Did you ever hear anything from your friend. Is Matty in any kind of trouble?"

"No one knows of any trouble. Even Cormac has been a law abiding citizen lately. Kinda frightening in a way."

"Would you mind if I go over there and try to find Matty? I need to talk to him."

"Do you want me to go with you?"

"No, that might scare him away."

"Be careful, Annie."

Annie drove over to The Hungry Lion to find Matt. She parked the car, got out and noticed two entrances. She chose the one on the right and walked inside. Some guys drinking at the bar looked at her and made rude comments. She ignored them and walked up to the bartender.

"Hi! Is Mr. Sullivan or Matthew here by any chance?"

He wiped the bar with the towel that had been on his shoulder and asked without looking at her, "Maybe, who wants to know?"

"It's all right, Sean. This is a friend of Matthew's," Cormac

174

Sullivan said. "Hello, Miss O'Dell."

Annie turned around as she heard the voice. "Hello, Mr. Sullivan."

"What brings you down here, Annie?"

"I'm looking for Matt. Do you know where he is?"

Mr. Sullivan jerked a thumb over his shoulder. "He's working in the back. Want me to get him for ya?"

Annie shifted her weight back and forth as she stood with her hands behind her. "I don't want to disturb him if he's busy working."

"He can take a break. Come on back with me."

They walked into a back office and Annie saw Matt sitting at a desk with a legal pad and a textbook.

"Take a break, Matty. There's someone here to see ya."

He snapped his book shut and raised his eyes. "Hey, Annie. How are you?"

"Hi, Matty. I hope I'm not disturbing you. Are you doing homework or something?" She looked around the room and spotted a police scanner sitting on a shelf.

"Yeah, I'm taking an accounting class when I get to New York, and I was just getting a head start. What's up?" Matt asked as he stood up and walked around to the front of the desk. He sat on the front edge, reached out and grabbed one of Annie's hands.

"I want to invite you to a party on Saturday. It's a graduation party for Derrick Keasling. I'm invited and I can bring a guest."

"I'm sorry, Annie, but I've got to work all day on Saturday," he answered as he squeezed her hand tenderly.

Matt's father had been listening. "Why don't you take Saturday off? You can work Sunday instead. That way you can have some fun with your little friend."

"Thanks, Mr. Sullivan. I appreciate it. I'll call you later, Matty. What time will you be home?" Annie asked.

Matt let go of her hand, stood up, walked behind the desk and sat down. "How about I call you when I get home?"

"Okay, do you remember my number?" Annie asked.

"Got it right here." He pointed to his head.

175

Matt called Annie three hours later.

"Hey, Annie, it's Matt."

"Hi, Matty. Are you home now?"

"Yeah, just got here a few minutes ago. Tell me more about this party. Where is it?"

"It's at the Keaslings."

"Don't they live in that fancy part of the city."

"The Barclay Estates. Why?"

"Are you sure they want me to be there."

"Derrick knows you and he doesn't mind. Why are you being so... defensive... or whatever?"

Matt shrugged. "I just don't want to be somewhere I'm not wanted."

"I want you to go with me. Isn't that enough?"

Matt was quiet for a moment.

"Matty! Don't you like me anymore?"

"All right. I'll take you."

They talked and made arrangements for Saturday.

"I'll pick you up at three, and we can leave whenever you want."

"Okay. Daddy will be at the station all day. He won't be home until late."

"How late?" Matt asked.

"After I go to bed."

"Should I stay with you until he gets home?"

"Why, Matty Sullivan, are you trying to be nice to me again?"

"I worry about you sometimes."

"I'm a big girl now. I haven't had a babysitter for a couple of years," she said as she raised the pitch of her voice.

"Okay, miss big girl. What are you gonna wear to the party?"

"I'm probably gonna wear a light dress. Kristen told me most of the girls would be wearing dresses."

"Do I have to dress up? Wear a tie and all that crap."

"Don't you have a suit to wear?"

"You are kidding, right?"

176

"Yes, you can wear jeans, but wear a nice dress shirt. No t-shirts. Okay?"

"Just for you. It will be nice to see you in another dress," he said as he smiled.

"You just wanna see my legs again," Annie said and then laughed. "I think I have a dress in the closet that comes down to my ankles."

"Go ahead. Doesn't matter."

"Do you think I should let my hair grow long like Kristen Keasling or Emmy Colasanti?" Annie asked as she twisted her hair around a finger. "They have such gorgeous hair."

"I don't think there's enough time before the party," he said seriously.

"Hah! Hah! You are such a funny guy."

"Would it still be all curly?"

"Probably not as much."

"Then keep it just like it is. I kinda like it. It's like that movie star."

"You mean Meg Ryan?" Annie asked as she tried to straighten out some curls.

"No, I was thinking Shirley Temple."

"I hate you, Matthew Sullivan!" Annie shouted into the phone.

He laughed and replied, "Yeah, I know."

"I don't look like Shirley Temple, and I don't hate you," she whispered a moment later.

"That's good, Annie. I wouldn't like it if you hated me."

Chapter Thirty

It was just after noon on Saturday and Detective O'Dell was getting ready for work. "What are you wearing to the party, sweetie?" he asked while looking in the mirror as he fixed his tie.

Annie walked into her father's room. "This old dress. Do you like it?" She held it up in front of her.

"It looks very pretty. Can you try it on for me?"

"Why?"

"I just want to see how it looks on you."

"You mean you want to see how short it is."

"I suppose so. Doesn't a father have any say in how his daughter looks anymore?"

"No! Besides, Matt has seen me in my bikini before."

"I could have gone without that knowledge," he said as he ripped off his tie and started over.

"Don't be old-fashioned."

"Please? Just humor an old-fashioned dad for a minute, sweetheart."

"All right. Give me a minute."

Annie went to her room and a minute later came out wearing her dress. She spun around for her father.

"You look adorable and I guess it's not too short. I've seen shorter dresses." He looked at her again. "Try not to bend over too much."

"Daddy! I will be wearing a bra." Annie tried to pull the neckline up.

He finished doing his tie, sighed and said, "It's times like these that I really miss your mother, Annie."

"Oh, Daddy. You are so sweet. I love you. Have a good day at work."

"I don't know what time I'll be home."

"Matty might be on the couch when you get home. I hope that's all right."

"I would rather see Mace on the couch, but as long as he's on the couch."

"Go to work, Daddy. I'll be fine."

Matt Sullivan arrived just after three wearing a new pair of black jeans and a new gray dress shirt. Annie let him in while still in her robe. She had just gotten out of the shower ten minutes before.

"I'm almost ready. Just have to put on my dress. Don't you look all sharp."

"Thanks. I aim to impress all the rich kids at the party."

"Derrick is nice. He doesn't flaunt his family's money like some kids do. I'll be out in a flash. Make yourself at home."

"Can I have a beer?"

"We don't have time for a beer. Maybe tonight when we get back."

"I was kidding."

"I'm not."

Annie ran into her room and returned in three minutes. She spun around to let Matt see.

"Well, how do I look?"

"Holy Crap! Has your father seen that dress?"

"Yes, and he told me I looked adorable in it."

"I wonder how adorable you would look out of it?"

"Matthew Sullivan! Are you going to behave or not?"

"I was just dreaming."

"Having a nightmare, you mean. We should get going."

It took almost twenty minutes to make their way to the Barclay Estates neighborhood where the Keaslings lived. Matt had never been in the neighborhood. Matt's father was far from starving, but he was small potatoes compared to the families who lived in the Estates.

"It's that one on the right. We can park in the street, or in the park just down a ways."

Matt pointed. "There's a spot."

"Grab it. We won't have to walk as far."

Matt parked the car and they headed up to the house.

"Rather impressive, huh, Matt?"

"I suppose so if you like huge houses."

"Don't be like that."

"Like what?"

"Smile, we're going to have fun if it kills you. This might be my only chance to see you all summer. I want to enjoy it."

"Where are we suppose to go?"

"Kristen told me the party would be in the back by the pool house, or on the deck. Let's just follow the sidewalk over there. I told Daddy you might be staying over."

They talked as they followed the sidewalk around the side of the house.

"Why did you tell him that?"

"Because you said you might stay with me. Don't you want to now?"

"Yeah, I do, but what if he comes home early?"

"It won't matter as long as we're not in my room."

"I've never seen your room."

"And you probably won't tonight. It's a mess. Dirty clothes all over. It looks like a guy lives there."

"My room probably isn't any better."

"Hey, look! There's Kristen."

They saw Kristen on the large deck off the back of the house.

"Annie! Hi, you made it. Hi, Matt."

"Hi, Kristen. Nice little place you've got here."

"You wouldn't say that if you had to clean it like I do," Kristen said. "My mother made me dust the entire first floor yesterday. It took forever."

"Is that a tennis court over there, Kristen?" Annie asked as she pointed.

"Yeah, Dad built that for Derrick a few years ago. Worked out kinda nice. He got a scholarship to play tennis at the University of Arizona."

"Must be nice!" Matt sounded sarcastic so Annie pinched his arm.

"Do you want me to show you around?" Kristen asked.

"Is it all right if we just take a look around by ourselves?" Annie replied.

"Sure. The pool is over there. There are trails back that way if you want to go for a walk. There's food and pop up here on the deck and some pop and water by the pool. We're gonna have some music later so we can dance. Derrick's around here somewhere with Emmy. She's got a dress kinda like yours, Annie. You both look so pretty."

Annie laughed as she smoothed out the front of her dress. "Dad told me I looked adorable—like I was a twelve-year-old kid."

"There are supposed to be a lot of kids coming. If you see someone you don't recognize, they're probably family. Most of my aunts and uncles will be here."

"Is your cousin Tony gonna be here?" Matt asked.

"No, he's in Indiana because his sister just graduated from Notre Dame. They were doing something in South Bend today. I don't remember just what."

"We're gonna go sightseeing. See you later, Kristen," Annie said as she tugged on Matt's arm.

"Okay, I need to mingle with my relatives. I'm really glad you came."

Annie and Matt walked around to check out the place. The pool was in-ground with a pool house and a large ceramic tiled area around the pool with outdoor furniture. The whole pool area was surround by a six foot high black wrought iron fence. Matt and Annie saw some kids from school but didn't know their names. They headed over to the tennis court and checked it out.

"Let's go for a walk, Matty. I see a trail over there. It looks like it heads into the woods."

Matt looked at the trail and then back at the house. "You won't get me lost, will you? We could be lost out here forever."

"I'll protect you from the wildlife. Come on."

They were walking up the trail when they ran into Derrick Keasling and Emmy Colasanti.

"Hi, guys," Derrick said.

"Hi, Derrick! Hi, Emmy! You know Matt, right?"

"Sure, we've talked a few times. Good to see you, Matt. This is my friend Emmy Colasanti."

Matt had seen Emmy around, but had never met her. He noticed her pretty blue eyes.

"Emmy, our dresses are almost the same," Annie said.

"Yours looks much nicer, Annie. Mine is getting old."

"It still looks very pretty on you."

"Thanks, Annie," Emmy said softly and then bit her lip as she looked up at Matt.

"We were just heading back to the house," Derrick said. "I've gotta mingle with my relatives and the other guests. We'll see you guys later."

"Where does this trail go, Derrick?" Annie asked.

"If you keep going there is a small lake. You can't miss it."

Annie and Matt kept walking along the trail as Derrick and Emmy headed back to the party.

"Do you know Emmy very well?" Matt asked Annie.

"Not really. I've seen her around school and I think we had a few classes together."

"How old is she? She looks really young."

"Yeah, she does. Lucky girl! We are the same age. I'm a few weeks older. I think her birthday is in July and mine is May twenty-ninth."

"How do you know that?" Matt asked. "Have you read her school file?"

"I've read everybody's file, Matt. Don't you know that?" Annie grinned. "Emmy's really smart, but kinda quiet and shy. She's got an older sister who is like the exact opposite. Diane is real friendly and outgoing. She was really popular in high school if you know what I mean."

"I've heard stories about her sister. Are Emmy and Derrick a couple?"

"I'm pretty sure they're just friends. Emmy is really sweet, and, like I said, the total opposite of her sister in so many ways."

"What do you mean by that?"

"Diane kinda had a reputation. I'm surprised you didn't know her. She was just your type."

"And what, pray tell, is my type?"

Annie shrugged and answered, "You know. Easy virtue, loose morals."

Matt looked at Annie. "Are you my type, Annie?"

182

"Do you want me to punch you in the... you know?"

"I was just teasing. Emmy looks even more petite than you. I didn't think that was possible."

"Yeah, we both have to shop for clothes in the children's department."

They kept walking and Annie told Matt more about Emmy.

"Her family is not very well off, if you get my drift. I always got the impression her parents spoiled her sister and Emmy just got hand-me-downs. They are very protective of her for some reason. Maybe I shouldn't say anything, but Lainey told me her father is an alcoholic."

"Don't say things like that unless you know they are the truth."

"I've heard Grandpa mention him a few times. They went to school together along with Carmen Lombardi."

Matt stopped walking and said, "I've heard that name before. I think my father knows him."

"Everyone in SoHam knows him," Annie said.

A little farther up the trail Matt pointed and said, "Annie, look. There's the lake. There are ducks and geese. They probably get fed by the people walking back here."

"There's a bench. I'm gonna sit down."

Annie sat and Matt joined her.

"We should have brought bathing suits. We could go swimming."

Matt looked at Annie and smiled. "There's no one around, Annie."

Yeah, but we aren't wearing bathing suits." Annie looked at Matt.

He grinned.

"No way in hell, Matty Sullivan!"

"Haven't you ever been skinny dipping before?"

"No! And I'm not starting today."

"Can I kiss you?"

"Maybe later."

"Why not now?"

"Because you might take advantage of my youth and

innocence with boys. I might not know when to stop you," Annie said as she smiled.

"I bet it's been a long time since anyone took advantage of you, Annie O'Dell."

"And I'm not letting you take advantage of me, either."

"I like it when you get all feisty. Your eyes sparkle and shine."

"Ain't working!"

"Has anyone told you you have nice legs?"

"Still ain't working."

Annie tugged her dress down to cover her legs more. Matt was quiet for a moment.

"Okay, I got nothing left. We might as well head back."

"Quitter!" Annie shouted. She jumped off the bench and took off running.

Matt watched for a second and then took off after her. She slowed down and turned around to let Matt catch her. He caught her and wrapped his arms around her waist and held her close. She put her arms around his neck and held on tightly. He kissed her and she kissed him back.

"You taste so good, Annie O'Dell. I could kiss you all day."

"Better not."

"Half a day?"

"That was all the kissing I'm doing today. I'm not Victoria Madison, or any of your other girls."

"I'm glad you aren't."

Matt took Annie's hand and they headed back to the party.

When they got back to the party, they noticed a bunch of kids behind the pool house. They headed back there and discovered the kids were drinking beer. They saw Bert Hodges, Dawn Matuzak and others they knew from school. Even Randy Braun had a beer in his hand.

"I don't wanna hang out with this crowd. Let's see if Lainey and Cindy are here yet," Annie told Matt as she took his hand and led him away.

"Okay with me."

They headed toward the deck. They were passed by a two

men. Matt looked at them and then told Annie, "That's Carmen Lombardi."

"Who's Carmen Lombardi? You mentioned that name before."

"Don't you know? I bet your father knows who he is. He's Derrick and Kristen's uncle for one thing."

Annie turned around to look, but the two men were around the corner and out of sight.

"There's Lainey and Cindy with Bryce and Mark." Annie waved to her friends, who were on the deck, and ran to join them. "When did you guys get here?"

"Just now," Cindy answered.

"Is Mace here yet?"

"Right behind you, girl!"

Annie turned around and hugged Mace. He glanced at Matt as he hugged her back.

"Did you miss me or something, Annie? You usually don't hug me like that."

"Sorry, I thought you were someone else," Annie teased.

"Oooh! Score one for Annie O'Dell." Elaine used her finger to add a point for Annie.

"Where's Trish?" Annie asked.

"She's inside with Kristen," Mace answered.

"Are you hungry, Matty?"

"Starving. I haven't eaten all day."

"Let's see what they've got to eat."

Annie took Matt's hand and the group wandered over to check out the food.

"Wow! It's like even better than Darby's," Mace said.

They loaded up their plates and headed over to a corner of the deck where there were empty chairs around a table. They were having fun telling stories about each other from school. Each one trying to out-embarrass the other.

Mace told this story. "When Annie was a freshman she walked into the boys bathroom by mistake. Instead of turning around and walking out, she went ahead and used a stall and then even washed her hands. There were guys in there the whole time."

"I wanted to maintain proper hygiene, so I had to wash my hands."

"Hygiene is very important," Cindy teased.

"Oh, like you've never done anything to be embarrassed about, Cindy Mackens."

Annie and Matt decided to sit on the deck railing while the other kids were still in the chairs. Soon they were joined by some other Roosevelt High kids. Damon Barclay and Diana Ahronson made an appearance. Grady Harris and Maris Miller stopped by and Maris showed off her engagement ring again. Rachel Lowery and Kyle Norris arrived. Derrick and Kristen popped in and out as they socialized with everyone. Marcus Bell and Phil McLeish from the basketball team brought dates to the party. Mace walked over to Annie and took her hand.

"I need to talk to you for a minute, Annie. Come with me."

Annie jumped down and went with Mace. "What is it, Mace?"

Mace put his hands on her shoulders. "Annie, I love you like the sister you might be one day, so don't get mad."

"I won't get mad. Why would I get mad at you, Mace."

"Girl, you gotta remember you are wearing a dress. Some of those guys don't think of you as a sister."

"What are you talking about?"

Mace reached down and touched her dress and her leg.

"You have good looking legs, Annie, and they draw attention. Especially when you're moving them around and sitting on the railing."

"I guess I just wasn't thinking, Mace. I suppose this is one more embarrassing thing people will remember about me. Thanks for telling me."

Mace and Annie rejoined the party, but now Annie sat in a chair and was careful. Matt noticed Mr. Keasling and Carmen Lombardi carrying some beer as they came around from behind the pool house. They had told the kids who were drinking to either behave or leave. Most of them left. Annie noticed most of the adults had gone inside, and the kids had the deck to themselves.

"Does anyone want to dance?" Kristen asked. "I'm ready

to turn on some music."

"Sounds like a plan to me," someone shouted.

Mace was always eager to dance and soon there were a dozen kids dancing. Annie noticed Emmy dancing with Derrick and a kid she knew as Barry... something or other.

"Are we going to dance, Matty?"

"If they play a slow song, I'll dance. You know I'm not very good with the fast songs."

"You don't mind if I dance with Cindy and Lainey, do you?"

"Go ahead, Annie. I'll be content just to watch."

Elaine, Cindy and Annie began dancing together.

"Do you know that kid dancing with Emmy Colasanti?" Annie asked.

Cindy looked to see who Annie was asking about.

"That's Barry Newton. He lives by Emmy. I think they've been friends for a long time." Cindy informed her as she thought about Barry. He had an acne problem and most kids thought of him as a nerd.

"Emmy seems to be having a good time," Annie said.

"Maybe she's got shorts on under her dress and that's why she's showing off her legs to Barry," Cindy said. "Or maybe she and Barry are really good friends."

Trish needed to take a break, so Mace asked Annie to dance.

"Did you see Emmy dancing?" Annie asked.

"Yeah, she was having a good time. She was teasing Derrick about Dawn Matuzak," Mace informed her.

"Cindy thought she might have shorts on under her dress. Maybe I should have worn shorts. This dress is rather short."

Mace smiled.

"You're glad I didn't. Shame on you, Mace." She smacked his arm.

"At least Matt was sitting next to you."

The next song was an old tune, "I Got You Babe." Kristen and Emmy began singing it to each other as they pretended to be Sonny and Cher. After the song was over, the kids clapped and hollered for an encore.

"They sound really good. Don't you think Emmy has an amazing voice?" Mace asked.

Annie nodded and replied, "Kristen told me Emmy used to sing with Kenny Colwell at his church and sometimes with Fridays At Five."

"She seems so quiet and shy, but she just came alive when she and Kristen were singing," Elaine added.

"I've heard you sing before, Lainey. You have a good voice, too."

"Not good enough to sing in front of people."

Matt came over to tell Annie. "I asked Derrick to play a special song so I could dance with you."

"Is it something slow and romantic?"

"It's slow. I don't know about romantic."

The music began and Matt took Annie's hand. They held each other close as they danced.

"How late do you want to stay, Annie? I'm willing to go whenever you want."

"How about we leave at nine? That will give us another hour here, and we will still have time to do something at home."

As the song ended, Annie looked into Matt's eyes.

He looked down at her and smiled. "What are you thinking about, Annie O'Dell?"

"I was wondering if you were going to try and kiss me again."

"You want me to kiss you in front of all these kids. What will they think? Remember, I'm the school bad boy. Your spotless reputation might be tarnished."

"Oh, that's rich. My spotless reputation. Most of the kids think I slept with the basketball team."

"You know you're exaggerating. There might be a few kids who choose to believe that crazy story, but certainly no one who really knows you."

"So you're not going to kiss me."

"Not right now, but the night is still young, Annie."

Half of the kids kept dancing while the other half talked,

munched on the food, which never seemed to run out, and drank the pop and water. Annie and Matt were talking and moving around on the deck when Annie backed into Emmy Colasanti.

Annie spun around. "I'm sorry, Emmy. I didn't see you."

"It's okay, Annie. I wasn't watching where I was going."

Annie and Emmy backed up to the deck railing and Matt stood in front of them.

"I heard you and Kristen singing. You guys are good. Especially you, Emmy. Isn't that right, Matty?"

"I thought you sounded pretty amazing," Matt said as he smiled at Emmy.

Annie added, "I heard that you have experience singing for people."

"A little, I guess. Most people are surprised when they learn I have sung in front of people. Everyone thinks I'm shy and quiet and I suppose I am. Kenny Colwell told me my voice was a gift from God and I should use it."

"I heard you sing in church sometimes. Is that true?"

"I used to sing with Kenny at his church, but I don't now."

"Well, I liked listening to you, Emmy."

"Thanks, Annie."

"Are you spending the night here?" Annie asked. "Oh! I guess that's none of my business."

"No, I'm not spending the night. Kristen and I are close friends, but I've never spent the night here. You might have heard that Derrick and I dated a few times. They weren't romantic dates. We're really just friends."

"Derrick kissed me once when I was twelve," Annie confessed.

"He did? Tell me about it. If you don't mind, that is."

"It wasn't a big deal. We were at a junior high dance and someone dared him to kiss me. It only lasted a second at the most."

"He kissed me once, but it was almost like kissing a brother. I don't have a brother, but sometimes I think of Derrick as my brother."

"I saw you dancing earlier and you were showing off or something."

"Oh God!" Emmy said and then put a hand to her mouth. "You saw that?"

Annie nodded.

"I'm so embarrassed about it now. I usually don't act like that. At least it was with Barry. He's an old friend and I was just teasing him about something Dawn Matuzak did."

Annie moved closer to Emmy and whispered, "Word is that Dawn Matuzak came up to Derrick, lifted her skirt and offered herself to him as a graduation gift. Is that true?"

Emmy nodded and had to stifle a laugh. "Yes! It seems so funny now, but at the time I was shocked. I don't know if you are friends with her or not..."

Annie shook her head. "No way! I think she's a slut."

"She walked right up to Derrick and did that in front of bunch of kids," Emmy said.

"I can picture her doing that," Annie said and then looked up at Matt. "Matuzak really has slept with half the school, but kids don't talk about her like they do me."

"Stop exaggerating, Annie," Matt said.

"Which half are you in?" Annie asked.

"I would never touch her," Matt said and then glanced at Emmy.

Emmy smiled shyly at Matt and then explained, "I was teasing Derrick and Barry about what Dawn did. Trying to act like her, but all I did was embarrass myself."

"I don't think too many kids saw you dancing like that," Annie said. "It's too bad we never really knew each other at school. I think we could have been good friends."

"Maybe we will see each other again, Annie."

"I would like that."

Matt stood next to Annie and whispered in her ear, "I'm ready to go."

Annie looked up at him. "Okay with me." She turned back to Emmy. "I think we're going to get going. I should say goodbye to Derrick and Kristen. I'm glad we had a chance to talk."

"I'll see you sometime, Annie. Oh, there's Derrick and Kristen." Emmy pointed to the other end of the deck.

190

Annie and Matt walked over to say goodbye. Emmy followed along behind them and stood beside Kristen.

"Thank you for inviting us to the party, Derrick. We had a great time."

"I'm glad you could make it, Annie. It was nice to see you again, Matt."

"Your parents have a beautiful home," Matt said.

"Thanks. Dad's business has done well over the years."

Kristen hugged Annie and Derrick shook hands with Matt. Kristen moved behind Emmy and put her hands on her shoulders and held her as Annie and Matt walked away.

"Derrick, are you surprised that Annie would be friends with Matt Sullivan?" Kristen asked as she ran her fingers through Emmy's long hair.

Emmy leaned back against Kristen and said, "I hate it when it gets tangled up."

"I don't know him all that well, but I would guess he's not as bad as people think. I know he's a lot smarter than kids give him credit for."

"He is good looking and knows how to charm the ladies," Kristen said. "What do you think, Emmy?"

"He is hot," Emmy said and then bit her lip. *Maybe not as hot as Rory though.*

"Emmy! How can you say that?" Kristen asked.

Derrick laughed and said, "You guys better stop thinking about Matt Sullivan. I think he might be hooked on Annie O'Dell."

Chapter Thirty-One

Matt and Annie arrived back at her house by nine thirty. He parked in the street, but they didn't go in the house right away. They got out of the car and Annie leaned against the passenger door. Matt came around the car and leaned up against the car right next to Annie.

"I'm glad you made me go to Derrick's party, Annie. I had a lot of fun and it was good to see you again before I have to leave."

"Tell me again why you're going to New York."

"My old man thinks I need to spend some time with Uncle Denis. He's an accountant for some people, and he's supposed to show me the ropes."

"So you aren't in any trouble here, right?"

"Maybe a little, but nothing you need to be concerned about."

Annie leaned against Matt and he put an arm around her waist.

"Are you gonna come in, Matty?"

"People might talk if they see us out here together. I would like to come in, if it's all right."

"Would I ask if it wasn't?"

"No, I suppose not."

Matt looked around as they walked up to the house. He heard a sound and it startled him.

"What's wrong, Matty?"

"Just thought I heard something."

"Something spooked you. You almost jumped out of your skin."

"It's nothing. Let's just go inside." Matt grabbed her hand as he looked around again.

They went into the house and Annie checked the phone for messages. There were two.

"Hi, sweetie. I should be home around midnight. You don't have to wait up for me."

Annie listened to the second message which was also from her father.

"Me again, Annie. I'm gonna be out all night. We caught a lead in the case I've been working on. I'll see you in the morning. I love you."

Matt had been listening to the messages with Annie. "Guess it's safe to stick around awhile. How about that beer you promised?"

"They're in the fridge. Grab one for me. I gotta use the bathroom."

When Annie came back, Matt was at one end of the couch with the TV on and two opened bottles of beer. Annie grabbed one. She sat at the other end of the couch and faced Matt. She tucked her dress between her legs, and they talked about New York again.

"Have you ever been to New York before?" Annie asked.

"I've been there a few times to visit family."

"What, or who, does your Uncle Denis work for?"

"He works for the mob." Matt stated matter-of-factly.

"Really? Just like your father."

Matt grinned. "I was just pulling your leg. They aren't connected or whatever people call it."

"Well, you better let go of my leg before I smack you," Annie teased.

"Uncle Denis works for this accounting firm in Manhattan. He lives in Brooklyn, and I'm going to be staying with him and his family."

They finished their beer and Matt asked, "Can I see your room?"

"It's a mess."

"I don't care. I just want to see it. I won't try anything."

"All right, but I warned you."

Annie led the way and opened the door. She turned on the light and let Matt in her room. The only other guy who had ever been in her room was Mace. Matt looked around. He saw the pictures of her as a younger girl.

"I assume this is you. How old were you?"

"I was ten in that one and twelve in this one."

"This must be you with your Mom and Dad."

"Yeah. It's the last picture of all of us together."

Matt didn't know what to say so he remained quiet. He looked around the room and noticed the clothes tossed everywhere.

"I told you it was a mess."

Annie sat on her bed and tucked her dress down farther. She watched as Matt checked out her room.

"Don't look over there!"

"Why not? Are you hiding something?"

"Yeah, my dirty clothes."

Matt looked and saw what Annie didn't mean for him to see.

"I like your room, Annie. It fits your personality."

"You think I'm a slob, huh?"

"You probably know where every piece of clothing is."

"I was going to do laundry tomorrow. If you come back tomorrow night, my room will be much cleaner."

"No stuffed animals anywhere?"

"I used to have my bed covered with them but I put them away when I started at Roosevelt. They're in the closet now. I figured it was time to grow up."

"Is your bed comfortable?"

"You'll never know, Matty Sullivan!"

"I was just asking. I didn't mean I wanted to try it out."

Annie moved onto her side and looked over at Matt. He didn't move closer to her so she felt safe.

"It's very comfortable. Sometimes I feel like I could sleep all day. Especially when there is a cool breeze coming in."

Annie sat up and Matt turned around pretending to look at the stuff on her dresser. He turned back to Annie.

"Maybe you should change clothes, Annie. You don't want your dress to get all wrinkled."

"You've seen my legs before," she said.

"Yeah, but you should change."

"I will if you leave the room."

"I'll be in the living room. Do you want another beer?"

"We can have one more but that's all. Now go and let me change clothes."

Matt left the room to let Annie change. It only took her a

194

couple of minutes. She came out to the living room and sat on the couch.

"Are you hungry at all?"

"Sorta. We had all that stuff at the party, but I'm hungry again. You got anything here?"

"I'll check the fridge, but don't hold your breath."

"We could go out and get something."

"We could have something delivered. Then we don't have to leave the house. Then whoever is looking for you won't see you." She peered intently at his face to see his reaction.

He didn't give anything away. "How about a pizza?"

"Sounds all right to me."

They decided on what kind of pizza to order and the doorbell rang forty-five minutes later. Annie answered it while Matt was in the kitchen.

"Hey, Doug! You're working tonight, huh?"

"Yeah, I pull all the Saturday night shifts," Doug answered.

"How much do I owe you?"

"Thirteen even."

"Here's sixteen, Doug."

"Thanks, Annie. See you around."

Doug handed Annie the pizza and took off.

"Do you know that guy?" Matt asked.

"Yeah, Doug Katakas. He just graduated with us. He works at Beggar's on the weekend. He's a good guy."

"If you say so."

"Yeah! I say so, now let's eat. Can you grab some paper towels from the counter by the sink."

"Can I have that second beer now?"

"Sure, you can have another one, but I just want pop. There's Dr Pepper in the door of the fridge. Can you grab me one, please?"

Matt grabbed the towels, his beer and a pop for Annie.

"Wanna watch a sexy movie? I noticed some the other day that are rated for mature adults."

Annie shook her head. "No! Certainly not with you in the house. We can watch this one. Daddy just picked it up for me."

"What is it?"

"It's called *Show Me The Money* and it's got Tommy Cruz in it. There's supposed to be a sex scene in it."

"Yeah, I bet all you see is the guy's butt."

"I hope so!" Annie said and then giggled.

"We can watch it, but then I get to pick out the next one."

"Okay, as long as it's not that one. You know which one I mean. The mature one."

They watched the movie as they ate the pizza. Matt finished his beer and then switched to pop. When the movie got to the sexy love scene, Annie paused it.

Matt sat up straight and pointed at the TV. "Look! I told you. All you see is that guy's butt."

"Doesn't it look so good though."

"I'm telling your father."

"Go ahead. He bought this movie for me in the first place. He knew this scene was in it because he saw it at the theater."

"Can you start the movie up again? I'm tired of looking at his butt."

Annie giggled, but started the movie. "I'm not, but I guess I can watch it again sometime." Fifty minutes later the movie was over and Annie was still laughing. Annie was sitting next to Matt and he put an arm around her shoulders.

"Show me the money!" Annie mimicked the actor from the movie.

"I think I heard that line somewhere tonight. Where did I hear it?"

"Which line? Oh, do you mean 'show me the money?' Do you think they over did it?"

"No, they only used it a thousand and one times," Matt whined.

"If you were a movie star, would you do a scene where you had to show your butt?"

"Hell no!"

"Why not? Don't you have a cute butt?" Annie asked very seriously.

"I don't know. I've never looked at it."

196

Annie put a hand on his thigh. "Didn't Victoria, or any of your other girlfriends, ever comment on it?"

"No, and why are you concerned?" he asked as he moved her hand away. "I'm not ever going to be in a movie. Would you do a love scene if you were in a movie?"

"If it was done tastefully and a necessary part of the story, I would."

"What a bunch of bull! You don't even like to shower with other girls around in gym class."

"How do you know that?" Annie poked his side.

"Victoria told me."

"She certainly had no problem with being naked! I'm sure you know that."

"I'm not going to talk about old girlfriends, Annie."

"Does that mean I'm your girlfriend now?"Annie grinned and put her hand back on his thigh.

"No, we're just friends."

"Do you want to kiss me?"

"I would if you would be quiet for a minute."

"So I have to shut up before you..."

Matt leaned over and kissed Annie. She kissed him back and they kept kissing each other for longer than Annie had ever kissed anyone before. Matt pulled her onto his lap as they began to get excited. Matt stuck his tongue in her mouth and touched her tongue. She had never experienced that before. They kept kissing and then Matt touched her breast."

"Don't, Matty!"

"Why not? Don't you want me to make out with you?"

"I want to kiss you, but I'm not doing anything else. Let me get off your lap."

"I wasn't going to try to undress you or anything."

"I'm not ready to let you touch me like that. If I did that, then you would want to keep going."

"I'm sorry. I won't do it again."

"Promise?"

"Yes, I promise."

Annie let Matt kiss her again and he kept his promise. He

kissed her but didn't touch her anywhere he shouldn't. They began French kissing again, and once again they were both getting sexually excited. Suddenly Matt moved Annie off of his lap.

"I need to go home, Annie."

"Why? I thought you were going to stay longer."

"If I stay any longer, I might not be able to keep my promise."

"We could stop kissing and just watch a movie."

"No, I need to go. I won't be satisfied with just watching a movie with you."

Matt got off the couch. He grabbed his wallet and keys and ran out the door. Annie didn't try to stop him. She wondered how far he would have gone if she had let him keep touching her. She wasn't sure she would have wanted him to stop.

Two days later Annie called Matt's house.

"Hi, Mr. Sullivan. This is Annie O'Dell. May I speak to Matthew, please?"

"I'm sorry, love, but Matty isn't here."

"Do you know when he will be back?"

"He won't be home until the end of summer. He's in New York with his uncle. Didn't he tell you he was leaving?"

"He told me he was leaving at the end of the week."

"He left yesterday, Annie. I'll tell him you called when I talk to him."

"That's all right, Mr. Sullivan, you don't need to tell him."

Chapter Thirty-Two

"Annie, I talked to my private investigator friend, Mike Bushell, today. He needs some help in the office."

"I thought he was an attorney."

"He's also a P.I. His secretary is going on maternity leave, and he needs someone to cover her part-time hours."

Annie put down the newspaper. "That sounds all right. There's nothing in the paper that looks remotely interesting. How many hours a week?"

"He told me it would be around twenty hours a week. Answering the phone, doing some filing. That sort of thing. You wouldn't get to do any snooping, I mean sleuthing, but it would pay better than babysitting or working at Burger Bob's."

"When would I have to start?"

"Monday morning at nine. Monica DeWitt will show you the ropes and get you up to speed. Interested?"

"Yes, it will probably be boring, but it will be good experience."

"It will give you something to do so you don't stay around the house and mope."

"I'm not moping. Whatever that means."

"It means you are still thinking about Matt Sullivan too much. He's gone for the summer, Annie, and you need to start having fun. That's an order!" Dad put a finger under her chin and raised her face.

"Should I go out and see if I can pick up some guy at the bar or something?"

"As long as he's a biker with tattoos all over and long greasy hair and missing a few teeth."

Annie laughed. "Would it be okay if he has some of his teeth?"

"A few, but not too many. Have you talked to Mace lately? Or Lainey or Cindy?"

"I should call them, but I've been too busy moping."

On Monday morning Annie showered, got dressed and had

breakfast. She was a little nervous. Understandable since this was her first day on a real job. She wore a skirt and top and looked very professional.

"How do I look, Daddy?" She spun in a circle to let him check her out.

"You look like a real secretary, honey."

"Thanks. Are you going to give me ride this morning?"

"Yes, but we were going to have to find a more permanent solution. There will be days when I won't be around to take you back and forth."

"I have an idea!"

"What is that?"

"It's like a thought that pops into your head out of nowhere."

Dad stared at her. "I know what an idea is. What's your idea?"

"How about we get a second car? That way I won't have to depend on you at all."

"Wow! That's a great idea."

"Really?" Annie's eyes opened wide as she bounced up and down on her toes.

"No!"

"Daddy! I'm out of high school now, and I need a car. I need some way of getting around."

"You still have your bicycle."

She slapped her forehead. "Of course! I totally forgot about it. Well, never mind about a car. I can ride my bike to the office in my dress or skirt. That would be totally professional."

Dad rubbed his jaw as he looked at her skirt. "I see your point. Actually, Grandpa and I were taking about a car for you. He's thinking about buying a new one so he doesn't have to drive his van all the time and thought you might like his old one."

"His Prelude? Sure, I'll take it. I've always liked that car."

"You will have to buy your own gas and pay insurance."

"I have some money saved up. I can pay the insurance."

"Grandpa said he would pay the first six months insurance, but then you're on your own. The title will still be in his name until you turn eighteen, but then it will be all yours."

"What about repairs?"

"Your responsibility."

"50-50!"

"Nope!"

"60-40?"

"100-0. Take it or leave it."

"Deal."

Annie shook hands with her father, and he took her to work.

"Good morning. You must be Annie. I'm Mrs. DeWitt. Please call me Monica."

"Okay, good morning, Monica."

Monica was Mr. Bushell's full-time assistant and had worked in the office for fifteen years.

"Mike told me this is your first job. Is that correct?"

"My first real job, I've been babysitting for years, and I take care of the house for Daddy a lot."

"When Mike comes in, I'll introduce you. For now I need to get you acquainted with the office and what Mike expects."

"I've already met Mr. Bushell. I've known him since I was a little girl."

"Of course, I forgot. Mike is a good friend of your father's. Shauna Bolton is going on maternity leave, and you will be replacing her."

Monica and Shauna took Annie under her wing and in a couple of days Annie knew her way around the office like she had been there for years. Her main responsibility was answering the phone and keeping track of Mr. Bushell's appointments. She learned the filing system and helped wherever needed.

On Wednesday afternoon Annie got a ride home from her boss.

"Thanks for the ride, Mr. Bushell. I'll see you in the morning." Annie hopped out and ran inside. She slammed the back door closed and saw her father in the kitchen.

"Hi, Daddy. When did you get home?"

"Just a couple of minutes ago. Did Mike bring you home?"

"Yes, you'll never guess what I got to do today." She sat on her stool at the island.

Dad opened the fridge and grabbed a beer.

"Can I have..."

"No!" he said curtly.

"I was going to ask for a Dr Pepper. Did you have a bad day at work?"

"Sorry, sweetie. I shouldn't have snapped at you." He handed her a can of pop and got a clean glass from the sink. "You could say it was not the best of times."

"Isn't that a line from a book. I think we had to read it freshman year," Annie said. "Tell me what happened."

"We had this suspect in those home burglaries, see..."

"You're doing that annoying impersonation again."

"Sorry. Anyway, we had this guy who looked good for the break-ins, but we didn't have enough to hold him. He lawyered up and we had to cut him loose. I know he's the guy." Dad took a long swallow of his Sam Adams. "Now what did you do that's so exciting?"

"Mr. Bushell had me call this medical practice and pretend to have a claim. He thinks they're filing bogus bills and defrauding the insurance company that is his client. I might have to make an appointment and go see a doctor."

"What are you going to use as a reason?"

She grinned. "I'm supposed to be pregnant."

"Oh, that should be easy enough for you to pretend. You can just stuff a pillow under a sweatshirt and they'll never suspect a thing."

"I'm kidding. The appointment is for bloodwork, and they bill the insurance company for tests that never get done."

"Maybe you should go with the pregnant thing," Dad teased.

"Oh, Daddy!"

Shauna didn't make it two weeks. She went into labor at home on Thursday and had a baby girl. Annie took up the slack without missing a beat.

Chapter Thirty-Three

Annie called Mace Friday afternoon and asked, "What are you doing today? I've got a three day weekend because the office is closed for the Fourth."

"Who is this? The voice sounds vaguely familiar, but I just can't seem to remember," Mace teased but was partly serious.

"All right. I know I haven't talked to you for a while, but you haven't called me, either. So what are you doing?"

"Nothing! I'm bored. Judge Eiffert took his whole family on vacation. Trish is gone."

"Wanna come over here?"

"Lainey told me you've got a car now. True?"

"Grandpa gave me his Honda Prelude when he bought a new car."

"That red one?"

"It's a 1993, but it's only got forty thousand miles on it."

"Pick me up and we can go somewhere and get into mischief. Have you stolen any files from the office yet?"

"Not yet, but I'm working on it."

"Lainey told me you have to dress professionally. Does that mean you have to wear a dress?"

"I do sometimes, but I have skirts and a couple pairs of dress pants I can wear."

"How soon can you be here?"

"I'll be there in ten minutes unless I get pulled over for speeding."

"I'll be ready."

Annie made it in thirteen minutes. She came inside and Keyshon saw her. He got excited so Annie talked to him for fifteen minutes. He showed her everything in his room even though she had seen it many times before.

"I've gotta leave now, Keyshon. I'll see you again."

"Bye, Annie. Come over again, and we can play some more."

"I will," she promised as she hugged him. She noticed he would soon be taller than her. She ran back downstairs. "Bye, Mrs.

Franklin. I'll bring Mace back later."

"Keep him for as long as you want, Annie. Just feed him once in a while."

"Anything in particular he likes?"

"Doesn't matter as long as it's cooked. He'll eat anything."

Annie laughed and she and Mace headed out.

"So how you been?" Mace asked. "Haven't seen you since Derrick's party."

"I've been working thirty hours a week for Mr. Bushell. Taking care of my father, the usual stuff."

"I heard Matt Sullivan's in New York. Heard he left the day after the party. Any truth to the rumor that you scared him out of town?"

"Yeah! I told him this town wasn't big enough for the two of us and he had better split."

"Is that your James Cagney impersonation?"

"It was supposed to be John Wayne."

"I was gonna guess him next."

Annie poked Mace in the side. They were quiet until she pulled in the driveway. They went inside and Mace plopped down on the couch and turned on the TV. He flipped through the channels until he found something that caught his eye. Annie opened a can of Dr Pepper for each of them and joined Mace on the couch. She kicked off her shoes and put her feet in Mace's lap.

"Did I ever tell you what happened the night after Derrick's party?"

"No, you haven't told me squat for the last two weeks. What happened?"

"Matty and I came back here. Daddy was on duty all night."

"If you're gonna tell me that you and Matt..."

She kicked him. "We didn't do that! We ordered a pizza and he had a couple beers, I had one. We watched a movie."

"Which one?"

"*Show Me The Money.*"

"You watched that so you could see Tommy Cruz's butt."

"I paused it and made Matty look, but the movie was funny.

After the movie we started kissing. I sat on his lap and he stuck his tongue in my mouth."

"Tell me you've done that before."

"Just who would I have French kissed, huh?"

Mace thought about it for a time. "No one, I suppose. Go on."

"We were making out. Just kissing! Kissing a lot actually."

"Tell me you weren't still in that dress!"

"Oh, I should back up. Before we started..."

"Yeah, I got that part."

"I showed him my room. He looked at the pictures of me when I was younger while I was on my bed."

"Still in your dress?"

"Yeah, anyway, he looked around. He saw my dirty laundry."

"And your underwear was on top as usual!"

Annie smacked Mace on the arm.

"At one point I was moving on the bed and he turned around and told me I should change. It was after I changed that we were making out. I guess we were both turned on."

"I can guarantee you that he was." He grabbed her feet and moved them off of his legs.

"I was on his lap and he touched me. Let's say he touched the same part of me that you did that time..."

"Yeah, Yeah. I get the picture."

"I told him to stop and he did. We kissed again for awhile and then he got up and left. He said he had to go before something happened. He ran out and I haven't seen or talked to him since."

"You're lucky he left. Why did he go to New York?"

"He's working with his uncle Denis. Just between you and me, I think he got into some kind of trouble, and his father made him leave."

"Do you think he'll come back when college starts?"

"I don't know for sure. Maybe. It wouldn't surprise me though if he stays in New York and goes to college there."

"Hey, did you hear about Victoria Madison?"

"You mean, do I know she's pregnant?" She moved her feet

back onto his legs.

"I guess that's old news to you."

"She claims the father is Jason Agresta. If I was him, I'd make sure I had a paternity test done to be sure."

"You don't think it might be Matt Sullivan's baby do you?" Mace asked.

"Not if she's only two months along. She would be showing a lot more if it was Matthew's."

"What have you got to eat around here?"

"You know where the fridge is. I'm not your mother."

Mace grabbed Annie's feet and started tickling her. He pulled her closer and tickled behind her knees.

"Stop it or I'll kick you!"

Mace turned her over on her belly and then sat on her legs. She tried to get away, but couldn't, so she stopped trying.

"We used to play like this all the time when we were kids. Do you remember?" Annie asked.

"I remember you used to try and wrestle me."

"Sometimes I would win, too!"

"Only if I let you."

"Are you looking at my butt?" Annie asked.

"Maybe."

"Well, stop it. I don't look at yours. I want to turn over so I can see what you're doing."

Mace let Annie turn over on her back, but he was still sitting on her knees.

"Are you still ticklish on your sides?"

"You know I am."

"I won't tickle you anymore. Will I be safe if I let you up?"

"No! I'm gonna get you back somehow."

"Then I guess I'll just have to hold you down."

Mace leaned forward and placed his hands on either side of her. She looked up at her friend.

"If you try to kiss me, I will scream."

"If you try to kiss me, I will scream louder," Mace said.

They smiled and began laughing. Mace lifted up so Annie could move her legs. She sat up facing him.

"I made Matty stop that night because I didn't know how far he would go. I didn't know if I would be able to stop him. What's even worse is that I'm not sure I would have wanted him to stop. Does that mean I'm a slut?"

"No, Annie," Mace answered softly and then added with a grin, "Screwing the whole basketball team does, though."

"I heard it was just the starting five."

"If it was, then you left one out. When do I get my turn?"

"I'm not doing anything for the next ninety seconds."

"Great! I'll have thirty seconds left over."

They grinned at each other.

"I was serious. What do you have to eat around here, girl?"

"Fine! I'll check the fridge myself."

Annie got up and Mace swatted her behind. She shook it at him and then stuck out her tongue.

"Keep that thing in your mouth. Who knows how many guys you've used that on."

Annie looked at Mace with a frown.

"I meant French kissing," he said. "You've got a dirty mind sometimes, Annie Mercer."

Annie fixed tuna salad sandwiches and fed Mace before he starved to death. She ate half a sandwich.

"Will that hold you for an hour or so?"

"If it has to. Where's your father?" he asked.

"He's working today but has the rest of the weekend free. Let's go outside and do something. It's too nice a day to stay in the house."

"So what do you have in mind?" Mace asked.

Annie led the way as they went outside. She walked into the garage and brought out a basketball.

"I thought we could walk over to the park and shoot some hoops."

"Hoops are out of season. We'll have to shoot something else," Mace said and then grinned.

Annie dribbled the basketball a few time sand then stopped, looked at him and asked, "Was that supposed to be a joke?"

"Yeah! I thought it was funny."

"You should stick to playing hoops, and I'll tell the jokes."

"All right, Ms. Comedian, tell me something funny," Mace said as they walked down the driveway.

He grabbed the ball and started dribbling like Marcus Haynes of the Globetrotters. Annie watched as Mace put on a show. She was impressed as he did all kinds of tricks and showed off his ball handling skills for a couple of minutes.

"Where did you learn to do that?"

"Have you ever heard of the Harlem Globetrotters?"

"Yeah, we saw them play when we were kids."

"They always have a guy on the team who can handle the ball like a magician. I would practice doing some of their tricks."

"You don't do that in games."

"Coach would kill me if I started showing off like this. Sometimes I would goof around in practice if Coach wasn't looking. I used to throw passes to Marcus when he wasn't looking. A few times I hit him right in the face with the ball." Mace chuckled as he remembered. "He soon learned to keep his eyes on the ball and be ready for a pass at any time."

When they got to the park, there was a pick-up game going on. Mace was asked to play. Annie watched while the guys played. When one of the guys had to leave, she stepped in and was able to run up and down the court with the guys, but she mostly stayed out of the way. One time Mace passed her the ball, and the guy guarding her let her take a shot. She surprised everyone by swishing it. After twenty minutes of playing, Annie felt exhausted so everyone took a short break.

"Good job, Annie. I didn't think you would be able to keep up."

"Neither did I. I know I'm gonna pay for this tomorrow," she said as she leaned over with her hands on her thighs.

The other players came over and talked to Mace. They knew he played for Roosevelt and many of them had seen him play 'real' games at the school. After a break, they started playing again. This time Annie was a bit more involved in the game. She even stole the ball from the other team. If she got the ball on offense she tried to get rid of it right away. She would pass the ball to Mace.

Eventually everyone was ready to quit. Mace and Annie headed back to the house.

"You did all right, girl." Mace gave her a high-five.

"Thanks."

"You do realize those were grade school kids, right?"

"So? They were bigger than me even if they are just kids."

"A couple of those kids have some real talent. If they work hard, they have a chance to play ball in school. Maybe even in college."

"That one kid was almost as tall as you."

"He's going to be a monster when he grows up."

"What was his name? Do you know?"

"Russell Chamberlain, and he's only twelve."

They got back to the house and Annie ran inside. She brought out a couple cans of pop. She and Mace sat outside on the picnic table in the sunshine. They listened as the birds sang and some unseen crickets chirped. A light breeze rustled the leaves of the large walnut trees. Annie remember playing with Mace in a long since gone sandbox under the tree closest to the house. The old wooden fence had turned gray with age. They went back inside and Mace turned on the TV. They sat on the couch and watched baseball. They killed enough time that Mace was hungry again.

"Would you like mostaccioli for dinner? I can make that and a vegetable and a salad. We've got garlic bread in the freezer."

"When did you turn Italian?"

"My mother had a little Italian in her."

Mace almost said something naughty, but didn't. He knew Annie would be upset if he said something nasty about her mother.

"Do you need any help?"

"You can help with the salad if you want."

Mace got off the couch and helped Annie with dinner preparations. They talked about Keyshon and their parents' future plans. They bumped into each other and Annie almost fell down, but Mace grabbed her just in time. He held her and they looked into each others' eyes.

"We need to find a house with a bigger kitchen, dear," Mace joked.

"Yes, we do. I've been telling you that for over a year now, my darling husband. If we're going to start a family, we need more room." Annie checked the mostaccioli.

"You know I want babies, angel face. Six of them. Five boys and then one girl for you. I want my very own basketball team."

"We better get started right away then, my sweet sugar dumpling. Dinner can wait. Just take me now. I think it's the right time," Annie said as she leaned against the counter.

"Shouldn't we use the bed, my little plum pudding."

"No, we don't have time. I'm all yours right here, big guy."

Neither of them had heard Annie's father when he walked in the front door.

"I think I'm gonna be sick to my stomach," he said to get their attention.

Annie looked at her father and screamed, "Daddy! How long have you been home?"

"Just a minute or two, my sweet sugar plum pudding."

"We were just making dinner."

"It sounded like you were putting dinner on hold to take care of more pressing matters," Dad said as he winked at Mace.

Annie turned to Mace and told him. "I guess we will have to wait until after dinner now, sweetie pie."

"Just my luck," Mace replied.

"I didn't know you were coming home for dinner."

"I didn't think I could get away, but I'm playing hooky, Annie."

"I was gonna make mostaccioli with a vegetable. Mace was gonna try to make a salad and we've got garlic bread. I can have it ready in fifteen or twenty minutes."

"That's sounds perfect, my little love bunny."

"Oh, that's sick!" Mace grimaced. "Please tell me you don't call my mom that, Detective O'Dell."

"I'm just teasing, Mace, though I should write down some of the terms of endearment you were calling each other."

"Daddy, go sit on the couch, and I'll call you when dinner is ready." She pushed him out of the kitchen. "Mace and I can get the foreplay out of the way while I make dinner."

Mace nearly fainted as he held his breath.

"Okay, sugar dumpling, just don't burn the mostaccioli."

Annie had dinner ready as promised and the three of them sat at the island to eat.

"What do you kids want to do tomorrow? Elisabeth and I thought it would be fun to do something together. All of us."

"Do you guys ever go hiking?" Annie asked.

"We like to take walks together. I don't know that we would call it hiking. Is that something you and Mace would enjoy?"

"Keyshon would love it. He loves spending time with Annie," Mace said with a mouthful of salad.

Dad suggested, "Maybe we can go to the park and have a picnic."

"You mean with ants and bugs and all that?" Annie clapped her hands together as she asked.

"Annie, since when have you been bothered by ants or bugs?"

"I'm not, but Mace is."

"Whatever you and Mom decide will be all right with me. Going to a park might be a good way to get rid of Annie. I'm just kidding, sir." Mace teased.

"Too bad. I was going to help you, Mace."

Annie glared at both of them and stuck out her tongue.

"What did I tell you about pointing that thing at me, sugar blossom? And with your father here to see it. Shame on you."

Annie tried to kick Mace but hit the chair instead. "Ow! Crap! That hurt."

"Serves you right for trying to kick your darling love machine, Annie," her father teased.

"You would take his side."

After eating, Dad had to get back to work.

"Thanks for dinner, sweetie. It was delicious. The salad was just perfect, Mace."

"When will you be home?" Annie asked as she put the small amount of leftovers in the fridge.

"I should be home by midnight. Are you gonna stay here tonight, Mace? I'm not sure I want Annie taking you home real late at night."

"We'll see how it goes. If it gets too late, I'll just keep Mace prisoner here with me."

"I could always walk. It's only fifty miles."

"Have fun, kids."

"Be safe, Daddy!"

"I always try."

Annie gave her father a hug and a kiss as he headed back to work.

Annie watched him back out of the driveway and then asked, "Are you gonna help me clean up the kitchen, sweet cheeks?"

She giggled and then ran as Mace looked at her with a devilish grin. Mace caught Annie and threw her over his shoulder. He carried her into her room and dumped her on the bed. She landed on her back and looked up at him.

"Now what were we getting ready to do before your father got home? Oh yeah! I remember. I want to get started on my basketball team."

"Fine! Go ahead and use me, but I want three daughters so I have cheerleaders for your team."

"Maybe I would rather have a football team. Hmmm. Tough decision."

Mace moved next to Annie on her bed and kissed her cheek. They lay quietly side by side for a minute—both of them on their backs. Annie moved onto her side and put a hand on Mace's stomach.

"Do you think you and Trish will get married someday?"

"I would like to, but I don't think she wants to get married until after she's all done with college. She wants to be a doctor, you know."

"I know. Man, you would be almost a hundred by then."

"Yeah, probably too old to have babies with her. I guess I'll have to be satisfied with making babies with you, Annie."

Annie leaned closer and quickly kissed his mouth.

His arms and legs flailed as he scooted over toward the edge of the bed. "What was that for? What did I do to you?"

"I just wanted to try it once."

"Give me some warning next time. You didn't get the whole Mace Franklin experience."

"Should we try again?"

"Shouldn't we clean up the kitchen or something?"

"The kitchen can wait."

Annie moved on top of Mace and leaned down to kiss him again. This time he kissed her back. She stuck her tongue in his mouth and he responded. She relaxed her body and was right on top of him. He moved his hands to her butt. She could feel his need. They kissed like they had been practicing for years. They stopped to catch their breath and Annie moved off of Mace.

"Was that the whole experience?"

"If you weren't such a good friend, and I wasn't such a gentleman, you would have received the whole experience."

"I can be so naughty, huh?"

"I hope you don't plan on doing that with the rest of the basketball team."

"I already have, remember? Come on, let's go clean the kitchen. Maybe we can take a shower together later. I think you need a cold shower." She looked at his jeans. "I hear they can cause shrinkage."

Annie got off the bed and ran into the kitchen. Mace stayed on her bed for a couple of minutes thinking about what just happened. He got up and joined Annie in the kitchen. They made quick work of the cleanup and went into the living room and sat on the couch again. Annie acted like nothing had changed between them, and soon Mace forgot about it, too. They watched TV for a while before Annie took him home.

"See you tomorrow, Mace."

"See you, Annie. Thanks for dinner."

"You're welcome, sugar plum."

Chapter Thirty-Four

The breeze blew just enough to keep the eighty-five degree air moving. It promised to be one of those days that made a person want to stay indoors in the air-conditioned air, but at the same time feel the urge to go outside and enjoy the sunshine. Keith and Elisabeth were both off for the weekend and wanted to spend some quality time with the kids. They were growing very fond of each other but weren't ready to make the deep commitment to combine the families yet. Elisabeth was not quite sure she could adjust to Keith's unpredictable work schedule. Neither one was ready to leave their own home, so for the time being, they were keeping the status quo. Annie was talking to Mace about the plans for the day.

"We're going to pick you guys up and go to the park for a while and then come back to our house. Dad is going to grill some burgers and chicken breasts, maybe some Italian sausage. We've got corn-on-the-cob, too."

"Mom is making some potato salad and some other thing. I'm not sure what she calls it, but it tastes good. Keyshon wants to see the fireworks later. I told him we would take him. You don't mind do you?"

"Not at all. We can go to the stadium and watch. Keyshon will enjoy it."

Dad was ready to go and hollered at his daughter, "Annie, I'm ready to go. Are you ready?"

"Just a second. I'm in the bathroom."

Mace asked, "What are you... never mind! I don't need to know."

Annie finished in the bathroom and was ready to leave. She had fixed her hair differently, just for Mace.

"Daddy, is that what you're wearing?"

"Yeah, why? Is something wrong?"

"You can't wear those socks with sandals. Get rid of those socks! Throw them in the garbage. If you're going to wear sandals, then no socks. If you want to wear socks then put on your tennis shoes. Understand?"

"What would I do without you, honey?"

"It's a good thing you have to wear a suit to work."

"You did something different with your hair. It looks very pretty."

"Thank you. Mace showed me a picture he liked so I thought I would fix mine differently."

"So you fixed your hair for Mace?"

"I just thought he might like it like this."

"I see."

"What are you thinking?" Annie wondered.

"Nothing. I try not to think too much. I get headaches if I try to figure you out."

"I'm not that difficult to understand, am I?"

"No dear. Not any more than understanding Einstein's theories of relatives."

"Relativity, Daddy. Not relatives."

"Are you ready to go now?" Dad asked.

"I've been ready. I was just waiting for you!"

He shook his head and threw his arms in the air.

Detective O'Dell drove over to pick up the Franklins. Keyshon saw Annie and dashed to her with a big smile on his face.

"Hi, Annie! I'm going to the park with you. We can go hiking and feed the birds in the pond."

"That will be fun, Keyshon. Do you have your hiking shoes on?"

"Do you like them? Mom bought them for me. They're called, they're called... I can't remember what they're called. Mace, what are my new shoes called?"

"Air Jordan's."

"That's what they are, Annie. Air Jordan plays for the Bulls. He's not as good as Mace, though."

"I think you might be right, Keyshon. Are you ready to go hiking with me?"

"I'm ready! Come on, Mace. We're going hiking with Annie."

After the short drive to the state park at the edge of town, Keith found a parking space close to the main trail.

"Now, Keyshon, you have to stay with Mace and Annie all

the time. This is a big park, and I don't want you to get lost. Do you promise you will do what I asked?" Mrs. Franklin asked.

"I promise, Mom. I'll stay with Annie and Mace."

"I'll keep an eye on him, Mrs. Franklin," Annie said. "He can hold my hand, and we will have fun."

Keith and Elisabeth watched as Mace, Keyshon and Annie headed up the trail.

"Annie is so good with Keyshon. She has so much more patience than Trish Eiffert."

Keith responded, "Being with Keyshon is just as good for Annie as it is for him being with her."

"Are you ready for a walk, Keith?"

"I think I can manage a short walk with you. I think there is a bench up the trail a short distance."

The kids were moving along at a brisk pace until Keyshon tripped.

"Are you all right, Keyshon?" Annie knelt to check on him.

He looked up at her. "I hit my knee, but it's not bleeding. I was watching the birds and tripped. I'll be more careful."

"We can slow down." She rubbed his knee and then stood up. "We don't have to be in such a hurry. You can watch the birds all you want."

Mace and Annie talked as she held onto Keyshon's hand. They reached a spot on top of a hill with a view of the river.

"Keyshon, you can sit on the bench and watch for birds," Mace suggested.

"Okay, I'll tell you if I see any." Keyshon sat and faced the river.

Annie and Mace stayed on the trail behind the bench.

"I like what you've done with your hair today, Annie. Did you do that for me?"

"Maybe."

"Well, it doesn't matter. I like it anyway."

"Do you like it enough to kiss me?"

"I would have to like it an awful lot to do that," Mace teased.

Keyshon heard Annie say something about a kiss and

216

turned to watch her.

"Well? Do you?" Annie asked.

"I suppose I like it enough for one kiss."

Mace took Annie in his arms and kissed her as Keyshon watched. Although it was supposed to just be one kiss, it turned out to be more. Mace and Annie kept kissing, using tongues and holding each other.

"Annie, are you gonna marry Mace now. I think you should marry him because I like you better than his other girlfriend."

"Sorry, Keyshon, but Annie and I aren't going to get married. We're just friends." Mace waved at Keyshon and said, "Come on. Let's keep hiking."

They had been walking for an hour when Keyshon stopped and refused to take another step. "I'm getting tired and hungry. Can we go back to the car now?"

"We can turn around if you want, Keyshon. Did you enjoy the hike?"

"Yeah, but I've seen enough trees and birds for one day."

They hiked back toward the car and saw Keith and Elisabeth walking toward them. Keyshon ran up to his mother.

"Mom! Mace and Annie were kissing. Mace had his hands on her butt, and they were kissing for a long time. I think they should get married so Annie can live with us. She can stay in my room, and we can play together everyday."

Detective O'Dell walked up to Annie and stared at her. She put her finger in her mouth to look innocent as she looked up at her father.

"Am I grounded again," Annie asked.

Dad shook his head, sighed and said, "I wish your mother could tell me what to do."

Mace put a hand on Keyshon's shoulder. "Keyshon, you weren't supposed to tell anyone." He looked at Detective O'Dell to see if he was upset.

"Will you marry Annie, please?" Keyshon asked. "I like her better than Trish."

"I'm not old enough to get married yet, Keyshon."

"Oh! Guess what I saw, Mom." Keyshon ran to his mother.

217

"What else did you see?" Elisabeth asked.

"I saw some birds in a tree, and I think they had a nest with baby birds."

Keyshon had already forgotten about Mace and Annie kissing. They returned to the car and made their way to the O'Dell home. Grandpa Liam was already there, sitting on the front porch, when they got back.

"Where have you guys been? I thought we were supposed to eat at noon."

"Oh, Grandpa, we were enjoying the beautiful weather," Annie told him as she took his hand. "We went to Forbes Bend to go hiking."

"You could have let me know. I like to go for hikes." He put his arm around her waist as they went inside.

Everyone gathered in the kitchen.

"Mom, I'm hungry," Keyshon complained.

"It will take time to get everything ready. Can you wait?"

"Could I have some potato salad?"

"Okay, but then you will have to wait like everyone else." Mom spooned some potato salad on a plate for Keyshon. "Please sit at the table to eat."

"I suppose I should get the grill ready," Dad said as he kissed Elisabeth.

"That would help," Grandpa said.

Annie and Mace looked at each other and then all the men went outside.

"Can I go outside with Mace when I finish?" Keyshon asked.

"Yes."

Keyshon inhaled the potato salad and then ran outside.

Annie and Elisabeth got the burgers and chicken breasts ready. Dad started the gas grill and Grandpa supervised by watching over his shoulder.

"I think I can handle this without your help," Detective O'Dell said without turning to face his father.

"Just making sure."

"Go grab a beer or something."

218

"I'm waiting until we eat."

Detective O'Dell sighed and gave up. He let his father keep an eye on the grill. Grandpa watched the grill for a time and then headed inside.

"Okay, the grill is ready for the burgers," Grandpa told Annie. "Where's the meat?"

"Here's the burgers, Grandpa. Will you take them out to Daddy?"

"The chicken breasts will take longer. They should go on first," Elisabeth mentioned.

"I'll take them out," Annie offered. "Then I'll come back and get stuff to set the picnic table. I know the guys won't bother."

Mace and Keyshon tossed a softball back and forth while Dad and Grandpa kept an eye on the grill.

"How much longer before the hamburgers are done?" Keyshon asked as he retrieved the ball after missing a toss.

"Just a few more minutes, son. You need to be patient."

"I'm being patient, but my stomach isn't," he joked.

Eventually food, condiments, paper plates, drinks and everything needed for a picnic covered the picnic table. Keyshon sat next to Annie, and she helped him fill his plate.

"Can I have more potato salad, Annie?"

"If you eat all that, then you can have more, okay."

"Just watch me. I'll clean up my whole plate."

Mace watched quietly as Annie took care of Keyshon. The three adults talked among themselves.

An hour later Mace whispered to Annie, "Keyshon will have to take a nap this afternoon if he wants to stay up late enough to watch the fireworks."

"I don't need a nap, Mace," Keyshon protested.

"I think maybe you should rest for a while, honey. The fireworks aren't until after dark, and you want to be able to stay up and watch them, right?" Annie said.

"Can I sleep on your bed, Annie?"

"If you promise to rest and go to sleep for me, you can."

"I will. I want to see the fireworks later. Will you make sure I wake up before then?"

"I won't let you miss the fireworks, Keyshon."

She took him into the house. Fifteen minutes later he was out and sound asleep on Annie's bed. Annie rejoined the others on the patio.

"How did you get him to agree to a nap?" Elisabeth asked.

Annie smiled. "I read him a story and told him about how I grew up. So I guess I just bored him to sleep."

"Good job, Annie," Mace teased.

"Do you need a nap, too, Grandpa?" Annie stood behind him and put her hands on his shoulders.

He patted a hand. "I would like a nap, but I think I can manage to stay awake for the fireworks without one."

"Would it be okay if Mace and I take a walk around the neighborhood?" Annie asked her father.

"Sure, we'll hang out here."

Annie and Mace took off for a walk.

"Do you think we should get married so I can share a room with Keyshon?" Annie asked as they paused to cross a side street.

"Will you cook for me and bring me my slippers when I get home from work?"

"If I have to. Will you be satisfied with just kissing me and nothing more?"

"No way! If I have to marry you, then I want to be able to..." He paused because Annie was frowning at him. "Massage your feet at least."

"Then I guess I'll have to tell Daddy we're getting hitched." She couldn't keep a straight face any longer, so she laughed. "Are you busy tomorrow?"

"I think we have to get a license first."

She ran across the side street. "Never mind then. If we can't get married tomorrow, I don't want to get married at all."

Mace caught up with her. "Can we still fool around?"

"Just once a week. I have to keep the rest of the basketball team happy."

Annie had always joked around with Mace, but now it changed. The lightness and humor of their teasing became more serious.

"Oh, Lainey and Cindy are going to the stadium tonight. We are supposed to meet them on the north side around eight."

"Are their boyfriends coming with them?" Mace asked.

"I think so. Yeah, Lainey said Adrien would be there and Bryce is coming with Cindy."

"After the fireworks, Mom and your father are going to take Keyshon home. Maybe we can hang out with everyone then."

"Lainey said something about going back to her house afterward."

"Are her parents going to be home?" Mace asked.

"I don't know. Why? Does it matter?"

"Not really. I guess we can have fun even if they are home. I really appreciate how you are so patient with Keyshon. Trish gets upset with him sometimes."

"I've known Keyshon since he was born. Trish hasn't."

"That's not the reason. You would be patient with him if you just met him last week," Mace said. "Some people have patience. Some don't," he said and then shrugged.

"Sometimes I think I will get a degree that would allow me to work with handicapped kids. Others times I think I will want to work for the FBI."

"You're too young to decide, Annie."

"Have you forgotten? I will be starting college in the fall."

"Trust me," Mace said as he shook his head. "I haven't forgotten."

Keyshon slept until seven. When he woke up, he was ready to see the fireworks. Mom explained that he had to wait. Eventually, it was time to head to the stadium. Grandpa had seen enough fireworks in his lifetime and decided to go home instead.

"Good night, Grandpa. I love you!"

"I love you, too. Have fun with your friends tonight, but don't stay out too late."

"I won't be out past two in the morning."

"That's my angel. Do you have your fake IDs with you?"

"I don't know what you're talking about, Grandpa," Annie answered with a grin.

Chapter Thirty-Five

Mace and Annie searched through the rapidly filling stands of SoHam Memorial Stadium looking for their friends.

"I see them, Annie. They're up there at the top." Mace pointed.

Annie waved to attract their attention as Mace ran up the stairs. Keyshon hung onto Annie's hand for dear life.

"Don't let go. I don't want to get lost in this crowd."

"I would never let you get lost, Keyshon." She led him up the concrete steps.

"Annie, I'm glad you guys finally got here. I didn't think we were going to be able to holds these spots any longer," Elaine said as she moved her purse.

"What time did you get here, Lainey?"

"They let us in the gates around six-thirty and we've been up here ever since," Elaine said as she smiled at Keyshon.

"Are the fireworks gonna start soon, Annie?" Keyshon fidgeted as he looked around at the large crowd.

"In a few minutes, Keyshon. It needs to get darker." Annie kept talking to him to calm his anxiety.

Mace, Elaine and Cindy caught up on news about kids from Roosevelt High.

"Victoria still claims the baby is Jason's, but he isn't sure. He thinks the baby is Matt Sullivan's because Victoria was with him around the same time," Cindy explained the latest gossip she had heard.

"He told Annie he wasn't with her then," Mace whispered so Annie couldn't hear.

"Maybe he forgot," Elaine said to lighten up the serious conversation.

Cindy brought up an unpleasant possibility. "Maybe he was just lying to Annie."

"Adrien, Mace is going to North Park on a scholarship," Elaine said to change the subject before Annie heard them talking about Matt Sullivan.

"A basketball scholarship, right?" Adrien asked.

"Yeah, I chose North Park so I could stay close to home. Mom needs help with Keyshon sometimes. Lainey said you are almost finished."

"One more year to go and then I'm off to Kansas City for seminary school. Annie seems to be very good with Keyshon."

Mace glanced over his shoulder at his brother and Annie. "Yeah, Keyshon loves her like a sister."

"Are your mother and Annie's father still dating?" Cindy asked.

"Still are. They're here tonight. They're going to take Keyshon home later so Annie and I can come over after the fireworks."

"Where's Trish anyway?"

"They're on vacation. Trish won't be back for another two weeks," Mace said. "Thanks for reminding me, Cindy. I really appreciate it."

The fireworks started and the conversations ended because of the loud noise. Keyshon became more and more excited as the fireworks lit up the night sky with every imaginable color and formation. Annie appeared to be just as excited. She acted more like a kid whenever she was with Keyshon. An hour later the fireworks ended with a massive display. Annie held Keyshon's hand as they looked for his mother. Keyshon saw her first.

"Hey, Mom, did you see the fireworks, too?"

"Yes, I did. Weren't they great?"

"I didn't like the loud noises, but I didn't get scared. Annie held my hand. Are we going home now?"

"Yes, baby. It's time for you to get to bed."

"Good night, Annie. Thanks for bringing me to see the fireworks." He hugged her and then grinned. "You can go with Mace now so you can kiss him again. Good night, Mace."

"Good night, little man. I'll see you in the morning."

Keyshon went home with his mother and Detective O'Dell. Annie and Mace headed over to the Novicki house. Her parents were home, but they went to bed early. They had to work in the morning. The kids hung out in the backyard.

"How's work going, Annie?"

"I like it. The work is easy enough, and I'm getting thirty hours a week. How has your job been, Cindy?"

"It's okay. I like teaching little kids, and since Bryce works for the park district, we see each other every day."

"I can't wait for college to start. Just think, all of us will be at North Park. Has anyone heard where Diana Ahronson decided to go?" Annie asked as she sat close to Mace. "The last I heard she was not sure she wanted to go to Princeton."

"She ruled out Stanford. I know that," Elaine answered.

Cindy nodded in agreement. "She might end up at North Park. Her grandparents both graduated from there."

"Isn't the new science building named for them?" Bryce asked.

"Yeah, they donated something like five million to the college," Elaine said as she walked over to a bench and sat next to Adrien.

Cindy sighed. "I hope Diana ends up at North Park. She would make a good roommate."

"I thought we were going to room together?" Elaine asked as she frowned.

"Oh, we are."

"Are you going to live on campus this year, Adrien?" Mace asked.

"No, I've got an apartment with two other guys."

"How about you, Bryce?"

"I'll be living in Asner Hall again, but I'll have a new roommate."

"All of us girls will be living in Howe Hall," Elaine said. "Freshman girls live there unless they join a sorority."

"Have you decided what you're going to do, Annie?" Cindy asked.

"I'm going to live in a dorm for the first year. Then I'll decide if I just want to commute. Kristen Keasling is going to North Park after she graduates."

"Yeah, I heard that and I was surprised. I figured she would go to an Ivy League school."

"Anyone else going to North Park?" Mace asked.

"Matty Sullivan maybe. If he comes back from New York," Annie answered.

Cindy said without thinking, "He might never come back if Victoria's baby looks like him."

"What do you mean by that, Cindy?" Annie's voice thickened. "I thought the baby was Jason Agresta's."

"Jason claims it might be Matthew's."

Annie shook her head. "He told me it couldn't be. He wasn't with her after the night at the party."

"Annie, you need to face the fact that Matt might have lied to you," Cindy said.

"I don't think he did. He admitted to being with Victoria once so why would he lie?"

"Because he wanted you. You can be so naïve when it comes to boys, Annie." Elaine looked at Adrien as he slipped his arm around her shoulders.

"Isn't Randy Braun coming to North Park. His brother Christopher goes there," Bryce mentioned.

Cindy held Bryce's hand and said, "There are a lot of local kids who end up at North Park College."

"The ones who can afford it. The rest of them go to Paul Frank Junior College." Mace tried to hold Annie's hand, but she slapped it away.

"North Park isn't cheap." Annie thought of Emmy Colasanti as she said that. She assumed Emmy would have to attend Paul Frank if she could even afford to pay for that.

"That's why some of the local kids commute and don't live on campus. We're lucky Cindy and I have partial scholarships. Mace has a full ride. Must be nice," Elaine said enviously.

"I'll have a lot of pressure on me, though. The alumni and boosters will be expecting us to win the NCAA tournament with me on the team."

"Dream on, Mace Franklin," Annie teased. "We would settle for winning the conference and getting into the tournament."

"Do you think you'll join a fraternity, Mace?" Bryce asked.

"I haven't even thought about it. Trish will probably join a sorority."

"She'll get in and so will Diana if she comes to North Park," Cindy said as she scooted closer to Bryce.

"How about you, Annie? Want to join a sorority?" Adrien asked.

"No way! I think all those girls are stuck up."

Elaine frowned. "My mother was in a sorority at North Park, Annie. Do you think she's stuck up?"

"No, sorry, Lainey. I guess I shouldn't stereotype people like that."

Elaine stood up. "Is anyone thirsty? We have pop or water. There's a bag of ice in the freezer, too."

Everyone got something to drink and they talked more about the coming year at college. Just before midnight, the cozy little party broke up and everyone headed home. Adrien stayed so he could be alone with Elaine. Bryce walked Cindy across the street, kissed her good night and then left. Annie drove Mace over to his house. She stopped in front of the house and threw the transmission into park.

"Your father is still here, Annie. I think that means he's spending the night. I don't want to invade their privacy."

"You can crash with me, Mace. Daddy won't mind if you do."

"Are you sure it's all right?"

"What can he say? He's spending the night with someone he's not married to." She shifted into drive and floored it. "Crap! Sorry, Mace. I don't mean it like that."

"I know what you mean, Annie."

"Do you think Matt lied to me about Victoria?" she asked as she took the corner without slowing down.

Mace grabbed the dash. "I don't know, Annie. You know him better than I do."

They got back to Annie's house and Mace plopped down on the couch.

"I'm going to get ready for bed. Be back in a minute."

Annie returned in a couple of minutes in a t-shirt and gym shorts, plopped down next to Mace and asked, "Are you tired?"

"Not really."

226

"I'm not either. Let's go outside and look at the stars."

"You can look at me. I'm a star."

"Yes, you are. In fact, you're a legend," Annie said.

"I am?" Mace tilted his head.

"Yeah. A legend in your own warped mind."

"Are you dissing me?"

"No! Whatever gave you that idea? Now come outside with me."

Annie grabbed a glass of water, and they went out to the patio. They sat on the picnic table and looked up at the beautiful night sky.

Mace looked all around. "Where are all the stars? Aren't there supposed to be stars out tonight?"

"It's hard to see them in the city sometimes. It's easier out at Grandpa's place—not as many lights out there."

They sat and talked for a few minutes and then they heard a boom.

"Was that thunder, Mace?"

"I think it was and there's the lightning."

"Cool! We can watch some more fireworks."

"Aren't you afraid of storms?"

"No, why should I be? Are you afraid of thunderstorms, Mace?"

"Not unless they involve tornadoes. Was that a raindrop I just felt? We should go in."

"Why? Are you melting? I felt one, too, and it felt good."

"I'm not gonna melt."

They stayed on the table as it began to sprinkle harder.

"Shouldn't we go inside now, Annie?"

"In a minute. The rain feels good."

"I'm going to get under the porch, at least, so I don't get soaked." He jumped down and ran for cover.

"You big fraidy cat!"

"Names will never hurt me. Just hail and lightning strikes."

"It feels good, Mace."

Annie stayed on the table as the rain let loose. She was soon soaked to the skin and ran over and stood by Mace. They

227

didn't go inside but watched the rain as it came down in buckets.

"Put your arms around me before I get chilled."

Mace wrapped his arms around Annie as he stood behind her. It started to hail and in a couple of minutes the yard was covered in hailstones the size of marbles. Annie ran out and scooped some up in her hands. She tossed them at Mace and grabbed more.

"Annie, you need to come inside with me before you get chilled."

"Okay. If you insist, Daddy," Annie teased him.

They went inside and Annie shivered. Mace grabbed a towel from the bathroom and wrapped it around her. He rubbed her back to try and warm her.

"I'm gonna put on some dry pajamas. You left a t-shirt here. Do you want it?"

"Sure. Good thing I left it here."

Annie went to her room and found the t-shirt. "Here it is."

She tossed it to him and then closed her bedroom door. She changed into dry pajamas—another t-shirt and gym shorts. Then she came out to the living room.

"Don't you have any real pajamas?"

"Yeah, but I can't wear them in front of you." she said. "You might see something you shouldn't."

Mace touched Annie's hair as they sat on the couch. "You should dry your hair."

"And ruin this perfect look. Doesn't it look like I just had it styled at a fancy salon?"

Mace laughed. "Yeah, by a blind gay hairdresser named Maurice."

"Does Maurice do your hair, too? I always wondered about you, Mace."

"You're gonna pay for that remark."

Annie took off running with Mace right behind her. She ran into her room and tried to close the door, but Mace was too fast. Annie squealed as Mace grabbed her and tossed her on the bed. She waited on the bed to see what he was going to do. Mace got on the bed next to her and started acting like he was gay. Annie

228

started laughing.

"I always knew deep down you were gay. That's why we are such good friends."

"I'll show you how gay I am."

Mace moved close and kissed her.

"That was a gay kiss if I ever had one."

Mace kissed her again.

"Still pretty gay."

This time Mace moved right up next to Annie, who was on her back now. He kissed her long and deep. He used his tongue and she responded. Annie pulled Mace on top of her as they kept kissing. Soon their hands were touching each other intimately. Mace didn't try to put his hands under her t-shirt, but he could tell she wasn't wearing a bra.

"Should we get under the covers?"

"I don't think that's a good idea, Annie." He sat up. "You would end up doing one of the guys on the basketball team for real."

"You and Trish have done it, haven't you?" she asked as she turned onto her side.

"Are you sure you want me to answer that?"

"Yes!"

"Okay, we have. There you know."

"I figured you had, but Trish would never say anything."

"You won't mention that I told you, will you?"

"No, as long as you kiss me some more."

Mace leaned close and kept kissing Annie until she wanted to stop.

"Let's stop for a second, Mace."

"Okay. I need to catch my breath anyway. You are getting very good at kissing, I must say."

"I have an experienced teacher."

"Thank you, Annie. I must say I am pretty good."

"I didn't mean you. I meant my teacher, Mr. Kolinski."

"That's gross! He's an old man."

"Yeah, but can he kiss. Now get off the bed for a minute."

"Why?" Mace stood up.

"So I can pull the covers down," she said as she hopped out of bed.

Mace didn't say anything as Annie pulled the covers down. She got in bed and waited. Mace wasn't sure he should, but he got in next to her.

"I won't go all the way, but you can put your hand under my t-shirt."

"Annie, we shouldn't be doing this."

"I know we shouldn't, but I want to."

She kissed him again and moved closer. She took his hand and placed it on her stomach. She reached down to touch him.

He quickly grabbed her hand before it reached her intended destination. "I'm sorry, Annie, but I can't do this. We need to stop and think about this."

Mace got out of the bed and looked down at Annie.

"It's Trish, isn't it? You feel guilty because of her," Annie said as she moved onto her knees.

"I feel guilty because we're friends. Your father trusts me and if he came home right now, I would lose that trust and your friendship. Not to mention being shot dead."

"I'm sorry. I wasn't thinking straight. I don't want to lose your friendship, but I do like you. Can we agree to take a step back and see what happens. If you and Trish stay together, then I will not interfere, but if you split up, I want to give us a shot at being more than just friends."

"We need to take more than a step back. We need to take cold showers."

"That sounds like fun!" Annie jumped out of bed.

"I didn't mean right now and not together, girl."

"Are you afraid to let me see you naked?" she grinned as she asked.

"No, but I'm not sure how I would feel about being in the shower with you."

Annie moved closer to Mace, but they didn't touch.

"Don't you like the way I look?"

"You look amazing, Annie. God! If we weren't good friends, it would be an easy decision."

"Do you really think I'm pretty?"

"Is the Mona Lisa just a painting?" Mace asked as he backed up a step.

"Yeah! A famous painting, but it's just a painting. What's your point?" Annie asked as she moved closer.

"I have no clue."

They both started laughing, and Mace gave Annie a hug. He held her tight, and she put her arms around his neck. She could feel his body body pressing into her.

"Someone is still excited."

He broke off the hug and took a step back. "Can't help it when someone else is not wearing any underwear!"

"Should I put on my flannel pajamas?"

"I think I need to move to the couch."

"I suppose you're right. I'm sorry for being so easy."

"You don't have anything to be ashamed of, Annie. I shouldn't have given you my good kisses. You weren't ready to handle the best game of Mace Franklin."

"That was your best game?" she asked. "Guess you lost, huh?"

"Maybe we can say the game was called because of rain."

"So, we will have to make it up at a later date, right?" Annie asked as she pushed Mace toward her open bedroom door.

"We might have to, Annie girl. It might even be a doubleheader."

Annie pushed him out into the hallway and closed her door. "You can sleep on the couch, Mace Franklin. I don't like baseball that much."

Chapter Thirty-Six

The months of July and August passed quickly for the recent graduates of Roosevelt High as they anticipated beginning their college experience. Annie passed the time working for Mr. Bushell and taking care of the house for her father. Mace took care of Keyshon while his mother was at work and played ball in the evenings with friends. Elaine and Cindy worked for the park district's summer reading program. Trish returned from vacation with bad news for Mace. She found someone new and broke up with him. On August thirtieth, the last Saturday before school started, Annie joined her friends at the Novicki home for a last get together before the start of school.

"Hi, guys! Sorry I'm late. Couldn't find anything clean to wear so I had to do laundry. Now I can see the floor in my room again," Annie explained.

"It can't be that bad, Annie," Cindy said.

"Yes it can! She's not exaggerating," Mace said.

Elaine added, "Your room isn't much better, Mace."

"You haven't seen it lately, Lainey. I cleaned it up."

"That must have taken a couple of days," Elaine teased.

Annie looked at Elaine and then Mace. She hadn't seen Mace since the Fourth of July weekend, but they had talked on the phone. She wondered why Elaine would have seen Mace's room.

"Have you talked to Trish at all lately, Mace?" Cindy asked.

"I tried calling her a few times, but she told me not to bother her anymore."

"Did you break up with Trish?" Annie asked.

"Don't you know, Annie?" Elaine asked. "Trish found a new boyfriend on vacation and dumped our buddy."

"Sorry I never told you, Annie. I never told Lainey or Cindy, either. They got the news from Trish," Mace explained as he looked at Annie.

"I'm truly sorry you broke up with Trish," Annie said as she twisted her hair.

Mace shook his head. "I didn't break up with Trish. She

dumped me. Can you imagine? She dumped me for some other guy."

"That must have hurt. Do you still have feelings for her?" Annie asked.

"I'm starting to get over it. You know me. Always got a smile on my face."

"You should have told me, Mace," Annie said as she touched his arm tenderly.

"I know but after that night at your house, I thought we both needed some space. If I had rushed over to see you after Trish dumped me, I might have taken advantage of your feelings. I couldn't have been sure the attraction between us was genuine or just a rebound."

"You were always a good rebounder, Mace," Annie said. "For a guard!"

"What are you guys talking about?" Elaine asked.

"Nothing, Lainey."

"You were talking about something, guys. Are we keeping secrets from each other now?"

"We were just talking about Trish."

"Fine! You don't have to tell us, Annie." Elaine sounded miffed.

"So, are you guys ready for school to start?" Mace asked.

"We are going to be roommates. Do you know who your roommate will be yet, Annie?" Cindy answered.

"Not yet, but I have my class schedule. I have classes every day but nothing earlier than nine o'clock."

They talked about school for a time and then Mace and Annie were ready to leave.

"Do you need a ride home, Mace? I've got my car."

"You mean Grandpa's car. Can I drive?"

"Sure, as long as you stay under the speed limit."

"Can't make any promises. See you girls later," Mace said.

"Bye, Mace. See you later, Annie."

"I'll call you later," Annie hollered over her shoulder. "Maybe we can do some shopping before classes start. I need to buy some new clothes."

"That would be fun, Annie. Call me."

Annie and Mace took off. Mace liked driving her car and she didn't mind letting him drive today.

Elaine looked at Cindy and asked, "Do you think there is something going on between them?"

"Who?"

"Mace and Annie? Who do you think I meant?"

"Are you kidding?" Cindy chuckled. "Annie would never be attracted to Mace like that. Geez, Lainey, if her father marries his mother they will be brother and sister."

"I suppose you're right, but I had the feeling... Did you see the way Annie looked when she learned that Trish dumped him? I could almost swear she was trying not to smile."

"I think you are letting your imagination run wild, Lainey. We need to make a list of all the things we need for our dorm room..."

"Is it time for that makeup game?" Annie asked Mace as he pulled into his driveway.

"I'm not sure, Annie."

"Let's go to the park. We can go for a walk and talk about us."

They drove to the park, parked the car and went for a walk. Annie held Mace's hand as they walked together.

"Are we still friends, Mace?"

"Of course we are, Annie. I'm sorry I haven't been much of a friend lately. I had a lot on my mind."

"You really liked Trish, didn't you?"

"We were good together."

"I suppose you are talking about more than sex."

"You even have to ask?"

"Sorry, Mace. I know you how you felt about her. We all liked her. Will you feel weird if Trish is still friends with Lainey, Cindy and me?"

Mace jumped up and smacked a limb of the tree. "I don't expect you to stop being friends with Trish, but don't expect me to be her friend."

Annie stopped walking and looked at Mace.

"If I was Trish and we broke up for whatever reason, then you're telling me we couldn't be friends anymore. Is that right?"

"It would be different with you because we were friends before. If we became more than friends and that didn't work out and ended, we could go back to just being friends."

"Are you sure about that? I need to know."

"I can't give you a hundred percent guarantee like you get at Marshall Field's, but I'd like to think we could still be friends."

"What should we do, Mace?"

"Right now, I think we should kiss."

Mace leaned close and kissed her tenderly. Just once.

"We can wait and see what happens when school starts, Annie. We both know the physical attraction between us is there. We found out that night."

"After we get settled in a routine at North Park, maybe we can go out and take things real slow. Lainey and Cindy will be surprised, so maybe we shouldn't tell them anything for awhile."

"They might already suspect something, Annie."

She frowned and poked him in the side. "Did you tell them about that night? I will hate you forever if you did."

"No, of course not. I've never told anyone. Not even Keyshon. You know if we do become a couple, Keyshon will be overjoyed. He really loves you."

"Do you love me, Mace?"

"You know I love you, Annie. I'm just not sure how."

"We will have to figure that out at North Park, huh?"

"It is an institution of higher learning so maybe we can take a class to figure it out."

"Well, we will have four years to try!"

Annie kissed Mace on the cheek and they held hands as they walked back to the car.

"I think I'm going to enjoy college very much, Mace Franklin," she said as she squeezed his hand.

"It certainly will be interesting with you there, Annie Mercer O'Dell!"

www.ingramcontent.com/pod-product-compliance
Lightning Source LLC
Chambersburg PA
CBHW050034180626

46810CB00002B/719